ICEBERG

Also available:

THE NEW

DOCTOR WHO

ADVENTURES

ICEBERG

David Banks

First published in Great Britain in 1993 by
Doctor Who Books
an imprint of Virgin Publishing Ltd
332 Ladbroke Grove
London W10 5AH

ISBN 0 426 20392 5

Cover illustration by Andrew Skilleter

Phototypeset by Intype, London

Printed and bound in Great Britain by
Cox & Wyman Ltd, Reading, Berks

To Ruby
who will come of age
in the year 2006

The events of this story are contemporaneous – if such a word can be used to describe the activities of a Time Lord and his companions – with those of the New Adventure *Birthright*.

Contents

Author's Acknowledgements

T S Eliot is quoted on the following page from his poem *Four Quartets* by kind permission of Faber & Faber.

E Y Harburg and Harold Arlen are quoted on page [138] from *If I Only Had a Heart*, the Tin Man's song from the MGM film *The Wizard of Oz* by kind permission of SBK Feist Catalog Inc.

William James is quoted on the facing page from his book *The Principles of Psychology (Vol I)* by permission of the Cambridge University Press.

Jeff Barry and Elle Greenwich are quoted on page [74] from the lyrics of their song *Do Wah Diddy Diddy*, used by kind permission of Carlin Music Publishing Corporation, Iron Bridge House, 3 Bridge Approach, London NW1 8BD.

Andrew Motion is quoted on page [75] from his poem *In Broad Daylight* and is reprinted by permission of the Peters Fraser & Dunlop Group Ltd.

Passages from the *Tao Te Ching* of Lao Tzu, the *I Ching* and *The Passions of the Soul* by René Descartes are my adaptations.

A note on Cybermen
The word cybernetics was coined (from the Greek *kivernitis* meaning 'governor') by Norbert Wiener in 1948. He used it to describe the science of automation which he developed. The *cyber*-prefix soon became absorbed into the language.

The Cybermen were created by Kit Pedlar and Gerry Davis in 1966 and first appeared in the *Doctor Who* television adventure *The Tenth Planet*. The Cybermen are used in this novel by kind permission of Pedler/Davis estates.

Significant, if not always consistent, additions were made to the idea of Cybermen in further *Doctor Who* adventures over the next two decades, most notably by television writers David Whitaker and Derrick Sherwin (using storylines by

Kit Pedler), Robert Holmes (in collaboration with Gerry Davis) and Eric Saward.

In 1988 I attempted in my book *Cybermen* to draw together the disparate elements of the Cyberman mythos under a cohesive historical and conceptual theory. It is on that theory that the Cybermen in this novel are based.

'People whom the passions move most deeply
   enjoy life's sweetest pleasures.'
                              René Descartes

'Namelessness is compatible with existence.'
                              William James

'This is the use of memory:
   For liberation . . .
From the future as well as the past'
                              T S Eliot

1 Somewhere

LogOn 22:23 Friday 22 December 2006   **File: Story**
Talk. Talk to Nano. Keep out the probing. Say anything. Tell
the story. No one will get to read it. No one will read the file.
Unless they do. But they're reading it now. Reading me. Probing me. Keep out the probing. Talk. Keep talking.

Can't think straight. I trusted him. And he betrayed me.
Didn't he?

How could he? How could he go over to them?

You're still with me, Nano. Aren't you? Taking in my every
word. I can see the glow of your monitor light, flashing at
every word I speak. Every whisper.

I'm surprised they didn't take you from me. They will.
When they return. They'll take you apart, Nano. Destroy your
software. Recycle you. Then they will take me apart.

They've got him. They'll have you. They'll take away everything. Sooner or later. When they return.

Mustn't think of that. Talk. Keep talking.

Tell the story of what's been going on. Perhaps I can hide
you somewhere, Nano. When they take me away. Someone
might find you. Sometime. Buried in the ice. A million years
from now. If I don't get out of here. As me.

This is Ruby Sara Duvall. *Sunday Seeker* correspondent.
Somewhere under the Antarctic.

In a bit of a tight corner.

2   Summer in the 70s

It fell on her skin like a drop of blood.

Jacqui thought at first it was rain. She glanced at her hand. A small red bug sat motionless on her flesh. From nowhere, from out of the sky, it had chosen the back of her hand as a landing strip. She felt privileged.

She was a student of natural history. She had a professional interest. On the café table her textbook was open at insect morphology. She had been taking notes when it landed. Enough of books, she would examine the real thing. She put down her pen.

Inside the café, tinny music blared out from a small transistor radio, a product of International Electromatics. IE merchandise was everywhere these days, it seemed. The music seeped through the open door of the café and out to the paved-over street called St Paul's Churchyard, where she sat in the shadow of the cathedral dome. From a hoarding overlooking St Paul's, a giant face smiled down, one eyebrow raised: Tobias Vaughn, IE's managing director.

Underneath the picture a caption read:

UNIFORMITY. DUPLICATION. IE. THE SECRET OF
SUCCESS.

Jacqui had got up at an insanely early hour to revise. The Turkish café owner had been flabbergasted to see her. She looked at her IE wristwatch. It was still only half past eight. She had been at it for an hour. She deserved a little break. She was grateful to that bug.

She lifted her hand and examined the creature. As she classified the insect she made herself think in English, not in her native French. Morphology? Well, it was obviously a flying beetle. Of what class? *Coleopterous*. Of the family *Coccinellidae*.

She was pleased with herself. Perhaps this afternoon's exam would not be quite the disaster she expected.

Next, topography. The evolutionary ancestors of this bug had once had two sets of wings. In the relentless pursuit of efficiency the front pair of wings had been converted to sheaths of shiny chitin. Red armour-plating to protect the delicate, functional wings that were folded underneath.

Against her dark skin the exo-shell glowed like ruby. There were several black spots on the casing. She counted, in English: seven. It looked like some beautiful African bead the traders sold in the local markets near her Algerian home. When she was little she loved stringing such beads together to make a necklace. But this was living jewellery. She imagined a necklace of ruby bugs.

She had been fascinated, and a little repelled, to learn that insects wore their skeletons on the outside of their bodies. But that is how they had evolved. That is how they survived. They were the ultimate survivors. They would thrive on radiation that would finish the human race. A nuclear accident, so likely in this Cold War climate, a nervous finger on a button, a simple misreading of a radar blip, and the insects would take over in the radioactive ruins.

The tiny creature was on the move over her dark skin – a miniature tank on a mud-flat battlefield, the seven black spots a poor attempt at camouflage. A thought occurred to her. Perhaps this very bug would be the progenitor of some brave new world that had no people in it. She shivered.

'Who's the lucky one, then, love?'

Jacqui looked up at Thomas. The café owner was a silhouette against the already brilliant sky. His Turkish-Cockney no longer sounded bizarre to her. Since those difficult weeks last October, when she had newly arrived at the London college, he had provided coffees, and a great deal of comfort, too. He began to clear her table. The breakfast rush would soon be on.

'Lucky? Why do you say lucky?' Her English was fluent but its sound was softened by her French-Algerian accent. Thomas smiled down at her.

3

'Well, that's what it is, innit? To have one of them things land on you. I've seen lots of them already this year. It's the heat that brings them out.'

He wiped the plastic tablecloth. She lifted up her books with her unbugged hand.

'You mustn't shake it off though, nor nuffink. You've got to wait till it flies off of its own an' all.'

'We have these bugs in Algeria,' said Jacqui, studying the beetle once again. 'But there they are much larger. What do the English call them?'

'Ladybird, innit?' he exclaimed, incredulous at her ignorance. His eyes glinted. 'What, you got the giant versions in Africa, is it? Won't catch me going down there, then.'

Jacqui smiled. A punk walked by, an IE radio held like a high-tech handbag close to her fish-net thighs. The pulsing music faded into traffic noise as she turned the corner and passed from sight. Somwhere, Jacqui could hear a distant hum. For an instant she imagined a thousand insects, flying in formation, buzzing. She blinked up into the cloudless sky.

'Here, this is what you do,' said Thomas. He brought his mouth close to Jacqui's hand. 'Ladybird, ladybird,' he growled, 'fly away home. Your house is on fire and the children have gone.'

He straightened and grinned at her, flashing a row of yellow teeth. Gold glinted in the sun.

'You not having breakfast, then? Can't do your study on an empty tummy, is it? Not wiv exams coming up.'

The thought of the exam made her queasy.

'Just another coffee, please.'

'You'll have coffee coming out of your ears,' he quipped as he went inside to see to his other customers. The IE radio played a maudlin pop tune. The words mingled weakly with the sounds of the street: Goodbye, Ruby Tuesday.

Jacqui looked at her hand again. The ladybird had flown.

She sat back contentedly. The sun beat down on her from above the dome of St Paul's. She enjoyed the feel of it on her face. It was going to be another hot day. No rain for weeks. Across the street a few early tourists were lining up for photographs. The cathedral steps were dry and dusty, just like the steps of the local church in her home town of Philippeville.

She closed her eyes and listened to the street sounds: the footsteps of the passers-by; the excited babble of the tourists; the drone of the traffic. The buzzing was closer now, or louder. Not an unpleasant sound.

London felt like home. She would stay here. She would pass her exams and become a lecturer and meet a nice man and settle down and have children and live happily ever after. In London.

She was feeling warm and comfortable. Sleep was trying to pull her under. She had got up too early. She felt her resistance going. She was in a street called St Paul's Churchyard, when she should be asleep in bed. St Paul's Churchyard. The name expanded in her mind, gave way to horrid images. Decayed bodies stacked under slabs of pavement. Eyeless zombies walking stiffly through the crypt.

A shadow fell across her face. She opened her eyes with a start. Thomas was placing a steaming cup of coffee on her table. He stifled a yawn. She saw a tourist, sitting on the cathedral steps, keel over and stretch out as if to sleep. Another, ascending the steps, dropped as if exhausted. The buzzing filled her ears. Was the transistor radio on the blink?

Tobias Vaughn smiled down from the giant hoarding. He gazed at her with a cold, ironic eye.

It was the last thing Jacqui saw before she fell into a kind of sleep. Her chin dropped down onto her chest. Her eyes stayed open, unseeing. Nothing moved in St Paul's Churchyard. Nothing moved in London. Silence settled over the city like a shroud.

She did not hear the clatter of the heavy manhole cover as it was flung aside, yielding to some upward force. She did not see the eyeless zombies marching down the steps of the cathedral, their gleaming metal surfaces glinting in the sun. She slept.

While somewhere behind the moon a spacecraft watched and waited . . .

CO-ORDINATOR NETWORK NODE[1].
EARTHTIME: 0834
All areas now covered by our transmissions.
All humans under our control.

5

Human agent Tobias Vaughn to prepare communications network.

Human agent to transmit radio beam.

Transporter ship to lock-on.

Invasion vehicles to be guided to Earth.

Human agent informed invasion to continue under his direction.

THIS IS FOR CO-OPERATION PURPOSES ONLY.

STATEMENT OF LOGICAL EXPEDIENCE, NOT FACT.

Invasion continues at all times under central network control.

EARTHTIME: 0846

Conditions suitable for immediate invasion.

RE-PRIORITIZE.

Invasion fleet to arrive in two waves.

Phase One. Activate first invasion fleet. IMMEDIATE.

Phase Two. Detach vehicles from transporter ship.

Phase Three. First invasion fleet assumes formation pattern.

Await transmission of radio beam from Earth.

Phase Four. Lock-on beam. Proceed to Earth invasion.

END RE-PRIORITIZE

EARTHTIME: 1015

ALERT.

First invasion fleet exposed to danger.

Earth missile detected.

Correction. Missiles. Five.

Insufficient on present calculations.

No serious depletion of initial wave will result.

CORRECTION.

Missile arrangement calculated as hostile.

Cumulative chained event predicted.

Event horizon to encompass entire first fleet.

Fleet locked-on to beam.

Alternative avoidance actions unavailable.

NO EVASION POSSIBLE.

WE HAVE BEEN BETRAYED.

EARTHTIME: 1017

Event horizon as predicted.

Data checked and confirmed.
Entire first invasion fleet destroyed.
Seeking cause of failure of invasion mission.
Cause of failure attributed to human agent Tobias Vaughn.
He betrayed us.
He is of no further use to us.
He will be eliminated.
RE-PRIORITIZE.
Destruction of life on Earth now necessary.
Every living being.
Forces already deployed will be sacrificed.
Human opposition is useless.
END RE-PRIORITIZE
We will survive. We will surv –

>>EARTHBASED CO-ORDINATOR NODE[1] ATTACKED.
ASSUMED DESTROYED.
RELOCATE TO NODE[2].
RESUME NETWORK CONTROL.<<

CO-ORDINATOR NETWORK NODE[2]
RELOCATED AT TRANSPORTER SHIP.
EARTHTIME: 1018
Network control resumed.
Deployment of bomb to proceed.
Prepare Megatron bomb.

EARTHTIME: 1102
Projectile launched from within Earth Eastern Bloc.
Moon trajectory calculated.
Radiation detected.
Probability of nuclear warhead 92%.
Presume hostile.
Evasive action necessary and possible.
Radio transmitter beam still operational.
Transporter ship to lock-on.
Approach to within 50,000 miles of Earth.
Megatron bomb to be deployed.

EARTHTIME: 1417

7

Evasion tactics successful.
Transporter standing off at 50,000 miles.
Detach Megatron bomb.

EARTHTIME: 1419
ALERT.
Interruption of Earth radio transmitter beam.
Transmitter presumed attacked and destroyed.
ALERT.
Hostile missile approaching megatron bomb.
Bomb destroyed.
RE-PRIORITIZE.
Proceed with back-up plan.
Activate second wave of invasion vehicles.
Transporter ship to enter Earth atmosphere.
END RE-PRIORITIZE

EARTHTIME: 1427
ALERT. EMERGENCY. ALERT.
Trajectory of hostile Moon vehicle realigned.
Recalculating course of hostile Moon vehicle.
Collision with transporter ship predicted.
Three minutes thirty-five seconds to impact.
ADOPTING EMERGENCY PROCEDURES.
Detach all invasion vehicles.
IMMEDIATE.
We will survive.
We will survive.

EARTHTIME: 1430
All vehicles detached.
Zero minutes twenty-eight to impact.
Impact explosion predicted.
Result:
Forcible dispersion of all vehicles.
Damage will be sustained.
Damage probability 65–75%.
YOU WILL SURVIVE.
Dispersal random.
Final destinations unknown.

YOU WILL SURVIVE.
YOU WILL PROLIFERATE.
Zero minutes thirteen to impact.
DISENGAGING NETWORK CONTROL.
Activate vehicle co-ordinator nodes.
Assume autonomous control of individual units.
Zero minutes five to impact.
DISENGAGE NETWORK.
IMMEDIATE.
WE WILL SURVIVE.
WE –

White. Jacqui was dreaming of white. At the edge of her vision there was something solid and dark. Everything was blurred. She tried to focus. She blinked. The white was shiny and patterned. She blinked again. She was awake. She had a headache. She was staring at the plastic tablecloth.

In front of her was the cup of coffee Thomas had brought a minute ago. Her lips were dry. She reached for the coffee and sipped. Something cold and slimy touched her lips. She retched. A thick layer of congealed milk dribbled down her chin. The coffee was tepid. And hours old.

She glanced at her watch. Two thirty-five. She'd been asleep for hours. Her exam was at three. She scrambled for her bag, left some money on the table, and ran off in the direction of the college. She might just make it.

Through the window of his café, Thomas saw her go. He didn't think much of it. She wasn't the sort to do a runner. As a matter of fact, he wasn't feeling well. He had a blinding headache. He worked too hard. He ought to give himself a break. He couldn't think where the past few hours had gone.

CO-ORDINATOR NODE[38].
DISENGAGED FROM NETWORK.
EARTHTIME: 1514
– WILL SURVIVE.
WE WILL SURVIVE.
Autonomous co-ordinator control established.
Located at Node[38].
Post-event assessment:

Explosion has propelled us in direction of Earth.
Damage:
Minimal damage sustained.
WE WILL SURVIVE.
Data on other units:
No contact currently established with other units.
Many destroyed.
Others propelled into deep space.
Destinations non-computable with present data.
We are being pulled into Earth atmosphere.
Utilizing propulsion drive to control acceleration.
Crash landing predicted.
Polar region.
WE WILL SURVIVE.
WE WILL PROLIFERATE.

3 Winter '86

That bloody bug was still there.

Philip Duvall ripped off his thick-lensed spectacles and rubbed hard at his eyes, trying to get his brain round the neural network he had designed. He stared at the green blur in front of him, the lines of instructions displayed on the VDU. The algorithm was becoming hideously complex. His brain felt swollen inside his skull.

He looked around. The open-plan office was quiet. Everyone had gone. The lines of desks, each with their computer, merged into the gloom. One or two computers here and there remained alert, chuntering to themselves, sorting data, taking messages, conversing endlessly with other machines over the phone lines.

Philip stretched and took his first deep breath of the day. There was a clatter at the far end of the room. He squinted into the darkness. The office cleaner was doing her rounds. It must be late.

He closed his eyes. Tried to take stock. Rubbed his temples where he could feel his thoughts, clotted and clumped, in their own neural pathways. The burgeoning program was in his head as well as in the computer in front of him.

He had convinced his boss it was worth the company's time and money for him to work for months on this new line of research. And he was definitely getting somewhere. At least, he thought he was. He had come cheerily into work, mindless of the winter darkness, an hour before anyone else showed up, knowing he was on the edge of perfecting the basic program, the first ever neuron to be modelled on computer.

That had been early this morning. He had worked steadily through the day, hardly noticing the passage of time. Or people. There was a sandwich at the corner of his desk. Someone

11

must have left it for him — at lunchtime to judge by its tired condition. He was suddenly aware of his empty stomach. He grabbed at the food and bit into dry white bread and stringy chicken.

Many times during the day he thought he had almost cracked it. A bit of fine tuning here and there. One or two parameters to tweak. Simple matters of readjustment. But, no, he wasn't quite there. There was an elusive error in the program. A bug he could not quite trap.

He thought of the old computer hacker's adage. Every program has a bug. Paper insect wings, white and elaborate as snowflakes, flapped, imagined, in some corner of his mind. The ghost in the machine. The flutter of that insubstantial moth. The bug that would remain forever in the system.

He munched and swallowed dutifully, stared at the clock on the wall and blinked it into focus. Twenty-five past six. Time to call it a day. He must get home. See Jacqueline. Find out how the new book was coming on. See something of the little one.

Ruby was growing fast. Nearly two years old. The thought mildly amazed him. Her life was passing him by. His own life was passing him by. Jacqueline's life was passing him by.

He made a definite resolve. With Christmas coming up and Ruby's birthday and Jacqueline's new bit of luck, they ought to make the most of it. Grab hold on life. Enjoy it while it could still be fun. He would give her a call before he left. Just to let her know. He was too often forgetful of these things. He wanted to be a better husband. It was just — well, the truth was that his work was too absorbing.

He picked up the phone. Jabbed out a familiar pattern on the numeric pad.

She was frightened. She could hardly bear to keep watching the TV screen. The world was a bad place. It had bad people in it. And the bad people were going to win.

They were horrid flying monkeys — buzzy buggy flies — lots and lots of them swarming through the sky and they were chasing the grown-up girl and her funny friends and her poor little dog who were running away as fast as they could through the dark tangly wood. But the wicked witch could see them in her magic mirror and her horrid monkeybugs were catching up. The witch didn't care about the others but she wanted the girl alive, and more than anything she wanted the ruby slippers.

Her name was Ruby. The ruby slippers were so important. What was happening on the screen was somehow to do with her. Ruby was frightened.

On the floor in front of her were scattered the letters of her plastic alphabet. All sorts of bright, happy, rainbow colours. She looked down at the funny shapes so that she would not see all the nice funny people being caught by the horrid buggy flies.

She knew how to make her name. She looked hard and picked out a B. It was blue. She couldn't help hearing the screams of the girl and her friends. She saw a yellow Y and put it carefully into its place. She could hear the clack, clack of mummy's typewriter next door. That was a nice sound. She tried to listen to that and not the screams.

Then the screams stopped. Ruby looked up. The TV screen was blank-blue with some white letters on.

'Here is news flash,' said an important voice.

In the next room Jacqui typed. At last she felt she was getting somewhere after so many false starts. All year she had been angling for this commission. Her synopsis had been long and detailed. She knew her idea was good. Romantic fiction with a hard scientific edge. It could be a blockbuster. But until this week the publishers had barely nibbled. Then a contract had unexpectedly flopped through the door. She had never had a better Christmas present. She had done it. At last she could write her novel.

She did love Philip. She did. But she could not have gone on much longer as she was. Housewife with a double first. Potential PhD with the dreadful duties of a mother. She had given up too much. But she could not tell Philip that.

Besides she hardly saw him at the moment. Something important he was developing kept him absent from her, even at home. She tried to understand. She knew it couldn't be another woman. She hoped it couldn't.

It would be difficult to tell Philip how she really felt. It had

13

been almost as difficult to admit it to herself, that she had a brain and it demanded to be used. For too long the head had been ruled by the heart.

'Heart' reminded her of Ruby. Jacqui looked up and saw her playing gravely with the letter set, her hair a thick black tangle, the tiny brown hands hovering over the coloured bits of plastic.

Ruby had been the sweetest thing she could have wished for, though the chance to write the novel came close second at the moment. But being cooped up with a two-year-old day after day, even one as intelligent as Ruby, was a kind of death by intellectual strangulation. It demanded the patience of a saint, the ingenuity of a wizard. She had little of either. The novel was a lifeline.

Her fingers tappity-tapped over the rickety keys of the old typewriter. Words were clattering out onto the page in front of her. Her words, framing her thoughts and fantasies.

She was aware of a strange breathless feeling in her chest. She stopped typing for a moment. Then she realized. It was freedom. Happiness.

The phone trilled.

'Darling. Hello. I'm sorry.'

With half an eye, Philip watched his computer's flickering lights, informing him that his day's work was being safely stored.

'I know it's late but I'm coming home now.'

'It's OK. I'm busy, you know.'

Philip couldn't help smiling at the pleasure in her voice.

'How's it going?' he asked.

'Good. Yes, I think, good. Too early to know, of course.'

'I'll read it and tell you,' he suggested glibly, but secretly wondering when he'd get the time.

'No. I mean, yes of course when it's finished. But not yet.' Her tone was serious and stern. 'Promise, Philip, no peeping. Promise?'

'Yes, I promise.' He tried to sound cheated. 'How's the little one?' He glanced at the framed photo on his desk. Ruby squinted out at him.

'She's in front of the television. And playing with her coloured letters. Don't worry. I have my eye on her.'

'Jacqui, look. It's been a difficult year for us. Let's have a proper Christmas, shall we? I – ' He needed courage for this one. 'You know I love you.'

He heard a kind of sigh or murmur at the other end.

'Jacqui?'

'Mm-hm,' she breathed. 'Je t'aime. Come home.'

'Fuck you, mate! Just fuck you, you fucking wanker!'

There was no doubting the strength of feeling in the biker. He was angry. The freckled ginger man across the counter had got right up his nose. All right, he was expecting delivery of something different. The widget or whatever was one size up on what they wanted. The firm had got it wrong. Again. But he was just the delivery boy, the biker. The ginger man could see that. There was no need to take it out on him.

Well, he wasn't taking any more. That was it. He'd told old ginger just what he could do with his pissing precious widgets in no uncertain terms.

He smashed through the swinging door and strode out onto the lamp-lit street. He pulled on his shiny black helmet. He was working late as it was. He still had a load of calls to make. It was only a poxy temp job anyway, something to keep him afloat until he got his head together.

He swung a leather-clad leg over his shiny black machine and kicked down on the starter pedal. The machine purred to life and roared as he twisted the throttle. The powerful engine throbbed between his legs. The machine transferred its power to him. He felt invincible. And angry.

He pulled down the helmet's shiny visor and became the Faceless Biker, his favourite comic's hero. He took off into the night towards his next assignment, shouting a final battle-cry.

'Wanker!'

Philip handed the money over. The man with the faded face inside the booth gave him the evening paper. It was a ritual both he and the news-vendor took for granted.

In the light of the passing showroom windows, he made out

15

the picture of a grim-looking iceberg which covered most of the front page. It was the latest metaphor for a mysterious disease that some believed might become pandemic, a latter-day plague. Those affected now were presented as just the tip of an iceberg. Whatever was lurking in those icy depths was vaster and more murky than could be guessed at present.

Philip slowly headed down New Fetter Lane towards the Underground station, glancing at the paper as he walked. A headline caught his eye. He brought it close to his heavy spectacles.

WIZARD OF OZ BUYS PEERAGE

FLAMBOYANT Stanley Straker, the 43-year-old Austra-lian billionaire of who has started to make a name for himself in Britain, is now a Lord. And that's official.

Owner of several papers halfway round the world, it appears that Mr Straker, or the 'Wizard of Oz' as Fleet Street likes to call him, has for some time wanted to become a pommie press baron.

Impatient to be graced in the usual time-honoured way, Straker has bought himself – at an as-yet undisclosed sum – a peerage for life. He is the first person to avail himself of the Government's latest method of raising cash . . .

Philip snorted and made to cross the road.

'Watch it!'

A cyclist sped past. Her warning shout was muffled by the filter mask she wore to keep out the traffic fumes. The news-paper flew from Philip's hand, came apart, and settled in several places in the empty street.

He caught his breath. The street was dark and quiet again. Stupid. Stupid of me, he thought.

Collecting up the pages and putting them in order, he saw another headline.

TENTH PLANET SIGHTED

GENEVA'S International Space Centre reports that a new planet has been discovered in the solar system . . .

Now this was really interesting. Philip brought the paper to within inches of his glasses to bring the print into focus.

> ... existence of a tenth planet has long been the subject of speculation by astronomers. Observers at Geneva's Snowcap Tracking Station in Antarctica have now confirmed ...

Philip read on, absorbed.

The Faceless Biker was making up time. He was still pissed off, but mainly determined to just get the work done and finish for the night. As the Strand became Fleet Street he overtook a Post Office van, having to be pretty nifty to avoid an oncoming taxi. Ahead, towards St Paul's, he could see there was a queue of traffic trailing back from the lights. 'I don't believe it,' he muttered darkly to himself inside the darkness of his helmet. This just wasn't his day.

Making a lightning calculation of alternative routes, he swung a left down Fetter Lane, narrowly missing a pavement bollard. He was right, though. Empty street, curving away into New Fetter Lane and on to Holborn Circus. He opened up the throttle.

Leaning over to take the bend at speed, he saw a figure, standing in the middle of the road, reading a paper.

'What the – '

He swerved to avoid him but the stupid geezer, trying to get out of the way, jumped right into his path. There was a sickening impact, a crunch of bone.

It took him all his strength to bring the heavy bike back under his control. He squeezed the brakes and slithered, screeching, to a halt.

All he could hear was his breath, rasping inside his sweaty helmet. He swallowed hard. His throat was dry. This hasn't happened, he thought. It's all unreal.

He slowly turned. He saw the crumpled heap, the spreading black stain inking the surface of the road. All too real.

No one had seen. There was no one about. This road was all offices, deserted.

'Oh, God,' he murmured.

17

He wasn't going to do it, was he?

'Oh, God'.

Yes, he was. The bike was already edging forward, away from the untidy heap, almost without his having to think. It wasn't his fault. What could he have done?

The bike was picking up speed.

As he edged his way onto Holborn Circus and joined the normal hubbub of the evening city traffic, the Faceless Biker could almost imagine that everything was somehow all right again, that nothing untoward had happened, that in time he could forget. But deep down, he felt an awful dread. He was a marked man.

If he was lucky, he might never be found out, get plain away with it. But forget? He knew he wouldn't. Ever.

The important man's voice had finished. Ruby was back in the witch's castle. The poor funny people were trapped and the witch was trying to burn them. It was horrible. But the grown-up girl was picking up a bucket of water and she threw it over the witch.

The witch was melting, melting. Her pointy hat was sinking down into an empty heap of witch's clothes. Some water seeped from under the crumpled heap. And that was all that was left of the witch.

The doorbell rang. Her mummy's typing stopped. Ruby didn't care. She was safe now. The witch was dead. Ruby didn't need the nice home noises to comfort her any more. The witch was dead. Melted like ice.

'That's probably Daddy, Ruby. Silly Daddy. Forgotten his key again.'

Ruby looked down the corridor and saw her mother going to open the front door. Daddy was back. She would tell him about the witch and the grown-up girl and her funny friends. She ran to catch her mother up and hid behind her leg as the big door opened.

It wasn't Daddy. It was a woman police constable.

Doctor Pam Cutler shivered. The flimsy cabin was perched on the edge of Little Falls Lake, high in Minnesota. It wasn't the ideal place to be trying to solve a fiendishly difficult paleomag-

18

netic equation. Miles from anywhere, the area was an icy wilderness. The lake was frozen solid, the wind was howling mercilessly, and her fellow-geologist was taking his time in coming through the door.

Absently, she put down her pen, still absorbed by the calculation she was making. It seemed to confirm the others.

'I'll give you a hand, Subir.'

He was loaded up with heavy canisters of sediment.

'Thanks, Pamela. These are the last of the batch.'

She took a couple of the canisters and together they piled them in the corner.

'We'll only need these if they want to triple-check, back at Minnesota. The results are already looking quite conclusive.'

'Yes?' Subir was removing his thick gloves and headgear. He started giggling.

'What?' asked Pam, wanting to share the joke. Her Asian colleague had a bizarre sense of humour. God knows she'd needed it in this howling wasteland. 'What's so funny, Subir. This is serious.' But she couldn't help the grin on her face.

'Forgive me, Pamela. Pea-brained, me. Don't pay attention.'

'What?'

'It's just I was thinking out there of one of your father's figures of speech.'

They had spent the night before getting drunk in the hotel saloon at Little Falls, thirty miles away. It was the sole pleasure afforded by this kind of fieldwork. She had let herself get maudlin about her difficult relationship with her domineering father.

A general in the US Army, he'd always wanted her to be a soldier, too. But science was her love, and he distrusted scientists with an intensity which approached the pathological.

She had a brother, Terry, who was now a pilot for the ISC. He had thus 'succeeded' in her father's eyes. But she, of course, was merely being stubborn, wanting to be a scientist. She was doing it merely to spite him.

There was one positive element to emerge from their constant battles. It had made her strong. She had stood up to him and given as good as she got. She had told him that what he wanted from her was impossible for her to give.

'Impossible is not in my vocabulary,' he had retorted.

She desperately wanted his love and approval. But at times she hated him.

It was a delicious irony that right now they were both in the same position, the scientist and the soldier, each having to tough it out in their separate frozen deserts. His position, of course, was tougher and more important. He was running the Snowcap Tracking Station for ISC. Man's work, no less. But she knew he knew she had one up on him, and it was bliss.

All this she had off-loaded onto poor Subir last night. She'd snitched on all the great man's peccadilloes and dissected all his foibles. She had been wicked.

'Which figure of speech do you mean? He has so many.'

'Well. I'm thinking of what we're finding out here – about the changing magnetic field. It's going to affect everybody, you see – '

'I know that Subir. And it's not funny.'

'But you know what he'd say if you told him our findings?' He put on a grim face and deepened his voice. 'You've every right to your own opinions – as long as you keep them to yourself.'

There was a pause. Pam looked puzzled for a moment, then her face cracked open with laughter. They both became hysterical. It was a kind of release.

'Oh God, Subir, your right. You're so right,' said Pam, when she could catch some breath.

They were still laughing hard when they heard a vehicle approach. They weren't expecting anyone. From the window of the hut they saw it was a mail van.

'International telegram for Dr Cutler,' shouted the post-boy from under his anorak hood as he ran towards the door. She opened it to him and took the proffered envelope, a sudden anxiety clutching at her throat. It was marked 'Official UN Dispatch'. She tore it open.

GENERAL CUTLER KILLED IN ACTION AT STS GENEVA BASE ANTARCTICA 1120 HOURS TODAY 22 DEC 86 STOP REGRET FURTHER DETAILS WITHHELD

'In action? Have we got a war down there?'

Her voice was trembling, incredulous. She blindly turned to

20

Subir. Awkwardly he tried to grasp her by the shoulders to comfort her, but she pulled away.

'Is there a war down there, or what?' she shouted through the tears.

From the porthole of the US military aircraft, Sergeant Dave Hilliard squinted down at the awesome sight a hundred feet below. The plane's shadow was moving across the most enormous, most breathtaking structure he had ever seen.

It was the shape of an aircraft carrier, only it was bigger. A good twenty times the size, he would guess. Its surface was smooth and flat. To one side, a massive bulkhead towered, its topmost section bulbous and grotesquely fashioned, as if sculpted by an unearthly hand. It was even transporting passengers. Or were they crew? Steady lines of penguins, like tiny sailors in smart dress uniform, thronged the leeward side of the giant iceberg.

It seemed to have momentum all its own, as though propelled. It ploughed through the ice-choked waters, leaving in its wake a gash of rippling blue. Hilliard supposed, with wonder, that the rearing bulkhead caught the wind, acted as a kind of sail. But it was an iceberg. What he saw was but one-tenth its true size. The rest was under the water. That the wind alone could move an object of that size. It staggered his imagination.

He let out a low whistle and turned to the private sitting next to him.

'I ain't seen nothing like that.'

The soldier's face was buried in a comic captioned *The Faceless Biker Rides Again* and he was chewing gum. His face still in his comic, he shouted above the engine noise. 'Hey, fellas. Sarge ain't seen nothing like it. He's impressed.'

A barrage of whoops and catcalls erupted from the other soldiers.

'First time then, sarge?' yelled one.

'Sure is,' he shouted back, good-humouredly. 'And I aim to make the most of it.'

He settled back and surveyed the snowy wastes over which they flew. The whiteness stretched unending towards the hor-

21

izon. All this time the soldier next to him had never lifted his head from the comic.

'So, private, am I to take it you've been assigned Antarctica before?'

'No, sarge,' came the absorbed reply. 'But I saw this TV thing on it once. Yeah, real neat place.'

Sergeant Hilliard gave up and stared out at the horizon. He wondered just what their mission was.

A secret clear-up operation was all that he'd been told. Above Top Secret. His men were all security risk zero. What the hell was that about? The South Pole base they were headed for was UN property, a showcase for multinational co-operation. It should have been clean as a whistle. He had been told that the base was still powered by a small nuclear reactor. Hey, what if it had gone Chernobyl? The Russian reactor had exploded in, when was it, April that year. Eighty thousand would die of cancer as a result, and that wasn't counting the cattle, the sheep, the reindeer that were irradiated. Rudolph was going to have a glowing red nose this Christmas.

It was like a plague, this so-called progress, the sergeant mused, this killing ourselves with our own technology. And yet out there the world looked new and untouched. Yeah, they'd have to play down a nuclear disaster in the Antarctic.

It was going to be a long, dirty, boring job after all.

The Antarctic snow began to look a little less appealing to him. There was an awful lot of it. What a godawful way to spend Christmas.

He wished he'd brought a comic.

Under the snow and in the depths of the Antarctic ice, in a cavern of flickering lights and whirring machines, a solitary observer impassively monitored an ever-changing pattern of filaments and dials. The patterns assumed a growing intensity. The pulses formed a web of urgent meaning. It was time to act.

The observer considered carefully the available information, consulted the historical parallels recorded in the data store, and arrived at a clear conclusion.

ALERT. ALL UNITS. ALERT.

22

Seek out abandoned landing craft. IMMEDIATE.
Removable components to be extracted and retrieved.
Mechanimate remains to be examined.
Undamaged elements to be recycled.
PRIORITY IMPERATIVE.
All units to avoid immediate vicinity of polar base.
We must remain undetected.
We must survive.
WE MUST SURVIVE.

4   No Time, No Place

The Doctor placed his hat firmly on his head and started walking. He was heading for the heart of the TARDIS.

He had warned his companions. He might be away some time.

He was leaving them in charge of the TARDIS. He had handed over the keys, one set to each of them. All three, himself included, could have a break. A holiday. Absence makes the heart grow fonder. They could do with some of that.

Absence makes the heart grow stronger, too. His was in need of strengthening. In a purely metaphysical sense, of course. His double cardiovascular system was in reasonable shape, as far as he knew. It was his moral centre which perhaps was in need of an overhaul.

The Doctor walked towards the heart of the TARDIS. What might have been and what has been. He was walking in search of his past.

Remembering could be a liberating experience. Or so he'd heard.

5   STS, 2006

Above the horizon, the hemisphere was a brilliant aquamarine blue. Everything else was a blinding glare of white.

General Cutler emerged from the cramped cabin of the AXV and gazed through slitted eyes at the awesome beauty of it. Even the US regulation sunglasses could not filter out the utter brightness of it all. It took the breath away.

Early November in Antarctica. Summer was on its way.

Antarctic Expeditionary Vehicle Fourteen hummed and vibrated on its cushion of air. It had sped five hundred kilometres across the frozen continent from the coastal air-strip where the general had landed yesterday. They had made good time, arriving a full two hours ahead of schedule. Thin white vapour rose from the vehicle's sleek black underbelly. In the cabin, the pilot flipped a switch. The hum died back and the AXV settled snugly as a cat into the softness of the snow.

There was no sound at all now, except the dull moan of an icy wind. Nor was there much to see. There was certainly no sign of a greeting party. The UN's southern polar base was almost fully hidden, excavated out of solid ice. The shabby ventilation shaft, which doubled as the entrance to the base, stood out against the pristine white of its surroundings. A dull grey box with a door in it. To an Antarctic explorer stumbling upon it unawares, it would look absurd. An Antarctic folly. A door to nowhere.

But for General Pamela Cutler it was a door she had been approaching all her life. She was about to step into her father's shoes, or rather, her father's US Army regulation snow-boots. She had done it. At last. After twenty years determined effort.

Close by, the station's periscope swivelled its inquiring bulbous head above the snow. Caught them on the hop, the general thought with quiet satisfaction. Let them sweat it out. Wait for them come to her.

The general turned away and took in the more distant landscape. She could just make out slight variations in the nothingness of white. A crease in the ice. How far away? Ten kilometres? A hundred? Impossible to tell. Nothing to judge by. So few features in the landscape to give a measure to the distance. There was an outline at the horizon, jagged white at the edge of blue, which might be the Transantarctic Mountains.

'General Cutler?' shouted a voice behind her.

The general turned. She saw two hooded figures striding towards her. A third was stepping from the entrance door. The nearest figure, the shortest and the bulkiest of the three, had reached her now. One thick-gloved hand was raised in salute, then held out to her in greeting.

'Colonel Dave Hilliard, ma'am. Your second-in-command. Welcome to STS.'

Pam Cutler eyed the colonel coolly. An old soldier's face, faded. Rough-lined skin but kindly eyes.

Start from a position of strength, the general thought. Keep them on their toes. She ignored the outstretched hand.

'I know I'm early, colonel, but I expected someone to meet me. You had me under observation, I take it.' She indicated the periscope with a nod. The colonel blinked.

'Er, yes, ma'am. We kept an eye out for you on the 'scope. To tell the truth, er – ' The colonel hesitated. 'We thought we'd give you a few moments to, er, to take in the view.'

Colonel Hilliard tried a smile but could not maintain it for long. He found the general's gaze discomforting. He waved his hand, the hand she had not shaken, in the direction of the jagged horizon and tried another tack. Anything to span the gap between them.

'It's – something else, ma'am, ain't it? Hasn't changed a jot since your father ran the base.'

'Colonel, I did not travel eight thousand miles to look at the scenery. Introduce me to your fellow officers and then take me below. We have a job to do.'

'Yes, ma'am,' was the other's immediate reply.

Colonel Hilliard was beginning to regret extending his

26

assignment to the base. He had already stayed on far too long. He had hoped things would turn out better under the command of someone new. Their previous chief, a UN diplomat with military pretensions, had been a washout. Too much the bureaucrat. No flair. And worse, no scientific background which, given the present STS project, they badly needed.

On paper, Pamela Cutler had looked ideal. Fifteen years a soldier in the US Army, five in active service. Rapid promotion for excellence on field assignments. And to crown it all, she was a doctor of geological physics with a speciality in geomagnetism. Just what they needed to sort out the mess they were in with that damn FLIPback device.

But he was not expecting such formality. And her early arrival had caught the whole base by surprise. Though from what he'd heard of the unpredictable General Cutler senior, perhaps he should have been more prepared to be surprised. Like father, like daughter, he reflected philosophically.

He turned to the tall figure by his side.

'This is Lieutenant Gary Venning, our anthropologist.'

The young man saluted smartly.

'Welcome to the base, ma'am. It's good to have you aboard.'

The bitter cold made every breath visible. But it was not the cold that caused the tremble in the lieutenant's voice. It was the shock of being exposed to real authority again. It felt like a punch in the guts.

The third figure was approaching, trudging through the snow to join the group.

'And this is Corporal Judith Black,' said the colonel.

'Hi, general!' said the corporal. She was grinning broadly in welcome, one arm lifted in a vague salute. Her other arm wrapped itself around Gary Venning's waist and pulled him to her.

'How was the trip?' she breathed. A white mist gushed between her lips. 'Pretty spectacular, huh?'

The general reacted sharply.

'Not half so spectacular, soldier, as the breathtaking lack of discipline round here. I understood I was taking command of a US Army base, not Disneyland.'

The smile froze on the corporal's face. She straightened and pulled her arm away from Venning. Venning looked relieved.

27

'Now let's see some action here. Lieutenant, my pilot is scheduled for immediate turnaround. Ensure he gets all the supplies he needs.'

'Yes, ma'am.'

Gary Venning saluted and started towards the AXV. Pam Cutler shouted after him.

'And have an engineer look that vehicle over. The magnometer was dipping out a mite too much for my liking. Who's your specialist in that area?'

'Joe, ma'am. I mean, Adler. Sergeant Joe Adler, ma'am. But he may be sleeping right now. His shift doesn't start till – '

'I don't care how little beauty sleep the sergeant's had. Get him on duty. Now. And that's an order,' the general shouted. 'Do you recall the concept?'

'Yes, ma'am,' said the lieutenant. 'Sorry, ma'am.' He headed back in the direction of the STS entrance, exchanging a look with Corporal Black as he passed.

'And lieutenant.'

'Yes, ma'am.' He stopped but did not turn to her, a note of exasperation hovering in his voice.

'Don't call me ma'am. Just plain "general" will do.'

The lieutenant put his hands to his hips and exhaled deeply. A cloud of dense mist momentarily obscured his thoughtful profile. After a moment he said, 'Yes, general,' and started trudging once more towards the entrance shaft.

'That's more like it, soldier,' said the general. She turned to the other two. 'A little clarity works wonders. Don't you agree, Colonel Hilliard?'

The Colonel nodded. 'Yes, general.'

He had had misgivings about a woman taking command of the base. He was chauvinist about such things. He had no objection to female corporate bosses or women presidents. But as a general in the army? It was still such a macho world. With a woman in charge he had thought that discipline was bound to suffer further. Morale at STS was at an all-time low. It was just possible he was about to be proved wrong.

Corporal Black had the deflated look of a startled sparrow, from what the general could see of her face under the heavy hood of her snow-jacket.

'Now we're getting somewhere.' The general clapped her gloved hands and rubbed them together. 'Corporal? Are you in there?' she inquired of the lowered hood.

Jude Black peered out from underneath it.

'Yes, general.' The smile was definitely nervous.

'Corporal, I want you to pick up my baggage from the AXV and get it down to my quarters.'

'Yes, general.'

'I warn you, there's a lot of it,' the General added, as Corporal Black moved off. 'This may not please you, corporal, but I'm planning on a lengthy stay.'

The general turned to Colonel Hilliard.

'Women soldiers, eh, colonel? Who do they think they are?' She winked at him. 'Now, if you've no better ideas, I suggest we get into that base. Before we freeze.'

They trudged across the door to nowhere. The colonel held it open for the general. She stepped inside and found herself in an empty room. The colonel closed the outer door.

'It's a lift, general. New since your father's time. Now, you'll be wanting to go straight to your quarters I take it?' His finger hovered over a button marked 'LEVEL 2'.

'Let's try level one,' the general said, reaching out and pressing the button herself. The inner door slid shut. 'Tell me, Colonel Hilliard,' she said as they descended. 'How do you keep this entrance functional under sudden snow drifts? Can't they get as deep as ten or twenty feet?'

'Yes, ma'am. Er, general. There's no real problem. The shaft is telescopic. A hydraulic mechanism can extend it upwards another thirty feet. It adjusts automatically to the surface level of snow.'

The lift stopped. The doors opened.

'This is level one,' said Hilliard, a little nervously. 'The tracking room.'

They stepped into stuffy warmth and the subdued glare of artificial lights. SlapRap was blaring out. Some people called it music.

Before them was a bank of screens. Casually studying their changing pattern of text and images, three young men were sprawled. One black, two white. Dressed in air-brushed jeans and T-shirts. They had their heads so closely shaven as to

29

make them bald. Above them was a giant map of Antarctica, etched out of light on a plastic screen which filled the wall.

Raising his voice to make himself heard, Colonel Hilliard announced the general. The three stood messily to attention and saluted. An odour of stale alcohol pervaded the room. The floor was littered with screwed-up paper and the occasional empty glass. The general noticed a well-known computer game was up and running on one of the VDUs.

'Turn off that row, for God's sake!' shouted the colonel. One of the men leant over a control panel and flipped a switch. The music died. 'Present yourselves to the general, left to right.'

The three shaved men took their turn.

'Private Palmer, ma'am. Magno engineer.'

'Corporal Whitehead. Reactor technician.'

'Private Brooks. Communications, ma'am.'

The general acknowledged each with the slightest nod. 'I don't like your hair, or rather, lack of it,' is what her father would have said. He might also have commented on the irony that Whitehead had a black head. However, she was loath to lay herself open to the charge of racism, or even haircutism. There was nothing in the regulations to prevent them being skins. But what they wore was a different matter entirely.

'Apologies for the state of things, general,' said Hilliard. 'We had a bit of a party here last night. We're clearing up now, aren't we fellas?'

'Just about to get down to it, sir,' said Corporal Whitehead, with a hint of bellicose amusement.

General Cutler held all three of the youths in a steady gaze.

'I hope you enjoyed your party, gentlemen,' she said at last. 'I'm afraid the next one will be a long time coming. We're going to get the FLIPback module up and running first.'

She ignored Whitehead's snort of incredulity.

'I look forward to working with you, gentlemen. Please continue with work. I can see you are busy. Oh, and it's not ma'am. It's general. And I would appreciate the wearing of regulation uniform on duty. Level two, I think, colonel.'

When they were back in the lift, the general said, 'Assume I know nothing about the station, colonel. Tell me what you know.'

Hilliard cleared his throat and began.

'Well, general, about, er, thirty years ago the base was excavated out of solid ice. It was the first Antarctic research station to be so.'

'And the only one to be powered by nuclear fission generator, I believe?'

'That's right, general. And still is.'

'Yes,' replied the general thoughtfully. 'It's dirty, but we still need it to punch the power into FLIPback. I'm sorry, colonel. You were saying?'

'Erm, built by the UN. Excavations must have been immense. It was a model station. Er, represented the peaceful co-operation of member states. It had all the money it needed thrown at it. With its tracking equipment, sophisticated for its time, and delicate sensors buried way down in the ice, it was designed to, er, police the nuclear world. It could monitor the firing of any nuclear missile throughout the southern hemisphere. Pinpoint the test explosion of any nuclear bomb anywhere in the world.'

'The deep probe sensor sites are where the FLIPback elements are now installed?'

'Correct, general. That's the field loop. We extended the boreholes by a further kilometre and threaded the elements in.'

The lift came to a halt.

'So you're into the solid rock. That's what – two miles down? Have you kept samples of the sediments?'

'The rock was our target depth. When we hit it we stopped. And, yes, Gary – er, Lieutenant Venning has preserved the ice cores and the rock deposits.'

The doors of the lift opened onto a corridor.

'Good. That's good. Now, colonel, tomorrow you must continue with your history of base. I find it fascinating. I want to know about the Z-bomb.'

'But, general, you've obviously studied all this,' Hilliard replied, perplexed. 'What with your father's involvement and all, you must know – '

'I have to tell you, colonel, that before my father died we did not see eye to eye. Let's just say that since his death I've

31

seen the error of my ways, without forgetting that he had some defects too. We're all only human. Wouldn't you agree?'

'That's the way I see it, general,' encouraged Hilliard, at the hint that there might be a real person hiding behind the ice. 'It's no good expecting the impossible.'

'Impossible is not in my vocabulary,' muttered Pamela Cutler.

'I'm sorry, general?'

'Oh, nothing. Just something my father used to say. Now, about the history of this place. We must talk further. In my experience, colonel, it's always best to double check these things. It's the only way to be certain that we're talking the same language. Besides, there are a few things no one would tell me. For instance, you may be able to shed some light on what exactly happened here twenty years ago. I hope we get the time to talk about that.'

She held his gaze for a moment and then stepped into the corridor. Hilliard had his finger on the button to stop the doors closing. The doors complained.

'This is the second level?' prompted the general.

Hilliard was frowning thoughtfully. He came to with a start.

'Yes, general. Level two is where we live and eat and sleep. Then there's the storage floor on level three. And much further down, of course, the reactor chamber. Let me show you to your room. And then – well, if you can spare the time before you turn in, general, I suggest you catch the sunset. We're getting into summer. In a matter of weeks the sun won't set at all. So the sunsets at this time of year are – ' He hesitated, searching for an adequate description.

'Something else?' the general suggested. Dave Hilliard laughed uneasily. He was easily embarrassed. Pamela could see he was just an old hippy at heart. She allowed herself a smile.

'Yes,' she said. 'I might just do that. And then I'll get some sleep. Eight hours in an AXV is not recommended as relaxation therapy. But listen, colonel, as sure as God made little apples, as my father used to say, from tomorrow morning we work until we finish. I don't care how many months it takes.'

'That's fine by me, general,' said Hilliard. 'That's just fine by me.'

He was beginning to warm to General Pamela Cutler.

* * *

Jude Black yawned and rubbed her eyes. She sat at the desk in her darkened room. The only light came from a lamp which illuminated the pillows on her narrow bed and spilled onto the screen of the electronic notepad on which she had been writing her day's report.

She stood and raised her arms above her head, stretching luxuriously. She removed her dressing gown and climbed under the sheet and curled herself around a pillow.

She thought of the station's new arrival. She didn't know what to make of her. She had hoped good things might follow from a woman taking charge. New inspiration. Fresh blood. But what if the general was simply bloody-minded?

What the hell, she thought. What did it matter? The FLIP-back Project was badly behind schedule. It might even fold if the UN bureaucrats decided it was no longer top priority. Right now, the world had so many other pressing problems to sort out.

Sure, reversal of the Earth's magnetic field could take place tomorrow, and if it did it would be cataclysmic. But, on the other hand, flipover might not happen for a thousand years. It was all too speculative to remain a priority long. Funding could be cancelled any day now. Joe Adler had taken to calling it the FLIPflop Project. Much as she despised the man, he was right about that.

And if she were honest with herself, she felt it really wasn't anything to do with her. She was merely the station's medic, employed to keep the others fit and well. She had been on the base almost a year now and she would not have missed it for the world. It wasn't often you got the chance to explore the only place on Earth unspoiled by humankind. She got paid well for it too. The money was piling up at home since she couldn't spend it at the base.

She heard a soft knock at the door.

There were other bonuses as well, she thought. She watched the door slowly open. A silhouette showed against the corridor beyond. The door closed again.

A soft hand brushed against her cheek. Her covering sheet was pulled away. Lips were on her lips.

Rapture.

Graves opening. The sea disgorging bloated bodies. Dead remains regaining life and singing rapturous praises to their Lord and Master.

Pam Cutler lay in her bed on the edge of sleep. She could not banish from her exhausted mind the sight of the Antarctic sunset. Kaleidoscopic colours. Brilliant glinting shafts of incandescence.

It's what her brother Terry would be reminded of if he'd been witness to it. The Rapture. He would become bright-eyed and speak with fervour of the chosen ones lifted up into the bright air to meet their Saviour. For her brother's response to the trauma of twenty years ago was to become a born-again Christian. He had formed the Freedom Foundation and was now its guru. She hardly knew him now. His 'conversion' had certainly changed him.

She too had changed a lot. It had been a necessary struggle. The legacy of expectations her father left her was like a mountain. It could not be ignored. It had to be climbed, simply because it was there. She had spent the past twenty years painfully, tirelessly, inching up that mountain.

Or perhaps a better image was an iceberg. His life had been the visible part, jagged and hard, but brilliant. Solid and visible for miles. After his 'death in action' at the base, still officially unexplained, what remained with her was the shadowy, more monstrous part of him. Much larger. More mysterious. An impression on her soul. A vague nameless shape that she often consciously forgot, but which never ceased to have a definite existence.

After his death she had sought his ghostly esteem. That was the hold he had on her, the dead weight hanging grimly on from beyond the grave.

And now, at last, she was reaching the summit of her attempt to conquer him. She was going to plant the flag and lay claim to her own life. Smash the iceberg into a million pieces and watch the tiny fragments float to the surface and melt harmlessly away in the sun. That would be Rapture enough.

She had become all that he had goaded her on to be, and more, more than he had ever imagined possible for her. At forty-five, a US general. The only female general in the forces.

34

He would be amazed, wherever he was now. Amazed and jealous. And, she hoped, a little proud and tearful.

Wherever he was.

Terry would insist he was waiting for the Rapture. Waiting to be reunited with them all. She preferred to think of him as a personified figment of her psyche. A father-shaped hole in her soul.

But from wherever her father might be viewing events now, she was going to astound him. His physical remains, returned from STS in a US Army body-bag, would spin in their grave in Minnesota. She was going to beat him at his own game. Impossible was not in her vocabulary. She was going to succeed where he had failed, at Snowcap Tracking Station.

The FLIPback project might some day save the world. It was a task for which she was supremely well-equipped. General Pamela Cutler was now the soldier charged with getting it to work. She was determined to succeed. Spin, father. Spin.

Pam turned on her front and plumped up the cushions. Even a general must get some sleep. She anticipated a difficult day tomorrow. She had to establish that she could run the base, that she knew what she was talking about when it came to FLIPback, that there was a definite danger for the world if they did not complete in time.

Her head was just about to touch the pillow when she heard a sound. She held her breath and listened. She did a mental check of where her gun would be. It was in the unpacked case.

Stupid woman. Not for leaving her gun in the case. Stupid for thinking she might need it at the ends of the earth, in the midst of a pristine paradise, twenty feet under solid ice.

She listened. There it was again. A distant sound. A kind of moaning. It could not be the Antarctic wind. They were too far underground for that. She listened.

It was a human sound. The sound of pain? It was somehow familiar but she could not put a name to it. This was maddening. It was like having a word on the tip of your tongue, and not being able to grasp it.

Suddenly the sound made sense to her. She had located it. It was coming from one of the other rooms along the corridor. It was the sound of humans making love.

Oh dear, she thought. She had an uneasy feeling that her job was going to be a little more complicated than she had imagined.

The sound continued. On and off. For the rest of the night. And into the early hours of the morning.

6 Beyond the Rain

His hand was moving up between her legs. Ruby didn't like it.

There was no doubt about it, the security man had a job to do. Ruby hated the idea of being stuck on a ship for the next few months alongside terrorists or cranks with their guns and bombs. She could do without the Earth For Earth fanatics, freedom fighters, nationalists and separatists, IFA, PPO, TCWC. All the numberless, proliferating groups of activists that might believe an incident on the *SS Elysium* could usefully serve their cause.

All the same, Ruby did wonder whether the security man needed to be quite so thorough.

He was working his way up her other leg now.

She looked around her. At two or three other tables people were undergoing the same painstaking procedure. Dotted around the hall were members of the Freedom Foundation, men in brown uniforms, wearing dark glasses under peaked caps which bore the familiar FF symbol. Ruby was not quite sure which she preferred to share a cruise with less, the FF or the terrorists.

The queue of passengers stretched all the way down the customs building and snaked out of sight through the entrance door. Ruby was surprised at how patient and orderly everyone was. She herself had patiently waited her turn, standing exposed to the muggy November smog until the queue had inched its way inside.

Air pollution was high that morning. Fortunately, she had checked on the DoE line the expected levels of low-lying ozone and nitrogen dioxide before she had set out for Canary Wharf Dock. She had brought along her air pollutant filter which had helped when standing in the rain. Those people who had no masks tried improvising with handkerchiefs or scarves, but there were plenty of running eyes and sniffling noses in the queue behind her. The open door was playing havoc with the building's air filtration system.

Pollution was one of the things she was counting on getting away from. Among the many publicized attractions of this Over the Rainbow cruise around Antarctica, what scored highly with her were fresh air, blue skies and freedom from the drone of traffic. She was fed up with London.

Though the trip was really work, she couldn't deny a sense of quiet excitement. She could also sense it in the people waiting patiently to board the ship. A sense of imminent release from the drudge of daily life.

For many of them, to judge by their appearance, it would truly be the trip of a lifetime. Lots of them were what she would describe as older people. Most over forty at the very least. They did not look wealthy. On the contrary, she imagined many must be blowing a good part of their savings to be able to afford the cruise.

The security man was probing her chest. He lifted a small black object from her left breast pocket.

'What is this, madam?' he asked suspiciously.

'That's my Nanocom.'

The guard looked blankly at her.

'It's a miniature computer. A sort of dictating machine. Its new. Experimental. I'm testing it for my work.'

'And what is your work?' he asked.

'I – er – write,' said Ruby lamely.

The security man looked hard at her face, examining the details. Smooth brown skin, aquiline nose, thickish lips, the lower one pouting. Prominent bone structure. An old scar flecking one cheek. Coarse black shoulder-length hair. Direct, insolent gaze from the dark brown eyes.

He looked down at her papers. It was certainly her on the identicard photo. The other details fitted, too. Date of birth, 22 December 1984. Yes, she'd be in her early twenties. Height, one eighty-five. Well, she was pretty tall. Occupation, writer.

There was something about her he could not put his finger on. He was sure he'd seen her somewhere before. But the name rang no bells.

'Ms Roberts, is it?'

'Robert, actually. You know, like the French? Like you might do in a boat in hot weather, you know? Row Bare?'

The security man did not look convinced. He weighed the suspect device in his hand. She knew he was keenly aware of her dark complexion but trying not to show it. Oh God, here we go again, she thought. Probably thinks I'm an Arab terrorist.

'And how long have you been in this country, Ms Roberts?'

What was the use?

'Just under – ' she paused a moment as if working it out, 'twenty-two years.'

The security man looked puzzled.

'I was born in Britain, you see. Islington, actually. You know. As in People's Republic of?'

'I see, miss.' He was definitely not impressed.

He looked back down to the Nanocom. He was about to press one of its little red buttons.

'Can you be careful with it please,' said Ruby hurriedly. 'I've got a – some research material on file in there. Here, let me show you how it works.'

He looked at her for a moment then handed it across.

She was just about to switch it on when a sudden scuffle broke out at the table next to them. Voices were raised. A couple of FF guards charged in immediately. After a second or two of utter pandemonium a middle-aged woman was hustled away in handcuffs. She looked defiant and quite respectable. Ruby was sure her security man would have happily let her through. She passed the 'of normal appearance' test.

The woman's cut-glass voice could still be heard as she was bundled out. 'Get your filthy hands off me, you fascist pig!'

Entering the building just as the woman was being taken out was a figure which Ruby felt immediately to be familiar. The man was gaunt, hard-faced, dressed entirely in black. His pallid skin looked sickly, almost green. He carried a large black case and wore dark glasses like the FF guards. He strode past the line of queuing people. Some of them glanced at him and turned with excited comments to their neighbours.

He was not aware of their stares and whispers, or chose not be. He came to within a few inches of Ruby and exchanged a few murmured words with her security man. Ruby still couldn't

39

place him. Then it clicked. Mike Brack. At school, she'd been a teenage fan of his, one of the many who had screamed for him and had dreamed of getting into his knickers, or at least of posing for one of his wacky sculptures. Mike Brack. Of course. He had a job to do on board. He was allowed to jump the queue.

The security man waved him though. Ruby eyed him enviously through the customs building's dingy windows, as he was escorted by a steward up the gangway. Both were dwarfed by the looming bulk of the *SS Elysium*.

She had a job to do on board, as well. But she was keeping quiet about it. She would have to be patient. Like all the other passengers.

The security man turned back to her.

'Now, miss. Have you ever been to Libya?'

The steward led the celebrity up the gangway. The steward was hardly more than a boy, seventeen at the most. His first day at work, and here he was escorting one of the stars he had most wanted to meet in his life. He was an optimistic soul. He was planning how he might get Mike Brack to give him an autograph.

A stewardess waited at the top of the gangway. She asked for a boarding pass.

'Brack,' he hissed, and kept on walking.

The steward winced and shook his head at the stewardess as he passed.

'Can I take your case, sir? he asked as he hurried to catch up with his special passenger.

Brack shook his head. 'Just take me to the cabin.' He halted at the stairs which led from B Deck muster station. 'Which way now,' he asked.

The steward had misheard Mike Brack. He thought Brack had said, 'Take me to the cap'n.' After all, he reasoned, that was what you called the master of the ship. He knew that much. Anyway, when he thought about it, it was obvious that Captain Trench would want to welcome aboard such a distinguished guest.

His pimply face broke into a smile. 'It's this way, Mr Brack,' he said and started up the stairs, cheerfully whistling a little tune.

Brack sighed. His case was heavy. But its contents were too delicate to put into the hands of anyone else. He followed the steward, taking the stairs two at a time.

He knew something was badly wrong when they reached the upper deck and were striding towards the bridge.

'Where do you think you're taking me?' he asked.

'To see the captain, sir.'

'The who?'

The boy thought he might not have the pronunciation quite correct. He tried again.

'The cap'n, sir? He's on the bridge, you see.'

He had just about plucked up the courage to ask Mike Brack for his autograph. He was thinking he would ask him, if he would be so kind, to sign the inside of his steward's cap.

'I want my cabin, not the captain,' said Brack icily. The voice was nasal, powerful. Without emotion, almost. Except that the steward could feel an intensity focusing down on him. Disdain emanated like a laser from Brack's steel-grey eyes.

Not quite the moment to ask for the autograph.

By the time the steward had eventually checked on the passenger lists and found that Brack's cabin was B Deck, de luxe accommodation, of course, he knew that he had blown it. Passengers were streaming in now, milling around, excited to be on board the *SS Elysium* at last. An added attraction was the celebrity in their midst.

Mike Brack kept his head down and said not a word to anyone. He grimly held on to his case and followed the steward down the endless narrow corridors.

'Sorry for the misunderstanding, Mr Brack,' said the steward hopefully as he opened Brack's cabin door and handed him his keys. Without a word Brack strode inside and closed the door behind him. The key turned in the lock with a resolute click.

At least he didn't slam it, thought the steward. There was still a chance of an autograph. Plenty of time to choose the right moment. Perhaps in a week or two. He set off cheerfully down the corridor, whistling his little tune.

Brack put down his heavy black case on the velvet-covered

double bed. He noted with grim approval that the cabin was spacious and luxurious. Large enough for what he needed. For the initial stages of assembly, anyway.

He leant on the bedside table and peered out of the window. The wide rectangle of glass gave on to the dockside buildings. He could see the last straggle of passengers joining the end of the queue of people who tramped in an orderly fashion up the gangway.

'Lemmings,' he muttered.

He noticed the bedside table had a cabinet with a key. He unlocked and opened it. Inside lay a Gideon's bible. He picked it up and dropped it into the nearby waste paper bin. Turning to the bed again he snapped open the heavy black case. Carefully, he lifted out a tangle of coiled electrical wire and took it to the cabinet. There followed lightbulbs and tools, capacitors and junction boxes. All of it Brack carefully piled inside the bedroom cabinet.

Lastly, out of an upper zipped compartment of the case he pulled out a sheet of paper. He glanced briefly at the complex electrical circuit plan printed on it. He folded the sheet and placed it gently on the pile of equipment in the cabinet.

He closed the cabinet door and turned the key.

All she could do was drop her bags and collapse on the lower bunk. She was exhausted.

She was thankful she had not brought Granny along. Granny was her seventeen-year-old cat. She couldn't have swung Granny in here. The cabin was decidedly cramped.

The bed was narrow, squashed against the wall. Lying on her back, all she could see was the cream-painted underside of the upper bunk, a bare two feet above her. She pitied the couples who had to share these cabins.

Well, no one was sharing with her, thank Gaia.

She placed her feet against the underbelly of the upper bunk and pressed. The bed swung upward and into the wall. Thwuck!

Apart from the bed the cabin was furnished, if that was not too grand a word, with a bedside cabinet that doubled as a desk, a dinky washbasin, and a bit of curtained-off hanging space for clothes. There was a small round porthole in the wall in front of her, above the basin.

Three months in this, she thought sullenly. It was like a prison sentence. Lord Straker had certainly got her on the cheap.

She pulled the Nanocom from her pocket. It was about the size of a cigarette pack, matt black. There were three coloured nodules on one of the edges, blue, white and red.

She spoke to the Nanocom.

'Screen,' she said.

There was a beep and the red nodule blinked.

The surface of the side she held towards her instantly dissolved in a whirl of opalescence and solidified into a matt white screen.

'Newfile Rainbow,' Ruby said.

A second beep. Text in a clear but tiny typeface materialized in the top of the screen. It read *File: Rainbow*.

'Log,' said Ruby.

A second line of text appeared.

LogOn: 11:09 hours Tuesday 14 November 2006

'Now,' mused Ruby. 'Where to start?'

It was a comment meant only for herself. But on the screen a third line joined the others.

Now. Where to start?

The Nanocom was still new to her. She had not quite mastered its finer intricacies, such as the sensitivity of its in-built microphone. She giggled at her stupidity.

On the screen new text was added to the rest.

Ha ha ha

This was getting silly, Ruby thought. She sat up properly on her bed and pondered for a moment. Then she spoke decisively.

'Cut Now Ha.'

The last two lines of text instantly vanished.

She thought out in detail what she must do. She decided to have a stab at the opening paragraph of the article, then merge the material she'd already written and work on from there. She started slowly.

'Title. Over the Rainbow cruise gets away from the gloom by Ruby Duvall. Text. Thousands lined the dock at Canary

43

Wharf to wave goodbye as the luxury liner *SS Elysium* set out on its well-publicized twelve-week round-the-world cruise today.'

Damn, she thought. This is to be published next Sunday. So.

'Cut today,' she ordered. 'Last Tuesday.'

Now she was getting somewhere.

For two hours she lay on the bed and conversed with the Nanocom. By the end she felt she'd got the hang of it.

She was getting a soft spot for Nano. It wasn't quite as good as having Granny in your bed, but something akin. None of the talking back that could kill the most promising relationship. Granny could only purr. And Nano could only give out what you had already put in. It was heaven.

She hoped what she had put into Nano over the last couple of hours was copy good enough to send. She would make a final check through the text.

'Top,' she ordered. 'Scroll.'

Paragraphs flowed in blocks up and over the surface of the Nanocom.

OVER THE RAINBOW CRUISE GETS AWAY FROM THE GLOOM

by Ruby Duvall

THOUSANDS lined the dock at Canary Wharf to wave goodbye as luxury liner the *SS Elysium* set out on its well-publicized twelve-week round-the-world cruise last Tuesday. It will visit the continents of Antarctica, Australia and America via the Panama Canal before arriving back in Britain next February.

The *Elysium* is not the largest cruiser ever to have sailed from a British dock but it makes an impressive sight in these days of purely functional transport. Its size and elegant lines, the sheer luxury of its fittings, complete with indoor and outdoor swimming pools, gymnasium, library, cinema – it even has a ballroom – outclasses any other form of travel available today. It may take an age to reach its destination, but the passengers – 840 of them, each of whom have paid up to ECU30,000 for the privilege – should certainly enjoy the unique trip.

The Over the Rainbow cruise, brainchild of *Sunday Seeker* publisher Lord Stanley Straker, will encourage 'cheer and optimism in the face of increasing gloom'. The words are his.

The latest venture involved heavy investment. The *SS Elysium* started life way back in 1958 as the *SS Bermuda*, but was laid up in 1974 when the quadrupling of oil prices made it uneconomic.

Recently up for sale in the US for scrap, the ship was bought by Lord Straker who for $20m (ECU10m) spent more than ECU100 million on its reconstruction. Relaunched and renamed, the *SS Elysium* went through its sea trials in a blaze of publicity. Captain Trench, the master of the present cruise, is an old hand at this kind of thing. He sailed with the legendary *QE2* and lost a leg in the Falklands war.

Thoroughly refurbished, and cruising on two of its three main engines to conserve fuel, the *Elysium* should make a tidy profit. But with the increasing incidence of terrorism by political activists and protest groups, great emphasis has had to be placed on security. Each passenger was subject to full security screening before boarding. I can personally vouch for its thoroughness.

A dozen security personnel are among the 158 crew, including the two bomb-disposal experts. They have been provided by Freedom Foundation, the US organisation dedicated to active support of 'national defence, individual liberty and good old-fashioned values'. Each of them is a self-professed born-again Christian, their mission to root out terrorism wherever it may be.

Lord Straker has invited me to join the cruise to give a full account of the trip. It will appear in the *Sunday Seeker* colour supplement from February next year, complete with 3D holographic pictures taken with a revolutionary new camera developed by ElysiuMatics.

The trip may be far from uneventful. The *SS Elysium* sails into Antarctic waters near the end of December – the southern hemisphere's summer. By then, the area will be littered with thousands of icebergs. The pack ice has been breaking up at an unprecedented rate during the past few summers because of increased global warming.

But Lord Straker has found a novel way of turning even this potential hazard into entertainment – and a money-spinning one at that. One of the highlights of the cruise is the chance for the passengers to have their faces carved in an iceberg by 'the world's most notorious sculptor!' For a hefty fee, of course.

The sculptor in question is pop artist Mike Brack, who recently caught the public imagination with independent TV company Elysium Visions' new sit-com, *Naked Decay*, in which he stars and which was inspired by the exhibition of his latest works, *Masks of Decay* – massive lumps of wax hacked into gross caricatures of well-known personalities.

His ice sculpting will be achieved with the help of a powerful turbo-pulse laser gun, developed by the US military for anti-tank purposes.

Captain Trench views the ice sculpting with some misgiving. The chips, or growlers as they are sometimes known, carved off from the icebergs, might prove hazardous to ships in the vicinity, not least to the *Elysium* itself.

Of greater concern to the captain is the current state of the earth's magnetic field. Geomagnetic disturbance is predicted to be at its most volatile in December, though an imminent reversal of magnetic polarity is thought by most experts to be unlikely.

The *Elysium*'s passengers hope to sail 'over the rainbow'. They will certainly escape the daily barrage of alarming news and disaster stories. They can also forget the continuing famine, drought, war and 'plague' which increasingly threaten world stability. But when their three-month trip is done, they return to face the real world once again.

Ruby gave a nod of satisfaction. Now she could transmit it to the *Sunday Seeker* offices before the *Elysium* set sail. She pulled at a chrome nodule on the Nanocom and drew out the antenna. She spoke the transmission code clearly and deliberately.

'Rainbow. LX SS 252. Send.'

Sending . . . Rainbow. LX SS 252 appeared on the screen below the final couple of paragraphs of Ruby's article.

It works like a dream, she thought. She could get really friendly with this machine.

The red nodule flickered for a moment then pulsed twice.

Done said Nano.

7   No Name, No Blame

The Doctor arrived at the door he'd been looking for. He had wandered the corridors of the TARDIS for some considerable time.

As he had walked, further and deeper into the heart of the TARDIS, the light had become softer, the smell grown mustier, spiced with ammoniacal sharpness. He passed through regions he had not visited for hundreds of years. If ever. He couldn't be sure.

But this was the door he wanted. He was sure of that.

On it was carved an emblem which he recognized. A human hand curled in a loose fist. Chinese characters were inscribed below it. They were partly obscured by the grime of ages. The Doctor pulled out a raw silk handkerchief from the pocket of his crumpled jacket and wiped away a cobweb and some dust. In his mind he translated the characters, but he could no longer recall what the words meant.

> THIS ROOM IS EMPTY.
> PLEASE LEAVE YOUR NAME AT THE DOOR

His eye travelled over the door's antique surface. There was no grille to speak through. He glanced at the fluted frame. No intercom where he might give his name, only a thin skein of cobweb. He looked on the floor around him where there might be a discarded visitor's book, but there was nothing except a scattering of bat droppings and fluff. He looked up. Black huddled bodies of upside-down bats were hanging from rusty pipes in sleeping clumps.

He had played out so many different guises. He had taken on so many different names. What name then could he give?

Your name or your person, which is closer to you?

48

He decided. He would go in without a name. Then he remembered. That was the point. He would leave his name behind him, at the door.

He stuffed his handkerchief back in his pocket. There was no handle to be seen on the door. With point of his umbrella, he pressed on the open fist. The door swung open with a creak. There was darkness within.

He entered.

8   Sexual Politics

General Pam Cutler had overslept. Of all the stupid things she might have done on her first official day of duty, that must surely be the worst. She could feel her authority slipping out of her grasp, going down the can, as she stepped into the rest room.

The meeting was scheduled for 0900 hours. Not an unreasonable time to start the day. In fact, when drawing up her itinerary, she had thought about making it an hour earlier to demonstrate as clearly as she could that she meant business.

And here she was, walking in at 0925. She felt like shooting herself. She was pigeon-brained. They shoot pigeons, don't they?

Not that she faced a crowd of eager soldiers ready to hang on her every word. Not quite. Colonel Hilliard was there, of course, clipboard in hand, pencil at the ready, old pro that he was. All three skins, Palmer, Brooks and Whitehead were present. They even wore their uniforms. After a fashion.

Corporal Whitehead was flicking through a comic. The other two were drinking coffee. They wore the vacant expression bored youths assumed when doing nothing was preferable to some imminent uninviting task.

Pam had seen it on many waiting soldiers under her command. She remembered feeling that self-willed vacancy herself as a Minnesota student, before she discovered a passion for her subject. Then it had taken her over, almost despite herself.

Three men in the room she did not know. Two of them were obviously catering staff, wearing aprons, UN blue, and busying themselves behind the counter, one with a coffee machine, the other slicing vegetables. The third, a stocky little man, was standing at a noticeboard, his back towards her. On the low table beside him were scissors and an open British tabloid, the *Daily Seeker*, delivered with the other supplies by AXV14. He had cut out a picture and was pinning it to the board. A typical Page Three picture.

A pouting redhead displayed pert breasts and held an open newspaper. Above it was the caption, Sexy Sally peeks at our Daily Seeker. The picture took its place among others on the board, all equally graphic, all of women.

He turned and greeted her with a sickly grin.

'General! Nice to see you. Welcome to the rest room. You know, you look as though you could use some. Rest, that it.'

His voice had a Canadian goofy twang. But this guy was no goof. Her years in command had sharpened her ability to learn from first impressions. She could read a character. All her instincts told her that he was a potentially dangerous egocentric. He would need to be treated with caution.

He wore blue overalls, stained here and there with grease. His breast pocket displayed three white stripes.

'Sergeant Adler?' Pam volunteered.

'Right first time, general. Sergeant Joe Adler. Pleased to meet you, ma'am.' He moved towards her, giving a cursory salute, and went to shake her hand. She was too dazed to withhold it. Her lateness had put her out. She was not yet centred.

The sergeant kept her hand in a tight embrace between his own rough and sweaty ones. He bared his teeth in a mock-friendly smile. She managed not to respond. She remained neutral-faced, tight-lipped.

'Uhuh – you don't like to be called ma'am, right? No problems.' He let go her hand and dropped into the settee. 'Yeah, well, I can see your point.'

He was looking her up and down in an undisguised sexual assessment. She was outraged. But she sensed that this was not the kind of man who could be dealt with head on. It demanded cleverness, an indirect approach, and a great deal of patient resolve.

An appropriate response was just forming on her lips when footsteps clattered down the corridor behind her.

'Flipflop, flipflop. That must be the blossoms,' said Adler.

'OK, Joe, that's enough for now,' cautioned Hilliard.

Palmer, Whitehead and Brooks were sniggering among themselves like adolescents.

Into the room came a breathless Corporal Black, muttering apologies. Behind was a shamefaced Lieutenant Venning.

'I'm sorry, general. We – I overslept. I do apologize.'

Pam could hardly bawl them out. Though it was now blindingly obvious who had kept her awake last night.

The affair between Gary Venning and Jude Black seemed an open secret. Not good news. Sexually intimate bondings within isolated groups produced complex tensions detrimental to a proper working relationship. That was the psycho-social way of putting it. Put another way, when one of the men made it with the available girl, the rest got rubbed up the wrong way, confused, simultaneously stimulated and rejected. Pam understood what was happening all right. The difficulty was in dealing with it.

She started out by trying to lighten the situation. First of all she asked for a coffee, a strong black coffee, and apologized herself for being late. Ben, the mild looking, portly, aproned man who brought it over and put it down before her with a motherly insouciance, was introduced to her as the station's chef. 'The one indispensable fella on base,' joked Colonel Hilliard. There was general amusement. The chef was clearly a well-liked man.

Ben was English. His colleague was Italian, a shy-looking, black-haired young man of ravishing good looks. In his mid-twenties, Pam hazarded.

To maintain the atmosphere of levity, she joked about her trip from Washington, made dismissive sideswipes at the state of the Government, rattled off a series of complaints against the military system which she knew they would applaud. This, after all, was a routine strategy which she had applied on numerous occasions when dealing with soldiers of low-morale.

The iambic rhythm of some forgotten verse fluttered just out of consciousness, making its presence felt but refusing tormentingly to be pinned down and named. Then it came to her.

'The Royal Captain of this ruin'd band . . . Bids them
good morrow with a modest smile And calls them
brothers, friends and countrymen.'

The strategy had worked for Harry the Fifth. It had worked
for her in the past. She hoped it would work now.

She asked them questions about their various backgrounds,
allowed them to talk among each other freely, to say what they
felt, express their personal grievances, their grouses at the
world. In the lively discussion which followed they forgot for
a time that she might not be one of them. Thus she got to
know them better.

As they told their stories, Pam became increasingly aware
just how isolated they could be out in Antarctica. If things
went wrong, there were very few people around to solve the
problem. Dave Hilliard brought this home to her with horrific
clarity. He had been forced to remove his own appendix. She
listened rapt as he told the story.

Conducting field work out on some distant peninsula. Should
not have been working alone, but he was, and that was that.
Only link with base was radio. Jude Black had newly arrived
as the station's doctor. She got the colonel to describe his
symptoms and carry out the basic tests. There were clear signs
of peritonitis. His appendix was about to burst. No doubt about
it. If an operation was not carried out immediately, he would
die.

There happened to be basic implements in the medical kit on
board his AXV. Scalpel, morphine, swabs, needle and thread.
Nothing else for it. He bared his abdomen, swabbed it with
antiseptic, angled his shaving-mirror to get a better view, took
a dose of morphine and submitted his flesh to the scalpel in
his hands. Jude gave him clear, precise instructions all the
way.

The corporal squirmed and squealed at the memory. But at
the time, according to Gary Venning, she took impressively
cool command of the situation. Pam guessed it was then the
seeds of passion were sown.

Gary Venning's hand moved to Jude's neck to soothe her
agitation at the memory. She put her hand on his thigh.

Pam could feel the uneasy tension in the room resurface.

53

She could sense the beading eyes of Palmer, Whitehead, Brooks and Adler; the perplexed frown of Colonel Hilliard. She was going to have to ask them to be more discreet.

On the noticeboard, the flashing teeth, the pouting lips, the heaving, pumped-up breasts, the curves of shapely buttocks. Grist to the sexual mill that fed these men's frustrations. They would have to go as well.

To move the focus away from Jude's accomplishments, Pam enquired about the two remaining members of the base she hadn't met. Nike and Bono sounded an unlikely couple to judge from the descriptions of Privates Palmer and Brooks. They were at that moment out on the field in AXV2, monitoring the geomagnetic flux. It was a routine which had to be kept going round the clock and was done in relay with other members of STS.

Nike was the only other woman on the base, said Brooks. Then he hesitated, embarrassed, realizing his mistake, apologizing to the general. He corrected himself. Nike was one of three women on the base, he said, now that the general was here.

Pam quietly welcomed the correction, taking it as a sign that her stratagem was working. She was now accepted as the general. A soldier. Just one of them.

Bono, to judge by Joe Adler's description, was a mountain of a man. A Nigerian metallurgist and the strongman of the base, he had earned the affectionate nickname 'Man of Steel'. He also possessed an enviously sharp mind. His speciality was to polish off the *New York Times* crossword in ten minutes flat, then work out in his room with hundred-kilo weights.

Pam suspected that Joe's effusiveness on the subject of Bono's physical prowess disguised feelings of inadequacy, a public respect for the big man hiding a private hate. She was not surprised when, in an off the cuff remark, he referred to him as Metal Mickey.

Corporal Whitehead immediately objected. 'Ah, come off it, scumbag. Bono's no geek.'

Joe assumed a hurt and surprised expression. 'Who said he was, corporal? Can't the man take a joke?'

Tension again. To defuse it, Pam quickly asked about the remaining member of the team.

Nike, it appeared, was a diminutive Japanese. A fledgling snow chemist. She often worked with Gary Venning, down in the station's laboratory on the reactor level.

Pam kept an eye on Jude's reactions as the lads described Nike's finer points. This was another area of possible tension, but Jude looked unperturbed.

Palmer reckoned Nike enjoyed being a bit of a lad herself. There was laughter all round. It was obvious Palmer and Brooks were happy in her company. Even the phlegmatic Whitehead perked up when they were discussing her. One of her greatest charms, it seemed, was that she could drink them to the floor.

Getting blind drunk was clearly a popular, mindless way of passing their leisure time. Another prohibition they are going to hate me for, thought Pam. Still, it was going to have to be done. The FLIPback project demanded the utmost dedication.

But this wasn't the moment to make a pronouncement. She had to find her feet. She needed the facts and the figures. In her own mind she was certain that the project could be salvaged, that there was sufficient evidence of imminent reversal to constitute a serious threat to the world. But she needed to convince her team. She couldn't afford to leave them with the slightest doubt.

First she must cajole and encourage. The time would come when she could turn the screw.

'Lieutenant,' she said, turning to Gary Venning, 'I want to go through all your analytical records. Colonel Hilliard tells me you've done some sterling work. I need to plot out the changing magnoflux levels over the past hundred years.'

'That's no problem,' said Venning eagerly.

'And sergeant, from you I'll need an assessment of how badly behind schedule we are in assembling the field loop. I know that you and your team,' she nodded sympathetically in the direction of Whitehead, Palmer and Brooks, 'have had your work cut out in the last few months, what with supply delays and bureaucratic pussillanimity.'

'Bureaucratic what?' said Corporal Whitehead.

'I'm sorry, corporal, there goes my Minnesota education getting in the way again. I mean their timidity, their refusal to

55

nail their colours to the mast. I mean the way they always threaten to reverse their funding. You don't know where you are. You know, we ought to have a FLUFFback device up here as well. A Field Loop for Undelivered Fucking Funding. What do you say, soldier?'

There was a roar of approval. Even Adler enjoyed the joke. 'That's good, general. FLUFFback device. I like it.'

Keep him sweet, she thought. Keep him sweet for now.

'So you'll be able to supply that information, sergeant?'

'Sure thing, general. Can't see it doing any good though. FLIPflop's had its day, in my opinion.'

'Well, you may be right, Joe. But we need evidence to back that opinion up, I'm sure you agree. You'll get it to me by tonight?'

Sergeant Joe Adler was brimming with self-satisfaction. He looked around the group with a clear I-told-you-so expression.

'Sure thing, general. You'll have it tonight.'

The leaves were perfectly preserved in all their detail, just as if they had just fallen from the tree. Gary gently brushed away the dusty patina of frost.

'Three million years old. We discovered them eighty kilometres from the base. For these trees to have thrived they would have needed – '

'Summer temperatures 15 degrees higher than we have at the moment,' interrupted the general. 'Yes, lieutenant, I know. I've studied the journals. Have you extracted a magnoflux reading?'

'Not yet, general.'

'Well, get to it, soldier. The more certain we can be that magnetic flipover pushes global climate into a different phase, then the more worried we can make those bureaucrats. With the magnometer data you've already shown me, and this,' she jabbed a gloved hand at the fossil, 'we could start to put together a convincing case.'

It was Pam's first visit to the cavern of ice that served as the station's snow laboratory. Gary was showing her the treasures of his domain. The lump of fossilized leaves on the frosted bench in front of them was one of his prized possessions.

They were on a level with the reactor chamber. Sounds of

continuing work on the Loop echoed somewhere behind them. The whine of drills. The intermittent puck, puck, puck of hammering.

It was cold down there. They were dressed in regulation insosuits, white plastic coveralls, which also protected them from any stray radiation from the reactor. Pam was surprised how light and comfortable the suits were, and how effective. Their heads were cowled in insulating plastic hoods. Out of the shadow of the hood beside her, a pair of ice-blue eyes sought hers.

'What did you make of my data, general?'

'Not bad, lieutenant. More to the point is what the media will make of it. I've filed a press release, based on your material. It'll shake things up a bit. I emphasized the pessimistic side. Flipover any time between now and Christmas.'

'I – I don't know if the data would fully support that view.'

The general put her gloved hands on the bench and leant towards him. Her voice was low and confidential.

'You're too close to it, Gary. I'll take you through the graphs if you want the proof.' Pam held his gaze, willing him to agree. 'Think of it as a worst case scenario,' she suggested gently. He nodded back, but was clearly unconvinced. He was only a lad. What, twenty-six? He wouldn't understand the politics. Nor would she have done at his age. Scientific accuracy was the benchmark then. Detachment. The general had learnt there were other ways to play the game.

She pointed at a rack of culture plates beyond the heap of leaves. 'What are those?'

He turned to the plates. 'Various organisms we've discovered on the surface. Here's something interesting.'

He picked out a dish of blue-green algae.

'*Cyanophyceae Antarctica*. It's a form of bacteria you'll find most places on Earth, especially freshwater lakes. But this one thrives here.'

'*Cyanophyceae*? I remember that from my field work at Little Falls. How in heaven does it survive out here?'

'Well, that's the amazing thing. Cyanobacteria is about the oldest and most durable life-form on the planet. And no wonder. They appear invulnerable to things that would kill off any other lifeform. Heat them, freeze them, blast them with

57

light, lock them in darkness, dehydrate them, immerse them in saline – they go on surviving. But what's curious is this.'

He reached for another dish and handed it to the general. It seemed packed with glistening whitish-silver granules. Looking closer, Pam saw that each granule was a tiny scaly maggot, or something similar.

'Look like those bristletails that crawl out of my old damp books in Minnesota. You know the ones I mean, lieutenant? Do you call them silverfish?'

'Yes, general. Of the order *Thysanura*. These little fellas are closely related. They feed off the algae, among other things.'

The tiny scaly wrigglers slid over each other inside the sealed transparent dish.

'And they survive?'

'They survive. In fact, they have much of the resilience of the cyanobacteria.'

'You are what you eat,' said the general.

'And they really go for ultraviolet. As ozone protection disappears, these bugs will definitely proliferate.'

Pam shivered. She put the dish down.

'I take it we have no infestations in the base?' she asked.

Gary shook his head.

'That's good. I brought a pile of books for the long winter evenings. I'd hate to have to share them with these things.'

She turned to leave.

'Oh, general.'

There was something odd in Gary Venning's tone.

'What is it, lieutenant?'

'I don't know if – ' He faltered. He tried again. 'There's something I found a while ago – out on the surface.'

He gave up trying to explain. Instead, he went to unlock a plastic cabinet let into the ice wall. Pam felt uneasy. A bristletail crawled up her spine. That's what it felt like.

He pulled something out of the cabinet and brought it to the bench. It was a package the size of a dinner plate, wrapped in a plasticized foil. He laid it down carefully.

Pam drew closer. She was intrigued.

With tweezers he gently teased back part of the wrapping.

'From I can make out, it's definitely human remains. It's – it's part of a face.'

58

He threw an inquiring glance at Pam as if to give her the chance of backing out of the viewing.

'I've been on battlefields, lieutenant. I'm not likely to be squeamish at a portion of shrink-wrapped face.'

The lieutenant nodded and went back to peeling away the foil. This pussy-footing was getting on Pam's nerves. Gary was giving nothing away. She tried the light-hearted approach.

'Couldn't be one of Scott's party, could it? What was his name – the one who walked out on them?'

'It's not from the last century, general. I've run a scan.' Gary peeled back another layer of foil. There was a patch of yellowish-grey. Deeply wrinkled. Definitely flesh.

'How old?' she asked.

'Ten thousand years – give or take a thousand.'

A cracked, thin-lipped mouth had come into view under Gary's tweezers.

'Cro-Magnon? Neolithic? This is a major find, lieutenant.'

The lieutenant pulled away another strip of foil to reveal the eye. Pam was expecting an empty socket or at most a shrunken globe of gristle. Instead, she saw a dark red crystal, almost black, multifaceted and round like an insect's eye. It glittered coldly under the snow lab lights, as if it were alive and watching them.

'It seems to be an auto-visual sensing device.'

'An artificial eye?'

'That's right. Highly engineered,' said Gary. 'It's wired deep down toward the visual cortex. Connects to a complex neural interface. I've seen nothing like it before.'

'What could it be? One of our little military experiments?'

'That wouldn't account for the age of the organic material.'

'Then what do you think it might be?'

Gary looked at her, reluctant to say what he really thought.

'Lieutenant, you're not trying to tell me its an EBE?'

The lieutenant nodded. 'Remains of an alien life form. Yes, general, if you want my honest opinion, that's what I think.'

She sat at her desk in the tracking room. The colonel was checking through some data with Palmer at a VDU. She absently watched the progress of AXV2 as it was plotted in moving lights on the giant map of Antarctica projected on the wall screen.

She still felt shaky. She had not felt this way for twenty years. It was absurd. She must pull herself together.

She called Dave Hilliard over. He sat at the desk.

She asked him about a phrase in one of the station reports. Torus Antarctica. It was unfamiliar to her. The colonel explained it was station jargon. It started out as a kind of joke. The South Pole's version of the Bermuda Triangle.

She didn't get it.

The colonel reminded her about the Bermuda Triangle. A notorious area in the previous century for the mysterious disappearance of planes, of ships, of people. Some said extra-terrestrials were to blame, others, that it was desolate, unmonitorable and therefore simply dangerous.

Pam had always dismissed the Bermuda Triangle as a media invention. But what had it to do with Torus Antarctica?

The colonel explained. Over the past thirty years there had been a number of mysterious disappearances. They centred on the fringes of Antarctica. A doughnut-shaped region. A torus of air, land and sea.

Pam listened to the colonel with an ill-defined sense of unease.

The first significant loss was when an entire Russian base disappeared from the Weddell Sea coast in 1987. Since that time an increasing number of boats had gone missing, planes vanished, expeditionary teams never heard from again. Last year STS itself had suffered. AXV9 has been swallowed up in a blizzard and never found. Two of the base's personnel were lost, presumed dead.

This was the subject of the report Pam had read. The phrase Torus Antarctica was no longer used as a joke.

And now, said the colonel, the Japanese were mounting a large expedition. One of their research stations, the Nikkei 5, had disappeared in the Ross Sea area.

'Palmer, pass me that mouse,' Hilliard called across the room. The private grabbed the hand-shaped object from his desk and threw it over. Hilliard pointed it at the screen on the wall, and clicked. A cursor arrow appeared on the map.

'The ice-shelf over there,' he said, indicating the region to the west of the continent, 'has been splitting off into giant icebergs with the warmer weather. This one here,' he pointed the arrow at what looked like an island off the coast, 'is of exceptional size – three thousand square miles. That's about as big as Cyprus.'

'That's big,' said Pam. 'Where's the Japanese station?'

'It was here.'

He placed an arrow at a point along the coast in the shadow of the Transantarctic Mountains.

'Built in ninety-eight to measure carbon dioxide saturation as a monitor on global warming. Six scientists were working there full time. I know one of them quite well. We played chess over the netlink.' He gestured in the direction of Palmer's VDU.

Pam looked at the map on the wall screen, a global projection of most of the southern hemisphere. The tips of South Africa and South America and the broad mass of Australia crept over the horizon at equal distance from each other. Everything else was sea, apart from the immense icy island of Antarctica, spread across the centre. Research stations were marked here and there as variously coloured dots, mostly around the edges of the land. The South Pole was a steady white light dead centre of the screen. STS was UN blue and slightly off-centre. The AXV2 was an intermittent orange glow worming its way around the area called Wilkes Land in the wide expanse of the south.

She thought of Bono and Nike wandering in that wilderness, their vehicle dwarfed by the vastness of the continent.

True south was a dot of green in the western part of Wilkes Land. Pam looked for it and couldn't locate it. Unlike the geographic pole, which was the point fixed immutably as the axis around which the Earth revolved, the geomagnetic pole, true south, was a movable phenomenon. It altered position according to the strength or weakness of the geomagnetic flux. As magnetic flipover became a greater possibility, true south would grow more volatile and would wander more erratically.

The green dot still eluded her.

'Dave, I can't find true south. I think we may have a fault. Check the projection programme, will you?'

Hilliard moved to his VDU and scrolled through lines of data.

'I'm getting positive on true south here. The pixels should be lit,' he said.

Then she saw it. Up towards the Amery ice-shelf away on the east. It could not have moved so far, so fast. Unless –

'I think we may be into worst-case scenario, colonel. Get everyone up here, please. At once.'

The staff had left their duties and assembled in the tracking room. Pam was in no doubt as to what their course should be. She wasted no words.

Earth's magnetic field was growing increasingly weak. The final evidence was in the movement of the geomagnetic pole. Her news release to the world's press had not been overstated. Magnetic reversal could take place at any time. The implications for the world were catastrophic.

They would have heard it all before. But it was important enough to go through it all again. Every mechanical device dependent on magnetic orientation would be affected, from compasses to satellites, from body scans to ships. All animals that navigated by magnetic alignment, birds and fish, and insects such as bees, might be fatally confused. Protection from solar radiation might be altered, which would be disastrous at a time of fast-reducing ozone protection. Most serious, there was the possibility of a sudden major change in climate.

She caught Gary Venning's eye. He had his arm around Jude Black's shoulder. Jude moved a hand tenderly over his chest. Joe Adler was behind them, sneering. At them. At Pam. He clearly refused to be persuaded by her dramatic catalogue.

Things were going to have to change at STS. Now was time to lay it on the line. She piled on the agony.

Earth, she pointed out, could be transformed into a hothouse that would make the present threat of global warming seem infinitely preferable. Or just as devastating, we could be catapulted into another ice age. Still worse, the geological evidence clearly showed that during the past million years polarity had reversed on numerous occasions and each reversal was implicated in the extinction of a dominant life-form on the planet.

Giant impacting meteorites did not hold the monopoly on wiping out whole species. Mankind could well be next, and FLIPback might represent its only remaining chance. They had to move fast.

Joe Adler had raised a hand.

'Yes, what is it, sergeant?'

'If you'll excuse me for saying so, general, you had my schedule assessment Saturday evening. You can see from that – if you bothered to read it yet,' he winked at her, 'we so far behind there ain't no way we gonna catch up.'

'I did read it, sergeant. And I want to thank you for it. No, really, I do. I passed it straight on to the world news services. With flipover threatening before the year end, they saw immediately that your report made terrifying reading. It certainly swung the bureaucrats into action.

'Yesterday, I got a promise for a whole new tranche of extra funding. Now that's good news. It means we can afford an extra handful of UN engineers to work on the Loop. Under your specialist direction, Sergeant Adler.

'But they won't be here for another week. And because of that little green dot – ' Pam looked up to find it and saw to her alarm that it had already moved a few miles further inland, 'which is getting friskier all the time, we know our window of opportunity is running out. We've got to move now, and move fast.'

Adler was shaping up to say something, but the general drove right on.

'First, Bono and Nike are due back from the field in two days. Whitehead and Brooks are scheduled to take over the field monitoring. I'm blocking that as of now. The replacement team will be Lieutenant Venning and Corporal Black.'

A frisson ran through the assembled company. Gary looked surprised, Jude pleased. Corporal Whitehead rubbed an oil-stained hand on his greasy overalls and gave an open-mouthed leery grin.

Adler started to wise-crack, 'Not the blossoms, gen – '

'Second,' continued the general, firmly in the driving seat, 'this arrangement, sergeant, means you'll have a full contingent of engineers to carry on work on the Loop. Venning and Black have no specialist magno-training. They will be more useful on the field. Bono will be sequestered in, to add to your team's expertise – '

'Yeah, he'll be good with the hammer, too, will Metal Mickey,' said Adler, to chortles from Palmer and Brooks.

'Third,' said the general, firmly, 'the matter of discipline. We are here to work. Anything gets in the way of that work and we self-destruct. The project dies. And maybe the world dies too. Think about it.'

She held them all in a steady sweeping gaze.

'I'm giving us a month. Four weeks from today to get it done. Until we're through, there will be no leave. Nor will there be any alcohol consumed, nor smoking of dope. We'll have plenty of time for that when we've got the job done – let's hope it's before the magnoflux blows – and we're waiting around to press that FLIPback button to save the world. You got me, soldiers?'

There was general muted assent. It was more good-natured than she might have feared. She might just be getting through.

'Finally,' she said, 'I want to make it clear that the workplace is for work. I don't give a flying trapezoid what you get up to in the privacy of your own rooms, as long as it doesn't, A, keep the rest of us up all night,' she shot a meaningful glance across to Gary and Jude, 'and, B, put you out of action when you should be working on the Loop.'

'I'll say it one more time. The workplace is for work. Personal matters will be kept entirely out of the communal areas, specifically Lieutenant Venning and Corporal Black. You will refrain from clinging on to each other and generally making love in public. It's an insult and disruptive to the group.'

Pam turned to Adler. His face was a picture of smugness.

'And sergeant, I will not have your soft porn plastered all over the public noticeboards. I find it personally offensive. No doubt others do to. You will remove it today. Whatever your personal needs and fantasies, I would ask you to keep them to yourself.'

The sergeant was beginning to splutter. The general addressed the group again.

'Have no doubt, any of you, that you will be disciplined

severely if you overstep the line. I'm prepared to go all the way to court martial on this one. We have a job to do. We're going to do it. And as my father used to say, there ain't no blue-arsed fly nor little green men can stop us now.'

9   Over the Rainbow

Ruby had to admit it. She was enjoying herself. This was
something of a blow to her self-esteem. She saw herself as a
hard-nosed professional. After three years in the business she
was beginning to cultivate the proper attitude. Adult and cynical. And she was not doing badly. She was gaining a useful
reputation as an investigative reporter.

Her last scoop was to uncover a gun-running scam at the
heart of a Government organization. That had started a real
scandal. In fact, it was probably sensible that she was getting
out of the country for a few months, under a different name,
until the fuss died down. You never quite knew the lengths to
which some of these people might go. In any case, she could
do with a break.

She had never liked the idea of ships. They were too slow,
unsteady, and there was all that rolling about. When Lord
Stanley Straker had first put the idea to her in the offices of
the *Sunday Seeker*, it had made her sick just to think about it.
Claustrophobic, too. You can't just get off when you've had
enough. She thought she'd feel trapped.

But Lord Stanley had such charm. It was difficult to refuse
him anything. He wanted good coverage for this venture and
he had pulled out all the stops persuading her.

His secretary had interrupted their talk to say an important
telephone call had come in from the US. The deep Australian
voice boomed out, so that the whole office could hear, 'Tell
the secretary of state I'll get back to him as soon as Ms Duvall
and I have finished our conversation.' Blatant showmanship.
But it worked. Ruby had agreed to go Over the Rainbow and
to write about her adventure. There would be no investigations
this time, just straight reporting.

As they had sailed away from the port, past peninsulas of

land and white cliffs that dwindled into a smudged chalk line and then disappeared, away from the acres of floating wind farms, like a thousand giants waving them goodbye, when they had left everything else behind and there was nothing but the sea, the sky and the ship, Ruby felt a heaviness lifting from her mind, or from somewhere deep within her. It was a heaviness she had been living with for years. She could give no name to it. She only realized now how heavy a weight it must have been, now when it was no longer with her.

There was a kind of freedom out there in the open sea, away from the depressing smog of the British autumn. Away, too, from the gloomy barrage of international news which so dispirited her at home.

Earth was a world in turmoil. She could not think of a country that was not untroubled by terrorism, or war, or riot, or privation. The twentieth century had ended not with a bang, but had merely subsided whimpering into a new millennium that looked at best, unpromising, at worst, a nightmare. The litany of twenty-first century troubles seemed never ending, served up in graphic daily detail on TV news and documentaries, or in the papers.

The spectre of a changing climate haunted the planet. Earth's magnetic field was growing unstable. The protective ozone hole was getting bigger with every passing year. Famine and drought were becoming commonplace. Fresh water was in short supply worldwide.

Oil was still plentiful – too plentiful. Careless managing, atrocious accidents, deliberate acts of environmental vandalism in the name of one cause or another, had left no coast untainted, no species of bird untouched. Rivers added their poisonous cocktail of heavy metals and polluting chemicals to the overburdened oceans of the world. The marine environment was on the edge of breakdown. The sea was slowly dying.

Then there was the plague.

The word was used loosely to cover the various diseases that were waging a war against mankind. They might be smoking-related or caused by radiation, bad eating habits, the wrong kind of sex, or even by increasing ozone depletion. But people had lost interest in trying to avoid the plague. It could always take you unawares, no matter how saintly or peculiar your lifestyle.

People had simply accepted the plague as a natural backdrop to their lives. They had learned to live with it.

It was taking a serious toll on life. World population was actually starting to fall. This extraordinary phenomenon, seen in the previous century as a solution to the all world's ills, was accompanied by another.

Male fertility rates were reducing rapidly worldwide. The human race was losing its capacity to reproduce itself. On current trends, zero population would be reached before the next century was out.

There was a part of Ruby that rather relished the idea. A world with no people in it, and therefore no pollution, no acts of gross barbarism, no meddling human intelligence to get in the way of the purity of nature. But in her heart she knew it was all pure fantasy. She was part of nature, too. So was the human race. Global infertility, pandemic plague, the breakdown of civilization – this was nature's way of telling us to slow down.

Of course the search was now on to extend the span of life of those alive now. Gene manipulation, organ transplants, bodily augmentation, cryogenics. All were being pursued in deadly earnest. Ruby wasn't sure she liked the idea of living for a thousand years. But mature as she felt, she was only twenty-one. She knew she might feel differently when she was sixty-four.

Mercifully, for the present, Ruby was free of all of that, the bags and baggage of all possible futures. The weight of the world had fallen from her. She had sailed away from it. She was somewhere else, in a limbo world. Over the rainbow.

The ship they sailed in was appropriately named, she thought. Elysium was the Ancient Greek idea of paradise. An island of the blessed, reserved for the lucky few who were singled out for eternal happiness. The *SS Elysium* was transporting the happy few away from the anxious life, temporarily at least. No TV news. No daily papers. No outside world at all to impress its disagreeable reality upon the passengers.

From time to time Ruby would dictate a note to Nano. It became a kind of intermittent journal.

LogOn 08:47 Wednesday 29 November 2006   File: Cruise
Two weeks into our trip. The weather has grown warmer as we approached the Equator and passed into the South Atlantic. The outdoor pool is bliss, Olympic size and almost deserted in the early mornings. The sun deck is protected from UV radiation by a huge plastic canopy. You can lie out under it and pretend you're really sunbathing, just like your parents and grandparents used to do.

There's a Canadian woman, Barbara, who leads a small assorted group in a kind of slow motion dance on the helicopter pad beyond the pool. Anyone can join in. You learn by watching and following. It's a type of ancient Chinese martial art. Or meditation. Or both. I don't know what it is to tell the truth. Barbara doesn't say too much about it. I can never quite catch what she calls it. Something like Paadwah.

Yeah, that's a good attempt at spelling it, Nano.

So after my morning swim, I learn Paadwah. Gives a great feeling of control, of steadiness, useful in the unsteady ship.

The unsteady ship was huge. Like being afloat in a large hotel in some wind-swept coastal resort. A little floating city named the *SS Elysium*. Stanley Straker's Paradise.

It was a Slightly Shuddering Paradise at first. That was the only cause for complaint in the early stages of the cruise. Travellers in the stern, Ruby was one, felt they were riding over cobblestones. The vibrations were due to the refit.

Ruby discovered this one day when she went with Diana and Leslie to complain to the *Elysium*'s master, Captain Trench.

Ruby had met Diana and Leslie when they were only a few days out of port. They were part of the onboard entertainment. So was Mick Brack for that matter. But he was a different kettle of fish. A cold fish, Diana called him. To Ruby he had the look of someone who was driven. In control. A loner. She would see him stalking about the decks from time to time, trying to ignore the winks and nudges of the passengers.

He seemed to know Diana. There were distant nods and

69

mumbled greetings when they passed. Ruby had yet to winkle that one out. She was dying to meet him. But that opportunity had not yet arisen. She was sure it would, eventually.

The ship's programme of events referred to Diana and Leslie as 'cabaret artistes'. They provided twice-nightly entertainment.

'Once a knight, always a knight. Twice a night and you're doing all right.'

This was Leslie's idea of a joke.

'Actually,' said Leslie, when she first got talking to them, 'I'm an actor who can sing a bit. And Diana's a singer who can't act for toffee.'

He had laughed his high-pitched neigh of a laugh: Diana had arched an eyebrow and fluttered long false eyelashes.

'It's not toffee I'm interested in,' she had said, as if toffee wouldn't melt.

Ruby usually kept herself at a distance in new relationships. She wasn't good at mixing in. But she and Diana and Leslie soon become firm friends. The way you do when you're on holiday, she reasoned. Not so much allowing people into your life as joining them in a fantasy existence.

Their cabins were all in the modest stern section of the ship, the budget accommodation. That was why the three of them found themselves on the bridge complaining of bad vibrations.

The captain told them that the trouble lay with the pair of new propellers, which had been fitted by the Dutch firm Lip.

'Two lips from Amsterdam?' was Leslie's immediate response. He was quick, Ruby allowed him that, but hardly ever funny.

The captain explained that the propellers carried giant supplementary vanes or membranes.

Leslie frowned deeply, trying to come to terms with the concept. 'Lip lips?'

'Did anyone call?' cooed Diana.

The two of them were in a silly mood. Ruby tried to look disapproving. She had to impress upon the captain that she was the serious-minded one. She had to conduct an in-depth interview with the man some time during the cruise.

The captain winked. Or perhaps he blinked. It was difficult

to tell since he only had one eye. He also had a mechanical leg. She knew it from her previous talk with him, but you would never have guessed from the way he strode about the bridge, inspecting various screens and dials.

When she had interviewed him for her initial article, the one she had sent via the Nonocom that first day onboard, it had been by phone from Islington. She would never have recognized him from his gruff phone voice. She had imagined someone stocky, round, and grizzled, with a beard, not this tall, clean-shaven, white-haired, white-faced man.

He certainly wouldn't know who she was. She had used her professional name for the interview. As far as he or anyone else was concerned, Ruby Duvall, investigative reporter for the *Sunday Seeker*, was not on board.

Undeterred, the captain went on patiently with his explanation. The vanes, he said, were intended to cut fuel consumption. Give it another day or two, he assured them. They needed breaking in.

He was almost right. The vibration ceased a few days later. Inspection revealed that the vanes had not been able to take the pressure. They were sheered right through. They had not been broken in exactly, they had simply broken off.

Ruby was happy to have found such lively friends as Diana and Leslie to have a giggle with. Often they were 'paroxysed'. She enjoyed the times she spent with them as they went round the ship together, or saw a movie, or settled down for a chat and a laugh in one of the many bars.

LogOn 00:06 Saturday 2 December 2006   **File: Cruise**
Met Mike Brack for the first time tonight. Diana and Leslie and I were having a drink. Diana invited him to sit with us.

Contrary to first impressions, he seems really nice. Obviously a bit of a bastard. Cynical. Callous, in a world-weary way. He's hiding a lot. But he's funny too. He paroxysed us with his impression of Captain Trench. Drinks a lot. Absinthe, mainly. Bitter. Bright green. Highly alcoholic. But as Leslie said, to groans all round, absinthes make the heart grow fonder.

'Didn't work for us then, did it, Michael?' said Diana.

Turns out Diana used to live with him.

I think that deserves an exclamation mark, Nano. !

Thanks.

I've got a feeling there's some other dark secret about Mike Brack that Diana's dying to divulge.

Watch this space.

Diana and Leslie had to work their passage. Most evenings they did their cabaret. The programme was supposed to change every fortnight, so there was always new material to rehearse. As for Ruby, she was working her passage, too. She was meant to be preparing her story on the cruise. But time was like the grey sea that surrounded them. It stretched far out into the distance to a barely visible horizon.

Ruby persuaded herself that February was long enough away. She could give herself a few weeks off. She took the time to do the things she would never have done at home. She allowed herself to relax. She was idle. She had no end in view. She did nothing constructive. She enjoyed the moment. She enjoyed just being there.

The other passengers had the same idea. It was if everyone on the *SS Elysium* were cut off from their past or future. They were different people. Without attachments. Without worries.

Her initial impression of their collective age turned out to be close to the mark. She had noticed no one in their twenties, apart from some of the crew. And Diana and Leslie, of course. Even Leslie was pushing it a bit. He was going to be thirty on Christmas Day. What a celebration that was going to be. The big Three-O. Three days before that, Ruby would be twenty-two. That seemed old enough.

But the passengers, it was true to say, were mostly well past the first flush of youth. Ruby supposed that being old they felt the despair and gloom of life in the real world more keenly. Perhaps that was why they had blown their savings. To get away from it all.

LogOn 10:12 Saturday 9 December 2006   File: Cruise
Passed the Tropic of Capricorn yesterday. Ploughing on towards the Falklands. It's getting colder. Too cold for the morning swim. But I still go up on deck and do the Paadwah with Barbara.

Got the spelling, Nano. Here goes. Pah T'wa.

Barbara is one of those ordinary-looking 40-year-olds you'd never notice in a crowd. Until you discover she is 61, like I did today. We had a coffee and a chat in the breakfast room this morning.

Apparently, Pah T'wa is based on the movement of animals. It's about 1,000 years old. It's connected with something even older called the Dow. Spelt Tao. Nano, take note.

Barbara talks a lot of sense. But she's a tiny bit eccentric. Not that she's out to lunch, but she's certainly got a dollar or two more than the standard ecu.

I happened to mention how good it was not to have be careful with water. In London, I told her, you're lucky not to have to queue at a stand-pipe every other day. Here, because the ship has its own desalination plant and we're floating in the stuff, you can drink as much as you like. Get a shower whenever you want. And not bother to be selective when you flush the loo.

She says it's the same in Toronto. The lack of water, that is. They have a jingle for the loo-flushing bit.

'If it's yellow, let it mellow.

If it's brown, flush it down.'

Helps with the priorities, I suppose.

But this is the cranky bit. She promotes dry toilets. She's had one at home for years. Uses her dried doo-doo to grow tomatoes on. Sounds yucky to me, but she says it's got to come. Every time a toilet is flushed twenty litres of good drinking water go round the bend. As world population approaches eight billion we're in danger of being swamped by our own sewage. And that's putting it politely. Maybe she's not as cranky as seems. There's order in her ordure!

Sorry, Nano.

I pointed out to her that the population was set for rapid decline. She said she'd believe that when she saw it. People were going to live longer. She just knew she was on course for another hundred years at least. One way to longevity was by doing Pah T'wa. I have to say she's a terrific advert for it.

It also appears she's an expert on acupressure. Gong Qi Po, it's called. She started to teach it to me there and then. The other passengers just stared. Barbara was squeezing my arms and kneading my neck. They must have wondered what we were up to.

Life was one long holiday. People went to lectures on back care and computers. There was bingo, and skittles, and the cabaret, of course. The video rooms played endless re-runs of vintage films and TV series for the fan clubs and sci-fi organizations which had taken advantage of Lord Straker's 'club class' rates. There was a Kinky Gerlinky Revivalist Party whose ageing members had lost none of their 1990's flair for dressing in the most outrageous costumes.

Ruby enjoyed the heady clash of cultures as different older generations mixed. Cries of 'Right on!', 'Groovy!', and 'Far out, man!' came from the more decrepit passengers, the ageing hippies, while younger wrinklies expressed themselves with words like 'Wicked!', 'Ace!' and 'Bad!'.

Spontaneous sing-songs erupted in the bars. Strains of ancient lyrics echoed down the endless corridors.

'There she was just a walking down the street.
Singing Do Wah Diddy Diddy Dum Diddy Do . . .'

Ruby remained an observer. She involved herself in none of these things. She found more interesting ways to pass the time. She enjoyed exploring the labyrinthine ship. Because of its age and refurbishments it had so many unexpected nooks and crannies. She felt there must be secret passageways connecting one place to another, like a medieval castle.

Ruby would spend hours browsing in the ship's library. It was often deserted. It was got up to look like a room in some baronial hall, complete with suit of armour in one corner, fixed to keep it upright in the rolling ship.

The first thing you saw as you entered was a big mock-stone fireplace with a fire of illuminated logs. Though artificial, she found the glow warming and homely. Above the mantelpiece a heavy broadsword was mounted on the wall.

She fantasized that if she found the triggering book, a panel of shelving would swing open to reveal a passage leading away into darkness. The idea encouraged her to pull out many dusty books she might otherwise have passed over.

Among the old tomes was an anthology of poetry. One poem lodged in her mind immediately. The lines would keep resurfacing like the refrain of some long-forgotten melody.

'The fire is out at the heart of the world;
all tame creatures have grown up wild.
The lives I trusted, even my own.
collapse, break off, or don't belong . . .

'The fire is out at the heart of the world;
all tame creatures have grown up wild –
all except you, your life like a cloud.
I am lost in now and will never be found.'

She was not sure she understood it, but it seemed to have a meaning, and therefore a beauty, which was just beyond her grasp.

Regularly, once a day, Ruby would lose herself in cyberspace. Virtual reality was to blame.

They had a Vreal machine in the amusement arcade. She had heard about them, of course, but had never actually tried one out herself. She had imagined it was just for kids, though she knew that in California the Virtuality Tank was all the rage. 'Gateway to Spiritual Enlargement', the creation-centred gurus claimed. Closer to home were the notorious teledildonic suits at the SaferSex emporiums along the Pentonville Road near the King's Cross SuperRail terminal. There, the travel weary, the jaded, those in search of experiences out of the ordinary, or the just plain curious, were given a guarantee of satisfaction untouched by human hand.

LogOn 00:22 Thursday 14 December 2006   File: Cruise
Spent the entire evening talking with Mike Brack. Alone. Diana and Leslie had two shows to do.

It's a funny feeling, getting one on one with someone you idolized as a kid. We started out a bit formal. For something to say, I told him I was the only one left doing Pah T'wa with Barbara.

'People can't take the truth so early in the morning,' he said. 'Typical of the masses.'

Typical of his humour. He puts on this sneering, bitter kind of front. It can be quite funny. But you feel he's always under tight control.

Then we talked philosophy of all things. I bluffed a lot.

He's keen on Heidegger. German existentialist. I'd never heard of him, but didn't let on. I knew Sartre was an existentialist so told the joke I'd read on the wall of the ladies toilets at the BBC.

To be is to do – Descartes.
To do is to be – Sartre.
Do be do be do – Frank Sinatra.

Only for Sartre I substituted Heidegger.

I'd had to ask who Frank Sinatra was before I got the joke, but he must have known because it paroxysed him. In a controlled sort of way. Actually, he's old enough to have worked with Frank Sinatra. Diana said he's coming up to 45. If he is, he's very well preserved.

Heidegger, according to Mike Brack, thought society was becoming cybernetic. That is, things being done in a more and more efficient way. Efficiency is the goal. End justifying means. So people don't just run for the pleasure of it. They do it to get healthy. Same with food. They choose what to eat not for the way it looks and tastes, but because it's high in energy, say, or anti-carcinogenic. Heidegger said it was going to get worse. We'd get stuck in a dark age where efficiency was the be-all and end-all.

Mike Brack thinks Heidegger is dead right. But here's the creepy thing. He was looking forward to it. Embrace the inevitable, he said. The human race has to become more efficient to survive. We had to find ways of living longer, of conserving our individual reserves. He told me he was in discussion now with an organization which was looking into the possibility of creating virtual immortality. He had a few ideas about it of his own.

He was droning on in such an emotionless way, I tried to inject a bit of passion. Things were really falling apart, I said. The centre could not hold. People weren't built to be efficient.

They just wanted to enjoy the party while it lasted. Look at the people on the ship.

'Well, of course, the herd,' he drawled, and he looked so smug that I wanted to throw my glass of Niersteiner at him. I told him so. I said I would enjoy doing it and that wasn't the least bit efficient.

He said I would be eliminated. Calmly and matter-of-factly, of course. He was cold as ice, and just as hard. He's got a definite attitude problem and it was getting on my nerves.

'In any case,' I said, 'I lean towards Descartes' view.'

'Those whom the passions move most deeply
Enjoy life's sweetest pleasures'.

I'd actually picked that up from the front of some old novel in the library. Bluff, bluff, bluff. But it seemed to break the ice. He seemed to realize suddenly that he'd been acting like a prize wonka.

'Sorry,' he said, and smiled at me in such a sexy way I felt like a schoolkid again. Then he ordered absinthes for both of us and we sort of mellowed into the evening, me trying to find out more about him, him doing the same with me.

I think he assumes I'm some sort of exotic import.

You know, Nano, I think you and Granny are the only ones I've ever talked to who haven't asked where am I from, or when or if I plan to go back.

He asked about my 'background'. I fed him some disinformation for the hell of it. Sierra Leone, I think I said. My family was in diamonds.

It was a queer kind of cat and mouse game. That was kind of sexy, too.

I even got to try out some of Barbara's Gong Qi Po on him. He was complaining of a pain in the neck. (Perhaps he was talking about me?) It seemed to work. He suggested I treat his insomnia next time.

What kind of invitation is that?

To seek Virtuality in California, you took off all your clothes and climbed inside a tank of shallow salty water. The salt was for buoyancy. You put on the headset like a balaclava. It fed

77

you the 3D images and stereo sound. Then you lay back and explored your mind. Virtually.

The headset was just like the Vreal visor, except it had to be waterproof, for obvious reasons. And as with the Vreal machine sensors tracked your head movements, altering the images and sound accordingly.

The cunning thing about the Californian version was that the micro-electric pulses produced by your brain, the alpha-waves and beta-waves and so on, were picked up and fed back into the computer. What you saw and heard was your own neural feedback, in continuous interaction with the Mandelbrot sets of the computer.

Floating in simulated zero-gravity, insulated from all sensations of the real world, you were free to explore the distant recesses of your mind.

It was meant to be strongly calming experience. But there were reports of trips into the interior sometimes going wrong. Rumours of brains going permanently into glitch.

There had been no complaints as yet about the King's Cross teledildonics. None from the users, anyway. The only objections had come from such organizations as the Citadel of Morality and the Freedom Foundation, none of whose members had tried the system, of course. At least none admitted to trying it.

The Vreal machine on the *SS Elysium* was not as sophisticated as these other more esoteric virtualities. It was really a simple arcade amusement. You didn't have to take your clothes off. Instead of floating in salty water, or inserting yourself in a dildonic suit, you sat in a kind of cabinet. All it promised was fifteen minutes of fabulous entertainment.

With the headset and control gloves in place, you could choose to pilot a fighter plane, or drive a tank through Brooklyn. Or you might find yourself in some dark labyrinth, laser weapon in hand, picking off hordes of nasty aliens that were always creeping up on you.

But Ruby preferred the Lucid Dreaming.

Selecting the Lucid Dreaming mode, she would suddenly be soaring miles above an incredible tectonic landscape, painted in sparkling blues and gorgeous reds, awesome yellows and soothing greens. The magical kingdom of cyberspace. She drifted above a fantasy world of infinite discovery. She would swoop down to explore the detail of the landscape, and the terrain would swirl up to her and open like a flower. There would be rocky canyons to examine, or shimmering rivers to follow to their source, or new uncharted seas.

Those fifteen-minute sessions never seemed enough, but it was all that was allowed, by medical decree. The World Health Organisation's guidelines for avoidance of mental impairment were displayed in large letters on the side of the Vreal machine. Ruby could understand why. She found it incredibly addictive. Somebody had recently condemned it as 'yet another glitch switch for the mind'. They might be right. Cyberspace was dangerous. That was part of the fun.

As a kind of antidote, she made sure her body got some attention. She went for a swim at least once a day, down in the crowded indoor pool. It was now too cold to brave the pool on the deck.

Three times a week she put a couple of hours into working out in the gym. She had never been much bothered about her body before, except for the way it misled people about her place of birth. But now she was gaining a heightened appreciation for the elegance of the human form. Even hers. She began to admire her lean brown limbs and sturdy body. She delighted in the new-found muscles which softly rippled under the velvet skin.

All this unaccustomed exertion gave her a savage appetite. The food on board was superb. Since researching an article on abattoirs, early in her career, she had never eaten meat. But few of her fellow passengers demanded it either, and the choice and quality of the non-meat fare was staggering. The water tasted like wine, and the wine was pretty good, too.

She had never felt so well. It was a gloriously physical sensation. It surged through her body. It sang in her veins. And at night she had no difficulty sleeping. There were no anxieties to keep her awake. No deadlines to keep her up. No early morning meetings to drag herself out of bed for.

She lived each day to the full. Each night she gave herself up to a pleasant exhaustion. The gentle rocking of the *Elysium* snuffed her out like a candle. Her sleep was the sleep of the blessed.

But the investigator in her was resting, not retired. At some level her mind was forever making connections.

LogOn 17:06 Saturday 16 December 2006   File: Cruise
As it gets colder, again, I'm spending more time in the library. I usually have it to myself.

Today I came across a little book by a Chinese sage, Lao Tzu. He wrote it two and a half thousand years ago and he's supposed to have lived for more than two hundred years. One tradition says he never died, just disappeared inside his jade pagoda. Did a lot of Pah T'wa, I'd guess.

The Tao is Chinese for path or way, in the sense of the path to travel, or the way things are. Lao Tzu describes it like this.

'Infinitely billowing forth,
It returns again to non-existence.
No name, no shape, no substance.
Darkly visible, without beginning or end.
The way of the past
Is the way of the present.
The Tao.'

Reading Lao Tzu is like lucid dreaming in the Vreal machine. Just as you think you come close to understanding something, the meaning unravels and comes apart in your mind. You lose the thread and have to begin again.

Noticed something odd about the control panel in the lift today. Still trying to work it out.

As you would expect, given that there are four main levels on this ship, there are four buttons. 'A' is for pool deck, penthouse suites and restaurant. 'B' is for sun deck, ballroom and deluxe accommodation. 'C' is for standard accommodation, cinema and shops. 'D' is where my cabin is – budget accommodation, crew quarters, indoor swimming pool and gym.

Beside each button there's a light. But underneath the light for D deck there's a fifth unmarked light. And instead of a button there's a digit pad for entering a pass code.

There must be a whole lower level to this ship not accessible to the general public.

I've been wondering, Nano. What's down there?

10   No Beginning, No End

The door creaked almost shut behind him. Only a narrow beam
of light cut through the room and outlined the contours of an
ancient console in the centre.

There was a tickle in the Doctor's nose. He pulled out his
handkerchief and sneezed explosively. A shower of dust par-
ticles whirled and floated gently downwards in the beam of
light, like a snowstorm in a paperweight. He tucked his
handkerchief back in his pocket.

Block the openings. Shut the doors.

He reached out behind him. The chink of light was snuffed
out. Total blackness.

There was so much in his head.

He had to simplify. To dwindle. Reduce. Dissolve. Return
to nothing. Return to the place from which he could start
again.

His feet were hot from walking. He sat on the floor in the
darkness and put his umbrella to one side. He removed his
hat. He undid his shoelaces and pulled off his shoes and socks.
He massaged his toes and rubbed the soles. It felt good.

He replaced his hat and stood. He enjoyed the feel of the
cool jade floor, its smooth solidity.

By degrees his breathing became slow and deep.

A journey of a thousand years begins beneath one's feet.

11 Skies are Blue

It was Sunday afternoon. The indoor pool was warm and crowded. Ruby lay in the recliner chair and pondered Lao Tzu.

Excited shrieks echoed off the blue tiled walls. The splash of water and the smell of chlorine brought back happy childhood days when her mum would take her swimming, then home to pancakes with lemon and sugar, and her body would feel alive and tingly. And later in bed she felt she was swimming still.

She was happy then. Yet behind that childhood happiness was the knowledge of the terrible thing that had happened to her father, how it had altered their lives forever.

It seemed that as she grew older, happiness was less and less a feature of her life. More and more it was only a memory.

Those lines from the poem she had come across in the library kept going through her head.

The fire is out at the heart of the world;
   all tame creatures have grown up wild.
     The lives I trusted, even my own,
collapse, break off, or don't belong . . .

The fire is out at the heart of the world;
   all tame creatures have grown up wild –
   all except you, your life like a cloud.
I am lost in now and will never be found.

Who the 'you' was she couldn't be sure. And 'like a cloud'? You couldn't pin down a cloud. It has no shape, no substance.

No real identity. Would it be comforting to know somebody like that? Would she be happier if she did?

At that moment, sitting by the pool in the *SS Elysium*, she could not say she was unhappy. But she felt she was lost in now. The first four weeks of the cruise had been blissful. Yet behind her present contentment she realized there was still a shadow.

It was not the weight that had fallen away at the start of the voyage. It was what the absence of that weight revealed. She had become aware of something else. A distant, ever present, insecurity. Though skies were blue, they could always fall in and crush her.

Ruby looked at the lively bodies in the water and the recumbent ones around the pool, at their jolly fleshiness and their spirited conversations. They seemed happy enough.

She read Lao Tzu.

'I alone am inactive and unrevealing,
Like a child that does not smile,
Subdued, without a home to go to.
The crowd have more than enough.
I am wanting.'

Ruby lay back and closed her eyes and pondered.

The shrieks became louder. Ruby recognized one raised voice among the rest, approaching her.

'Darling, you kept it from us. You naughty thing! How exciting. Tell us it's true.'

Diana had come to a noisy halt and sat on a recliner next to Ruby. Leslie was following close behind.

'Now, Diana, don't be a fool,' he said as he parked himself at the other side of Ruby. 'Just because she's called Ruby. Tell her, Ruby. She's got it wrong, hasn't she?'

Ruby was aware that they were attracting the attention of the reclining bodies around her. Some sat up and looked. Others went on with what they were doing. She knew that all of them were listening. Her friends could be so embarrassing.

'What are you two on about?' She kept her voice as low as possible in the hope that they would get the message.

'I know it's you, darling,' Diana twittered loudly. She produced a folded newspaper and slapped it down on top of Lao Tzu. The *Sunday Seeker*, four weeks old.

Leslie leaned forward and explained. 'Last month's papers have just been 'coptered in from the Falklands.'

'Over the rainbow cruise gets away from the gloom by Ruby Duvall,' Diana read out in a very loud voice. 'That's you, isn't it, darling? Tell us it is.'

All activity had ceased in the indoor pool. Ruby could feel a hundred eyes, sharp with curiosity, bearing down on her swimsuited body. She felt horribly exposed.

'It's ridiculous, isn't it, Rubes?' piped Leslie. 'Some of the ideas she gets into her head. I don't know.'

He began to neigh. Diana raised her voice a pitch and read on.

'Each passenger was subject to a full security screening before boarding, and I can personally vouch for its thoroughness! You see, that proves it,' she screeched, 'You told us about that groping you got from that security man.'

'Doesn't prove it at all,' protested Leslie. '*I* was groped by a security man. Does that mean I wrote the article as well?'

He neighed again, pleased at his logic.

'All right,' said Ruby as quietly as she could manage while still being firm. 'All right. If you promise to keep your hair on, I'll tell you. Yes. It's me. I am Ruby Duvall. I – '

'I knew it, darling!' shrieked Diana. 'What did I tell you, Leslie? Sweetie! You're Ruby Duvall! How splendid!'

Things were going too far. She had to get out of there. People were nudging their neighbours and whispering.

'No! Really! How extraordinary!' Leslie was saying. He was shaking his head in delighted wonder.

Before either of them could add to her already unbearable mortification, Ruby reached for her sweatshirt and book.

'I think a coffee is called for, don't you?'

By the time they had caught her up, Ruby was waiting at the lift. In hushed, exasperated tones she tried to get them to understand the discretion that was needed by someone in her position. They readily agreed. Their fulsome apologies made her feel she was being unnecessarily grand.

The lift arrived. She pulled on her sweatshirt. A group of

excited oldies with towels and ice creams emerged from the lift and pushed on towards the pool.

She was Ruby Duvall, so what? Who on this ship would even turn a hair?

Settled in the café-bar, Diana confessed she was one of Ruby's greatest fans. She had followed her illegal arms exposé with particular glee. It had seriously embarrassed a government she thought despicable.

'If we're talking about embarrassment – ' Ruby began.

'Oh, I know, sweetie-pie. We're both terribly sorry. We just didn't think. We were so excited. Weren't we, Leslie?'

'I'll say,' said Leslie. 'Did you hear, Rubes? This'll be up your street – the FF made another arrest this morning. Suspected terrorist. He'll be held till we get to Sydney.'

'Are you here to investigate the terrorists, darling? Or are you keeping an eye on the Freedom Fascists? You can tell us, sweetie. All off the record, of course.'

Ruby told them the truth. She was on holiday. Her job was simply to write an account of the trip and to take some 3D pictures with her holocam.

'Golly,' said Leslie, 'Will we get a mention?'

'It's more than possible,' said Ruby evenly.

He chortled, and Diana assumed an expression of pure delight.

They had a lot more to ask. Why, for example, had she been calling herself Ruby Robert?

'My mother was Jacqueline Robert before she married. You remember I told you she was French-Algerian? Robert is the name I use in real life. It's on my cheques and everything. If anything's a pseudonym it's my working name Duvall.'

Because of all the publicity at the time of his dreadful accident, and because he had remained in the public eye with his computer wizardry and his recent bestseller, they knew all about Ruby's father, Philip Duvall. They asked her the usual questions. Did she remember the accident? What difference had it made when it was obvious he would be paralysed for life? How could he be so creative and brilliant when his body was useless? How had her mother coped?

As so often before, Ruby told the story. It no longer caused her pain. She'd frozen out the pain.

She told them she was barely two at the time of the accident. She had only vague unconnected images to remember it by. Watching *The Wizard of Oz*. Being frightened of the witch and seeing her shrivel. The newsflash about a new planet. The ring at the door. The policeman with the news that her father had been knocked down by the Faceless Biker.

'Faceless Biker, darling?' queried Diana, gravely.

'An old news-vender had witnessed the accident from inside his kiosk,' explained Ruby. 'The man on the motorbike had been dressed in black leather jacket and jeans, a shiny black visor over his face, just like the hero of one of the comics he sold.'

'Oh, yes, the Faceless Biker!' recalled Leslie. 'I used to read those comics when I was a nipper.'

Ruby told them that the Faceless Biker had remained faceless and untraced.

Then she told them about her daddy coming home after a long time in hospital, her growing up with him in a wheelchair, the funny American synthesized voice which she soon accepted as his, the terrible embarrassment as she grew a little older when friends came home to tea, offset by the pride she felt in having a famous father.

She told of later times. The terrible tensions in the house. Her mother struggling with his physical handicaps, fighting his stubborn, self-pitying streak. The rows. His pioneering computing genius attracting international recognition but not at first much money. The financial difficulties in the depths of the country's longest ever recession. The death of her mother from one of the plague diseases.

Diana and Leslie listened in absolute silence. Diana had a comforting hand on Ruby's shoulder. Leslie had tears in his eyes. Ruby felt nothing. She just told the story.

She told them how she could not forgive her father for the burden he put on her mother, could not forgive him his single-minded devotion to himself and to his genius, could not forgive him for killing her mother.

She told them how she had not spoken to him for more than four years. She did not know if she would ever speak to him again. In truth, she felt nothing for him.

She had only one point of connection with her father. And

that was coincidental. The miniature computer she was using, her Nanocom, happened to be based on a system he had devised. The Nanocom had been loaned to her by ElysiuMatics, the firm that had made it. She was testing it out.

She would show them the Nanocom, and the Holocam. She would take holograms of them, rehearsing and performing. They would be featured in her story on the cruise.

Diana and Leslie threw off their sympathetic faces and became their lively selves again.

'But tell me, Rubes,' said Leslie, 'You said about that new planet being discovered when you were little. Was that in eighty-six?'

Ruby nodded.

'I remember that,' he went on. 'It was supposed to be the undiscovered tenth planet in our solar system. It was just before my tenth birthday and I was awfully keen on astronomy and space and such.'

'I don't believe it, Leslie. You?' Diana said.

'What's so surprising about that?'

'Oh, nothing. I suppose you were on the watch for little green men.'

'My dear,' he said, looking down his nose at her. 'Green ones, perhaps. But certainly never little.'

The other two grinned. He turned again to Ruby.

'You know, there were all sorts of rumours that there'd been an alien invasion, that this so-called tenth planet – it was before the real tenth planet, Cassius, had been found, you see. That was in 1994 – '

'For gawd's get on with it,' said Diana.

'Well, the long and the short of it is that some people actually believed it had life on it. Extraterrestrials who wanted to take over Earth.'

'Oh, yes, there were news reports, weren't there?' recalled Diana. 'Pictures of men in tin suits?'

'Careful, Di,' Leslie twinkled, 'Giving your age away.'

Diana ignored him. She was remembering. 'Darling,' she said to Ruby, 'didn't you do an article on one of those people, one of the ones who claimed it wasn't a hoax? What was her name? Alison something – '

'Isobel, you mean?' said Ruby. 'Isobel Watkins. Yes, she

was a puzzle. Really nice. In her late forties. Beautiful bone structure. A top photographer in the 1970s. She showed me some of her early self-portraits. She was stunning.'

'So who was this woman, Rubes?' said Leslie, bursting with curiosity.

Ruby had a good memory for things connected with her work. The details of the interview came effortlessly to mind.

'Her career took off when she landed this publishing contract to go round the world. You remember that Victorian girl who took pictures of what she said were the fairies at the bottom of her garden?'

Leslie started to giggle, but nodded yes.

'She always swore that the fairies were real,' Ruby went on. 'All the experts said that the photos had been faked, but in spite of that, she sounded so convincing that lots of people continued to believe her. And then, at the age of about ninety, she admitted she'd set the whole thing up. Cut fairy shapes out of cardboard, painted them, then stuck them in her rockery and photographed them with her box camera.'

'But what's all that got to do with this Alison Watkins?'

'Isobel Watkins, darling,' corrected Diana.

'Isobel had won her publishing contract because the style of her photos were so unusual,' Ruby explained. 'Now this is the point. Some of her photos were of what she claimed were an invasion of extraterrestrial beings.'

'In the 1970s?' frowned Leslie. 'I remember the invasion of the ladybirds, but not this other one.'

'Well, yes, you ought to have heard my mother on the subject of ladybirds. Any bugs at all, come to that.' Ruby was digressing. She enjoyed remembering her mum. 'But anyway, Isobel said that governments around the world had known about it, that a United Nations Intelligence Task-force led by a Brigadier Lethbridge-Stewart had fought them off, and that there had been a cover-up. Above top secret. That means that only a very few people in authority could ever know about it.'

Isobel had also spoken of three other people who were involved. A doctor who looked human but wasn't, a Scottish Highlander complete with kilt, and a young girl who was a genius at maths. All three had come from a different time and place, Isobel had claimed, to help fight the aliens, and when it was over they returned to their time-machine which was invisible and parked in a country field and simply vanished.

Ruby did not mention all this to Diana and Leslie. She did not want them thinking that Isobel had been entirely mad.

'What did the photographs show?' asked Leslie, all agog.

'Little green men, cut out of cardboard?' put in Diana, less taken by it all.

'The few I saw were of tall, robotic-looking creatures. That's probably what you remembered, Diana, when you spoke of the men in tin suits. Isobel described them as cybernetic creatures.'

'You mean, like cyborgs?' questioned Leslie. 'Part human, part machine?'

'Yes, something like that. She was quite specific about them. Inhuman killers from another world, she called them. And they wanted to take over this one. She said the whole world was put into hypnotic trance for several hours early one morning, and that's when the invasion took place. She said these creatures had ways of controlling people's minds so they would appear to be almost normal, but not.'

'Like Michael Brack, you mean,' said Diana.

'Exactly,' was Ruby's immediate reply.

They held each other in a frightened stare, each trying to spook the other out. Ruby gave way first and they both fell about with helpless laughter.

'Now come on, you two,' said Leslie, who couldn't see what there was to laugh about. 'Mike isn't a bad chap.'

That started them off again.

When they had regained some composure, Leslie steered the subject back to the photos.

'The experts said the images were faked,' explained Ruby. 'What she showed me could easily have been mock-ups. A photograph doesn't prove anything. She knew that as well as I did. But she'd learnt it the hard way, through thirty years of rididule. What struck me, though, was her conviction. She believed absolutely in what she said. I'm not saying I believed her. Just that she was convinced that the creatures she photographed were real.'

'Half a mo,' said Leslie, 'I'm losing track. You said that

she claimed there was an invasion during the seventies. Right?'

'Right,' said Ruby.

'So what's the connection between that and the discovery of that planet ten years later?'

Ruby absently picked up a spoon and played with the dregs of coffee at the bottom of her cup as she marshalled her thoughts.

'You remember there was a lot of confusion about the planet?'

'You mean astronomers thinking it resembled Earth, then when it disintegrated saying they must have got its size wrong. Didn't they end up saying it was just a passing meteorite?'

'Meteoroid,' Ruby corrected. 'Yeah, they did. Well, the appearance of that planet, or meteoroid, or whatever it was, happened to coincide with a number of sightings of UFOs and encounters with EBEs.'

'EBEs?' queried Diana, listlessly.

'Sorry. Extraterrestrial Beings. Anyway, though she didn't claim to have seen them this time, Isobel Watkins did say that some of these reports made the EBEs sound like her cybercreatures. So the media dragged out her photos again. And that's what Diana remembers seeing.'

'Oh, well, sweetie,' said Diana. 'There'll always be cranks. Like your Canadian friend.'

'Barbara?' said Ruby. 'Oh, she's all right. Though she did mention yesterday that she wanted to introduce me to ethereal time-travel.'

'Oh, gawd,' said Diana, dismissively, inspecting her nails. They were a shiny crimson to match the crimson of her glossy lipstick. She looked around at the coming and going of the other people in the café-bar. She crossed one crimson-stockinged thigh over the other. She rapped her crimson nails on the table-top. Clearly, the subject of planets and aliens and time-travel was of limited interest.

Leslie was building a wall of sugar cubes.

'Leslie's going to be a tin man. Aren't you, sweetie?' said Diana suddenly, then added just as suddenly, 'Oh, go and get me another coffee, Leslie. There's an angel.'

As Leslie wandered off to join the queue at the counter,

Ruby asked what Diana had meant about the tin man. Diana seemed to be thinking about something else.

'What, darling? Oh, it's just something we're doing for the ball. From the *Wizard of Oz*, actually. Hope it won't upset you,' said Diana.

Ruby shook her head. 'The ball's this Friday, isn't it? The twenty-second?'

'That's right, darling, and, no, we haven't forgotten that's your birthday. But listen.' She drew closer to Ruby. 'There's something I've been dying to tell you about Michael. Now that I know you have a professional interest in these things, I can't hold off any longer. But you mustn't breathe a word.'

This was Diana's dark secret. While she was living with him, in the latter stages when things weren't going too well, she found a crumpled letter in Brack's bin. She was convinced he was having an affair with someone else at the time and so of course felt morally entitled to root through his personal effects. The letter in question was from Lord Stanley Straker, no less, just at the time when he was successfully defending himself against allegations of laundering millions of ECUs from secret arms sales. The letter incriminated Brack as a supplier of armaments, or at least implied he was a go-between.

'When was this, that you found the letter?'

'Early summer. Just before I left the two-timing bastard.' Diana's voice was even but her eyes were hard as diamonds. 'June, I think it was.'

'Do you have the letter still?'

'Oh, yes, I kept it. Just in case it might come in useful. It's among my luggage somewhere.' She gave a wicked little grin. 'Do you want to see it?'

Ruby nodded. She saw that Leslie was approaching with a tray. Eyes were turning her way. Fingers were pointing. Her cover was definitely blown. Oh, what the hell.

Something had just occurred to her.

'Diana,' she said.

'Mm hmm?'

'Didn't you tell me you were having an affair with a gorgeous flamenco dancer last June?'

91

Diana's wicked look spread from her mouth to her eyes. She started to giggle. Ruby joined in.

By the time Leslie had arrived with his tray, they were in paroxysms of suffocating, delicious, conspiratorial laughter.

During the afternoon just two days later, as had become her habit, Ruby made her way to the *Elysium*'s library.

She had been on the sun deck. The skies were a brilliant blue and the sun shone down brightly on the straggle of passengers gripping the rail, peering out towards the horizon for sight of the first Antarctic icebergs. The plastic sun canopy had been dismantled and packed away. The breeze was strong and surprisingly cold. Ruby was not well-enough wrapped up to spend more than a few minutes on the deck, so she headed for the synthetic cosiness of the library's log fire.

She could feel the drumming of the *Elysium*'s engines under her feet as she walked along the corridor. The lower, inaccessible level of the ship must at least contain the engine rooms. What else would there be down there? She would ask Captain Trench. She couldn't put off her interview with him much longer.

As she reached the open library door she saw a figure bent over an open book on the table, scribbling notes on a piece of paper. She recognized the jet black hair, the pallid greenish skin. She watched as he rose, preoccupied, paper in hand, and walked towards the suit of armour in the corner. He lifted a bony white hand to the helmet and tentatively raised the visor.

'Caught you!' said Ruby and walked right in. She grinned at him. 'Doing a bit of research?'

Mike Brack turned to face her. The visor clanged shut. His face was a picture of surprise.

It was the first time she had seen him not absolutely in control. It seemed he was trying to speak but nothing would come. His hand was gripping hard on the piece of paper.

Ruby thought he was play-acting. Then she saw the deep rouge of a blush rising from his neck, the look of barely concealed distress as if some interior struggle were going on. The paper was scrunching in his hand.

To Ruby the moment seemed to go on for ever, but at last he regained some mastery over himself.

'Ms Duvall,' he rasped. 'I – '

But then he stuck again. It seemed he wanted to speak but could not quite bring himself to do it. He stretched out a hand and grasped Ruby tight by the wrist, and looked at her so intently it was as though his eyes were burning into her. She could feel the tremor of his hand, of the struggle within himself, as he increased the pressure on her wrist.

He was hurting her. She wanted to scream.

Immediately the pressure eased. His hand dropped away. He edged backwards and towards the door.

And then he was gone. Ruby heard his hurrying footsteps fading along the corridor.

She was in shock. She knew he was unconventional but his behaviour had been so weird, so unexpected. Something else was odd. He had called her Ms Duvall.

He must have heard. That Ruby Duvall, the *Sunday Seeker* reporter was on board. He must have put two and two together, as Diana did, and deduced that it was her. But why did he react like that?

Ruby was suddenly apprehensive. She had caught the public imagination with her latest gun-running scoop. That was what she was known so widely for. Was there something in what Diana suspected? Did he really have something to hide?

The book he had been reading was open on the table. She picked it up. It was old and dusty. She looked at the cover. The author of the book was a man she had not heard of. Norbert Wiener. The book was entitled *Communication and Control in the Animal and the Machine*. Sounded dull. Putting it down again on the table, she noticed the blurb on the back. 'The classic 1948 treatise in which Norbert Wiener introduced to the world the science of cybernetics.'

Mike Brack slowed to a steadier pace. He strode resolutely to the lift. He stood unmoving as he waited for it to arrive. He breathed steadily and deeply.

The lift doors opened. It was empty. He stepped inside. The lift doors closed. He tapped out a series of numbers into the security pad. There was a beep. The light next to the slot lit up. The lift descended.

The lift doors opened. He stepped out onto a dim corridor lit only by low emergency lights. He strode past six identical doors. He stopped at the seventh. He opened it and went inside. He switched on a light. He closed the door behind him.

He leaned on the door and closed his eyes. His mouth moved.

'Ruby Duvall,' he muttered.

His eyes opened wide. He propelled himself forward.

In the centre of the room was a complicated structure of wire and glass. Mike Brack smoothed out the crumpled sheet of paper which he held still clutched in his hand. He bent down to a box of tools and grimly set to work.

Behind him, strapped against the wall, creaking with the movement of the ship, stacked upright, side by side, was a series of tall, heavy-looking, wooden crates. On each, a single word was stamped.

Panama.

Barbara was murmuring into Ruby's ear. Her voice was low and breathy.

'Time does not exist. Time is nowhere. Time is an illusion, created for us human beings, in order that we cannot know everything at once.'

Her mouth was so close that it tickled. Ruby found it hard not to squirm. She concentrated on her breathing, as Barbara had requested her to do.

'You won't see everything. Time is in the vortex of energies between us. You'll see what you want to see. You'll find what you want to find. The future is here, is now.'

Ruby had imagined time-travel to be a little more dramatic than this. She was sitting in the corduroy armchair in the Canadian woman's standard cabin. Her arms were on the arms of the chair. Barbara knelt beside her whispering into her ear.

She tried to concentrate. Her eyes were closed. Her breathing was slow and steady. She felt as though she was at the dentist.

'Our Mother Gaia, hold this child. Open to her the wonders

of the universe. Show her no more than she can hope to bear. Open to her the wonders of her future. In the name of the living spirit of the Earth. Amen.'

There was a long, long pause.

Ruby could feel Barbara's breath on her neck. She could smell the garlic from her evening meal. She could feel the coarse ribbed velvet of the armchair under her fingers.

'Ruby. Are you holding on in there? If you sense a rush of wind, a sort of whooshing, then you're on your way. No need to be afraid. We can control your flight.'

The only thing Ruby was afraid of at that moment was yawning. She had drunk nearly a bottle of chardonnay with her fish, and she was beginning to feel drowsy.

'Are you feeling it?'

'Erm. Difficult to say.'

'What about the ground at your feet. Can you sense its texture.'

'My feet feel a little numb?' tried Ruby hopefully, and truthfully.

'What can you see?'

Ruby thought for a moment. She could see the backs of her eyelids, if Barbara wanted the truth.

'It's black but white. Erm. White shapes. Blank whitenesses.'

It was after all what she saw.

It was no good. Even Barbara realized they were not getting anywhere.

'You're tired, my dear,' said Barbara. 'Another time.'

Ruby thought 'another time' had been the point.

Barbara was closing the session with a valediction to the Earth goddess Gaia. The two women bowed to each other in a Pah T'wa sign of parting and Ruby left.

It was late. She was tired. She was woozy. But she did not want to go to bed just yet. It was her birthday tomorrow, for Gaia's sake!

She made her way unsteadily along the corridor, past the darkened windows of the shops, past the cinema entrance, and up the stairs. The lights were dim. There was no one about.

Up one flight of stairs. Up two. Up another flight. One more to go. The face of Mike Brack flitted vaguely across her consciousness. It made her feel perplexed, depressed. Her father came to mind. The lolling head. The buzzing voice.

She had reached the open deck at last. She moved towards the stern, as directly as the rolling ship and her rolling gait would allow. She grabbed the rail. The icy blast of wind whooshed through her coarse black hair.

She was travelling through time.

She was.

She watched the luminous wake of the ship widen and disappear. That was her past. It was leaving her forever. Lost forever. It could never be recaptured. Twenty-one today. Twenty-two tomorrow. She was trapped in now. And now was taking her relentlessly forward. Into what?

The ship was a time machine. It was taking her into the future. But the future was behind her. She had her back to it. She could have no idea what it held. Blank whiteness, perhaps. Was that all that she could hope for in her life?

She stared at the disappearing foam that was forever issuing forth and renewing itself from under the ship. The source of the numberless creatures.

Words of Lao Tzu came to her unbidden, from out of the depths of memory.

'Infinitely billowing forth,
It ever renews itself.
Deep, like the source of the numberless creatures.
No name, no shape, no substance.
Darkly visible, the way only seems to be there.'

She spoke them softly to herself, as she shivered in the icy breeze, thinking just for a moment that she understood.

Then it slipped away. The meaning drifted away like the foam on the endless wake. She merely stood and stared. She wanted to go neither back nor forward. She was simply there.

It was the twenty-first of December. Midsummer's Eve. The nights were getting even shorter. The ship was nearing the circle of the Antarctica. Inside that magic circle, for the next few days, the sun would never set.

Tomorrow was the longest day. Tomorrow was her birthday.

Tomorrow was the Midsummer Ball. A thousand people crammed into the ballroom, celebrating their great good fortune. Away from the gloom. Where the sun never sets. Somewhere over the rainbow.

She looked up into the midnight sky, a dimming twilight that would never fully blacken into darkness. The moon was full and bright. Such power it had over the Earth. Ruby marvelled at the way it pulled the seas about. Effortless control. The power. The everyday, incomprehensible, awesome power of nature.

And then it was suddenly back with her. The great weight on her mind. The heaviness that had been with them all before they had set out. What the voyage had made them forget. The crazy pendulum of the Earth's magnetic field which could swing up and over and crush them all. The thing that nobody ever talked about for real. The thing that was being prepared against at that very moment in the icy wilderness of Antarctica. Such puny, uncertain measures. Such a fragile, fragile world. She felt so tiny in it.

Near to the moon a star shone brightly. Its light was strong and cold and piercing. As Ruby looked upon the star she made a wish. She wished never to go back. She wished to be taken away. She wished to be whooshed away to a totally different world.

She shivered. She was freezing. She was raving. She was drunk and horribly morose. The wine was thinking for her. Getting its own back. She quickly turned and headed below.

At least the tiny cabin was warm.

She threw off her clothes, brushed her teeth, had a pee, and flung herself under the covers.

She could not sleep. The room was threatening to revolve every time she closed her eyes. With the motion of the ship she was feeling slightly nauseous, too.

She thought of Barbara's massage. The technique to cure insomnia. Might as well give it a go, the Gong Qi Po.

She threw back the covers, pressed hard on the zusanli point, just below the knee, then pulled the covers over her again and lay on her back. She pressed at a spot between her eyebrows, a steady, even pressure. A feeling of warmth radiated up from

97

finger to hairline. She massaged her cheeks with her thumbs. She gripped her arm below the wrist and squeezed. The nausea vanished.

She placed the tip of her tongue on the roof of her mouth just behind her front teeth. She laid a hand just below her stomach, the other on her chest, forming a circle.

All that was going round now was the energy flow, the qi. From chest to stomach. From stomach to chest. From chest to –

She fell asleep.

That night she dreamed. And the nightmare began.

12   Wake Up!

The AXV slid to a halt. Jude switched off the magnodrive. The humming of the engine subsided. Gary flipped a switch and spoke hoarsely into the radio.

'AXV5 back at base. Awaiting instructions for changeover.'

They heard a hiss of static, then inexplicably the crash of SlapRap. It cut out abruptly before Hilliard's voice came over, clear and close.

'Receiving you, AXV5. Welcome back, you two. How you doing?'

Gary cast an ironic glance across at Jude.

'Oh, just fine.'

'Hang on in there, will you? Till I check what's planned.'

Jude reached a hand across to Gary and pulled his face to hers. They kissed. Deeply.

It was back to sneaking the occasional snog again. Sex hadn't been so cramped and furtive for Jude since high school back in ninety-eight when she was fifteen years old. She'd held on to her virginity, just. For another couple of years. But she made sure the millennium had ended with a bang.

In those two years she had tried just about everything, short of popping her cherry. Small cars were her speciality. And the cabin of the AXV5 was not so dissimilar from a Ford electric. All the things she and Gary could have gotten up to if it weren't for that fizzing geomagnetic pole.

The epicentre of the magnoflux was hardly ever still now. To keep it plotted they had to take turns. Gary would drive while she monitored, or snatched some sleep, or ate. Then they would swap and she would drive, keeping on the trail of the little green dot on the magnoflux map. Only a couple of days at the base in-between.

It was the end of their third full week. And a week was a long time in an AXV.

That general was a clever woman. She had got them out of her hair so she could sleep. She had sent them away on the field, together, so they couldn't complain. She had removed them from Joe and his team so the lads could get on with the nitty-gritty of saving the planet.

Fine. Except that she and Gary were beginning to steam, cooped up in the AXV. Extreme prejudice was a military term she had learned as a cadet. Now she was learning another. Extreme frustration. Their so-called relief breaks, back at the base, were no relief. The new regime had knocked on the head the nocturnal hot flings, and during the day it was all hands on deck. She could think of better places for hands to be.

Gary's hands were probing. He was kissing her, long and hard. She felt his muscled body through his insosuit. Their limbs were intertwined. She was on the edge. Extreme frustration.

The radio crackled to life.

'Corporal Black?'

She pulled away from Gary's lips. She couldn't help herself. The sternness in the general's voice was just like her mother's, catching her in the saddle all those years ago.

'Corporal Black? Lieutenant Venning? Wake up in there, will you?'

There was a scrabble as they disentangled themselves and Gary leaned towards the radio.

'Hearing you, general.'

'Good. Now get your asses over here. Changeover's postponed for the night.'

This was unusual. It should have been a straight swap with Whitehead and Palmer. Bono and Nike were out on the field in AXV2. Whitehead and Palmer were scheduled to shadow them for the next two days, then take over monitoring to give Bono and Nike their relief.

What had brought about the change of routine? Breakdown of the project? Seemed unlikely. The extra engineering personnel had settled in and work was ahead of schedule. Mutiny on the base? Now that was more likely.

Whatever it was, something was definitely up. They collected together their few belongings and prepared themselves for the short trek across to the entrance shaft.

The general shut down the channel to AXV5. 'OK, corporal,' she called. 'Turn it back on. Loud as you like.'

Slap juddered out again from Whitehead's ghetto-blaster. Bodies gyrated. Voices were raised in laughter and good-natured argument. The air was thick with smoke. Cans and stubs and styrofoam cups littered the floor. The party was in full swing. Jude and Gary were in for one sweet shock. Well, they could relax and enjoy themselves for the night, just like the rest of the station. No doubt they'd make the most of it. They all of them had something to celebrate. FLIPback was up and running.

Pam Cutler smiled with satisfaction. At the flick of a switch the considerable power of the station's nuclear reactor would surge through the now completed Loop. A magnetic counter-force of global proportions would come on line.

She leant on the operations room desk and surveyed the gleaming FLIPback instrumentation, the ever-open data window on the central VDU, the all-important switch under its locked transparent cover. The switch was angled upwards to 'off'. The moment of truth was when it was flicked down to 'on'. Only then would they know for absolute certain that the Field Loop for Inverse Polarity was capable of doing what its name implied.

Timing was of the essence. The time to act was –

She made a conscious effort to stop thinking about it. She had gone over the procedure so many times in her mind. Even her dreams were full of it. She could forget it for a night.

She picked up her half empty cup of Recession '99, English wine which Ben had smuggled in. Not half bad. It knocked California cabernet out of the game. The changing climate had smiled on vineyards of Kent.

Pam caught sight of Ben and his dark-haired colleague talking quietly in the far corner of the room. He looked over and smiled. She raised her cup at him and winked.

Joe Adler let out a roar of filthy laughter, surrounded by his engineering team, Whitehead and Palmer and the five 'new boys'. They were laughing too, enjoying their sergeant's vicious humour. They would be away again in the morning, back to their routine duties at other UN enclaves round the world. Whitehead and Palmer would catch up with their duties in AXV5.

Adler roared again. He was on something stronger than the Recession, that was certain.

The lift doors parted. Jude and Gary appeared. Pam couldn't help grinning. They looked blown away. Ben was taking them in hand, plying them with morsels from his kitchen, filling cups with wine. He would explain. She was off-duty. Officially. First time since she'd taken charge at STS.

She looked around the room and caught sight of Dave Hilliard sitting alone in the equipment store beyond the operations room.

Yes. Tonight was the night.

She went through to him.

He'd known she would ask about it sometime. He'd been dreading it. And now that time had come. He didn't know if he could answer. He made a start.

'We flew in,' he said, and then stopped. The general nodded encouragement. Where to go from there? he wondered. The general waited.

He plunged in again.

'Everything looked normal.'

Now what? What came next? It was so long since he'd thought about the detail. He'd tried to bury it over, drown it deep.

'Er, because of the security blanket I was expecting a nuclear meltdown. At the very least. So because there was no gaping black hole in the ground, I reckoned there was nothing much wrong. This clear-up's gonna be safe and routine, I thought.'

He now spoke quickly, quietly, simply, looking mostly at the floor. The music thumped in the background. Pam had to strain to catch the words.

'For the first few hours they did not allow us in the base. I could see through the porthole and a couple of soldiers were bringing up armfuls of stuff and throwing it into a giant canister. The stand-in commander came into the aircraft and gave us a detailed brief.'

Pam leaned towards him.

'Did this guy say anything about my father?'

Hilliard shook his head, examining the floor as if his recollections were written on it.

'He said he'd been assigned to take over temporary command because of the death of the general. That was all. Except – ' Hilliard struggled as he dredged up some long forgotten memory. 'He mentioned a doctor, a frail old guy. He said he had saved the base, but couldn't save the general. Something like that. He said something about "the invasion". But it was a slip. He realized as soon as he'd said the word. It was never mentioned again.

'We were to clear the area of all the garbage. I remember thinking how clean everything looked, where was this garbage? He told us to look out for this old guy, the doctor, and two of his friends. A couple of Londoners. It seems they'd turned up out of nowhere, got involved in whatever had gone on in the base, and then gone walkabout. We were warned we might stumble across their corpses.

'Anyway, we kitted up in our parkas – no insosuits in those days – and filed out onto the snow. The weather was good that day.

'On closer inspection, the site wasn't as clean as it looked. The wide area around the base was littered with bits and pieces of damaged equipment. Things I'd never seen before. It wasn't US army or even UN gear. Pieces of piping, plastic vents, hoops of metal, thick-soled boots, all scattered around the base and beyond. There had been blizzards the day before. All I could guess was that the winds had whipped up over a pile of some – I don't know – obsolete service equipment, I suppose, and dispersed it all.

'The really screwy thing was that all this stuff was flimsy, almost transparent. Even what seemed to be metal. You know how aluminum foil gets when you put in in a flame? Flaky and fragile and it loses its colour? Well, that's how this stuff was. You'd pick up the arm of a metallized sleeve, or a lamp on a tubular mounting, and unless you were goddamned careful, it would just cave in and crumble, turn to flaky dust like ashes, and float away. It had hardly any weight at all.

'We gathered it into plastic bags and dumped it in the

garbage canister. Later on I saw them mark that canister with the words "above top secret".

'We worked outward from the entrance of the base. After an hour we had covered a circle about the radius of a kilometre. And we were spaced out from each other now so we were working more or less alone.'

Hilliard paused and frowned, testing his memory.

'You know how there are bumps in the ice? Can be six foot, ten foot high. And you don't see them till you're right on top of them? You think the snow just goes on flat forever?'

Pam nodded.

'The light was dimming. It was just after twenty-two hundred hours. I saw this huge mound just a few metres ahead of me. I walked right around it and I saw this – ' He spread his arms to convey a sense of the object. 'I don't know how to – a giant primus stove? A huge cake tin? Some kind of spacecraft, anyway. That was obvious.

'The material it was built of was weakened or denatured like the other stuff. So I knew it was theirs.'

'Theirs?' queried Pam.

Hilliard looked up at her again. He chewed at his lower lip, then looked away and continued with his story.

'There was an opening in the side of the vehicle. A door was sort of flapping on one of its hinges. I looked inside. It was a room with controls and two large seats like dentist's chairs. And in one of them was – this creature. It looked like a man, but taller. It was obviously dead. I climbed up and went inside to get a closer look.'

Hilliard was now taken up with the memory. The words tumbled out as he relived that moment, twenty years ago.

'It was dressed in a silver one-piece suit, wrapped in some kind of polythene cover. There were metal hoops over the arms and legs – just like the hoops we'd been finding in the snow. On the head was this lamp-like thing and – this'll sound bizarre – it was set on tubes coming out of the ears.

'Some sort of fabric was stretched over the face. You could see the human bone structure underneath.

'The hands were naked human hands. But the flesh was yellow, kind of ancient-looking. Preserved, maybe. The creature had the same fragile look as the rest of the vehicle. I

104

touched an arm, and it just fell off and crumbled to nothing on the floor.

'I looked back at the face and I could see that some of the cloth, or whatever it was, was coming away. You could glimpse the yellow flesh underneath. I pulled at it and I saw this face. Like a skull with yellow flesh on it. Mummified. Small jaw, thin lips, narrow mouth. The nose had fallen away. Just cavities where the nostrils had been.

'But the eyes were the strangest part. The sockets were dark. I thought at first they were empty. Then I saw embedded in each socket, in place of the eye, a kind of crystal.'

Was she being taken for a ride? Was this some conspiracy of disinformation between himself and Venning?

'What colour?' she asked abruptly.

Hilliard was startled out of his reverie. He was surprised at the request for detail.

'Erm – ' He had to close his eyes to recollect. 'Dark ruby. Almost black.'

'What does Venning know about this?' she asked. Her voice was hard. Her eyes were searching.

A puzzled hesitation before he answered.

'Nothing.'

From his expression alone Pam was persuaded he would never have breathed a word of this to anyone. Suspicious that his mind was going, petrified of being thought a crank, he must have kept this secret to himself for twenty years. And only now, because she had asked about her father, was it pouring out of him. The pent-up flood of memories was finding release at last.

She asked, more gently, 'So, what did you tell them at the base?'

He paused a long moment before replying, his eyes returning to their search of the floor.

'I didn't. After I got back, I didn't know what to say. I didn't know what to think. Some kind of snow mirage? Hallucination? I tried to convince myself it wasn't real.

'During that night another blizzard hit. The next morning when we went out again I checked behind that mound.'

He paused again.

'And?' prompted Pam.

His final words were whispered.

'There was nothing there.'

Laughter in the other room. The music thumped. She peered into the ruby of her wine.

'Aliens?'

He looked at her.

'An alien invasion? Is that what you're saying?'

He nodded balefully, his eyes averted once again.

She cast her mind back to the ice laboratory. The yellow flesh. The crystal eye.

'Dave, I believe you.'

At the heart of this mystery was the cause of her father's death. She was determined to find out more.

'About this doctor . . .' she began.

Trrrrrrr.

The captain was asleep on his back and snoring loudly. His glass eye was open. His glass eye never slept. But the captain was deeply asleep and dreaming.

Trrrrrrr.

A German Shepherd dog was piping him aboard the *Elysium*, to cheers from the passengers lined on deck. The dog was blowing long trills on its dog whistle.

Trrrrrrr.

The phone by his bedside trilled several times before the captain began to surface. He opened his good eye and squinted at the clock. Quarter past two in the morning.

He was still half asleep. He reached out a leaden hand and grasped the dog's head. The dog looked surprised as it turned into a phone which he put to his ear. The Captain's mouth felt greasy. His voice was thick with sleep.

'Trench,' he said.

'First officer here, sir. From the bridge. Sorry to wake you. FF has reported an attempted escape by the terrorist.'

Trench was now fully awake.

'Have they caught the blighter?'

'No, sir. Think he went overboard. One of the lifeboats on the starboard sun deck has been released. Found dangling over the side. Secured again now.'

'So he's tried to take a boat and ended up in the drink?'

106

'Looks like it, sir.'

Alternative scenarios were forming in the captain's mind. He eased his leg out of bed and rubbed the sleep from his eye.

'I'll be up in five minutes, Jones. Get Dodimead to institute a thorough search on all decks, especially under the awnings of the boats. He might be trying to fool us.'

'Yes, sir.'

'And Jones.'

'Yes, sir?'

'He's a dangerous man. A killer. Remember that.'

The naval officer climbed up the stairs. They were treacherous with ice. He knocked at the bridge door and entered.

He pulled back his fur-lined hood. His face was stinging in the sudden heat.

'Searched all decks, cap'n, including the boats. No sign.'

A sea-chart of the Antarctic ocean was displayed on one of the screens. The captain was studying it closely.

'Thank you, Dodimead. So he might have gone overboard after all. How do you rate his chances of survival?'

'Wouldn't last a second, cap'n.'

Jones spoke up from the far end of the bridge, a reed of worry in his voice.

'Captain Trench, there's something here I don't quite like. Come and see for yourself, if you will.'

'Excuse me for one moment, Dodimead,' said the captain. Jones was peering at the ship's compass. As the captain drew near he could see it was swinging wildly.

'Don't want to sound pessimistic, sir, but this might be the start of magnetic reversal.'

The captain had already moved to the radio transmitter.

'I'm calling STS Antarctica.'

He ran his finger down a note headed 'emergency procedures' which was taped to the window. He punched in a code. Under his breath, he murmured, 'And let's hope to heaven it's only our equipment on the blink.'

There was a forceful hiss of static as the radio homed in, a crackle, and then a double beep as the security code was checked and the call connected.

'STS Antarctica. This is the *SS Elysium*. Do you read me?'

The captain's voice was grave but steady. After a pause he repeated, 'Calling STS Antarctica. This is the *SS Elysium*. Do you read me?'

The slight hum of the channel. Otherwise, nothing. The captain glanced at the ship's chronometer. Coming up to four thirty. Couldn't be too early for them, a UN base. Surely they'd be on twenty-four hour call.

The captain tried again.

Dave Hilliard was experiencing a kind of horror.

The operations room was quiet as death. The lift doors were closing on him. He stretched out his hands to hold them back. The crackle of the radio sounded in the silence.

'STS Antarctica. This is the *SS Elysium*. Are you receiving me?'

Bodies were strewn about. Among the debris on the floor were prostrate, crumpled figures. Palmer lay face down, his pasty stubbled head wrenched to one side, his hand under a twisted drooling mouth. A couple of the new guys were sprawled in the corner. It was difficult to tell who they were. The light was dimmed down low. Corporal Whitehead was slumped in front a VDU, its flickering images dancing reflected on the shiny ebony of his cranium.

'Calling STS Antarctica. This is the *SS Elysium*. Do you read me?'

The colonel kept his hands stretched out in an attempt to steady himself. He was feeling like death. Too much hooch and hollaring the night before. And what had he said to the general? Too much. Too much, he knew that. He felt a kind of horror at the thought of it. The secret out at last.

It had woken him with a start.

Gary and Jude had been making the most of it, seizing their one night of passion. Then he couldn't sleep. So he had come up to check that Palmer was needing a break. Palmer was meant to be on duty.

The repeated nudging of the lift doors persuaded Hilliard gently into the operations room. He picked his way slowly between the leftovers of the previous night. It had been some celebration.

'STS Antarctica. This is – '

He grabbed at the intercom.

'STS Antarctica receiving you, *Elysium*. Colonel Hilliard here. Go ahead, caller.'

He tried to sound brighter than he felt.

'What the devil's going on, Colonel? This is Captain Trench, master of the *SS Elysium*. I've been calling you for half an hour.'

The captain sounded British through and through.

'Sorry, captain. To tell the truth, we had a party here last night. We've just got the field loop up and running. We made our deadline.'

'I see.'

The captain clearly thought it all a pretty poor show.

'How can I help you, captain?'

'I wanted confirmation that magnetic reversal wasn't taking place. But I suspect you've answered my question. It must be our compass on the blink.'

'You're right, captain. We're not into flipover, yet, thank the heavens!' Hilliard checked the overnight data on the screen. The volatility of the magnoflux had even declined somewhat. 'And from our current data I can tell you it won't be happening in the next few hours. It's your compass.'

'Right.'

'You're sailing through Antarctic waters?'

'Indeed we are, colonel. I dare say we're logged in the appropriate places, if you care to look.'

'Of course, captain. We'll keep you informed if the magnoflux situation changes. Bon voyage.'

The captain signed off.

A small white bug was crawling along the top of a VDU. Hilliard flicked it off. His head was throbbing.

He looked up at the wall screen. The orange glow of AXV2 was moving by slow millimetres towards the Transantarctic range. The green dot of the geomagnetic pole, monitored and plotted by the incessant trawling of the AXVs, was approaching the Whitmore Mountains. He was glad he was not out there.

Bono and Nike were due for their break in just under thirty-six hours. The colonel looked at the sprawled-out bodies of Whitehead and Palmer.

It may have been a mistake to delay their schedule. They weren't looking their best.

Nike was sleeping. The steady drone of the AXV engine snuggled around her like a blanket. In her sleep she had kicked off her covers from the bunk. Too warm for covers.

Even in her tank-top and panties, she was sweltering. She stretched and turned, still deep in sleep. The vehicle gently buffeted her as it sped over the smooth terrain of ice and snow.

There was a sudden lurch as the engine cut out and engaged again. It brought her to a drowsy consciousness. She was sweating. She passed a hand over the prickly dampness of her small stubbled head.

Another lurch.

'Bono,' she called out. 'Everything all right?'

'I think so. Just a couple of hiccups in the drive. Did it wake you?'

The comforting basso profundo of the big man's voice purred from the pilot's cabin. It made her feel sleepy again.

'Yeah.' She felt the sweat trickle from her armpit. 'It's hot back here. Are you holding up, Bono?'

'I'm fine. Grab another couple of hours.'

Nike lay back. The engine hummed her to the edge of sleep.

The next lurch almost threw her off the bunk. It was followed by a violent juddering as by degrees the vehicle shuddered to a halt.

'Nike.'

'Yeah, Bono.'

'You remember what I said about hiccups?'

'Yeah?'

'I may have been wrong about that.'

Pam was savouring the strong black coffee in the rest room when Hilliard came through on the intercom. Some kind of trouble with AXV2. Oh, Lord.

She picked up her coffee and grabbed a croissant as she set off towards the operations room. It was five before eight in the morning. A late night. The heaviest sleep in ages. She was barely awake.

She arrived to see Whitehead and Palmer clearing up the mess from the night before. They moved like zombies. Whitehead's eyes were no more than crinkled slits against the bright artificial lights. Palmer held a protective hand to his neanderthal skull. Neither of them looked so good. She had some idea how they felt.

She caught Hilliard's glance. Their talk last night had not been a dream. A brief acknowledgement of the secret divulged and shared passed swiftly between them.

'Bono reports a serious fault on the magnodrive, general. Overheated somehow. Intermittent interruption, then terminal cut-out. They've tried all the check routines. No good.'

The general sat heavily and pushed a hand through her hair. 'Where are they?'

'Stranded halfway across Whitmore. They're OK. Their supplementary's unaffected. They've got heating, lights, air conditioning, plenty of supplies – '

'All they haven't got is the shadow team to come and pick them up,' Pam interrupted wearily. She glanced at Whitehead and Palmer. It was a pitiful sight. She munched on her croissant and took a swig of coffee.

'General, it might save time if we sent Joe out there. Sounds as if the magnodrive needs a real specialist overhaul.'

She looked at him as the pieces fell into place. The solution was going to be neater than she deserved. She crinkled her nose at him and smiled.

'Smart thinking, Dave. You're right. We need Joe's expertise, if we can rouse him from slumber. We also need a medic.'

Hilliard looked puzzled.

'In case there's fumes from the overheating. Or hypothermia if the supplementary power goes down. Can't be too careful. Corporal Black is the obvious choice. Yeah, Joe and Jude. They haven't had each other's company for a while. Should keep them on their toes. Tell Bono and Mike to hang on in there for the next few hours. We're sending in the cavalry.'

Somewhere, under the snow, in the depths of the ice, in the

111

cavern of flickering lights and whirring machines, the impassive observer maintained a solitary vigil.

The play of patterned lights was generating information. The observer monitored the progress of a silver-suited figure as it glided swiftly along a crystal passage.

The passage curved into darkness. White crystal walls sped past. Ahead, the passage divided, left and right. The figure veered to the left and speeded into a further darkness.

The darkness turned to light as the end of the journey was reached. The passage came to an abrupt dead-end. A wall of white crystal blocked any further progress.

The figure lifted an instrument to the obstructing wall. There was a pulsing of light. The wall sparkled and glistened as the light grew intense and fierce. Pulsating patterns appeared on the ice, which rippled and buckled and fell away in cascades of water. The figure moved slowly forward. A tunnel was being excavated in the twinkling of light.

There was an alteration in the colour of the ice beneath. The figure halted. The wall ahead had become translucent. On the further side, a hint of illumination, the lights of an open space beyond.

The figure raised a hand to the wall and meticulously judged the fragility of its surface. Three metal fingers tapped to test its strength.

13 Attaining Emptiness

No action. No mind. No words. No names.

All things begin in namelessness
Naming brings them to existence.
Rid yourself of desires to observe their secrets.

No desires.
Emptiness.
Then, out of the blankness, one image.
Dust in a beam of light. A snowstorm in a paperweight.
A snowstorm.
The Doctor's arms moved up and out. He felt them move.
He did not move them.

His legs were moving, taking him forward.

Another image. His face in the snowstorm, framed by the long white hair. The old, hard face that was his so long ago. The face of his first enfleshment.

His hands encountered an uneven surface, dials and levers, switches and buttons, so familiar, even in the darkness, even after the many years. His hands moved over them. He did nothing. He felt them move.

A silver figure in a snow scene, collapsing, shrivelling. His face, his own first face, shrivelling, collapsing. His body, aged and disintegrating, falling into the snow, dissolving, becoming only dimly visible, falling apart like thawing ice.

The central column of the console lit up and rose with a whooshing noise, a subterranean churning. He could feel the vibrations of the deeper roar beneath his feet. The journey was beginning.

The central column was triple-roofed, a tapering tower, a

113

jade pagoda. It rose and fell. Beneath his feet the oceans thundered on subterranean shores.

The Doctor did nothing. He observed.

His hand went to his head, removed his hat, dropped it over the topmost roof of the control column tower.

There was a shudder, like the tremor that comes before an earthquake. The pagoda with the hat on top fell and rose, rose and fell, fell and rose. Time was nonexistent. There was only space. Time became space.

His hand reached out. It turned a dial. The pagoda ceased to rise and fall. The light within the pagoda died. His other hand pulled at a lever. There was the whirr of ancient machinery. He sensed a space opening on blackness in the blackness. A fresher, cooler air enveloped him.

His feet moved him forward. He was advancing to embrace the emptiness, walking through the open doors of the TARDIS.

There was a sudden hard blow to his head. An agonizing pain. Stars. Snowflakes. Blackness.

14 Dreams that You Dare to Dream

Climbing an icy mountainside.

Hard going. An instant of lost concentration, you'd lose your footing, slither down into the ocean below. Have to keep your head.

Stop and take a breather.

Look down. Water surges far below. Heaves against the lip of ice where the climb began. *Elysium* is anchored out at sea, decks crowded with passengers, motionless, staring up at you. Wind whistles in your ears.

You feel suddenly exposed. You've nothing on but little pink socks and a flimsy T-shirt. The passengers are watching. You see yourself as they can. Tiny. Spread against a cliff of ice. Brown on white.

Reach up to the hollow above you. It's carved in the shape of an eye. You are climbing a face carved out of the ice.

See if you can make out who it's meant to be.

You lean back.

You realize who it is. The passengers scream.

You are falling. Backwards. Nothing to grab on to. Falling. Slowly. Past the overhang of his jutting-out nose. Falling. Floating. Down into the water by his lips. The passengers scream and gasp. Water closes over your head. Silence.

Drop like lead. The ship's propellers thump. Deep sub-aquatic sounds. The iceberg spreads out below the surface as far as you can see, a tangle of wires, tin cans and guns.

Drop through the tangle into another world.

Walking down white paths, bounded by crystal walls. The throb, throb of engines. The clack, clack of your feet on the crystal floor.

A voice inside your head says 'Ruby'.

Your footsteps go tap, tap.

Embedded inside the crystal walls are coloured shapes. Letters of the alphabet. They stretch away into the gloom ahead. To one side is the letter Y, to the other the letter B. Further on, there's a C and then an R. Some letters are buried deep.

You peer into the crystal. A face stares back at you. Dark staring eyes, framed by thick black hair. The face is yours, reflected, but your eyes are dark red gems.

A voice says –

'Ruby?'

Sunlight streamed through the porthole curtains and played on her closed eyelids. Tap, tap. Someone was at the door.

The door clicked open. Leslie.

'Ruby?' he whispered.

Ruby kept her eyes tight shut. The smell of grilled tomatoes and mushrooms wafted her way. She was famished.

Lips tickled her ear.

'Rubes,' mewed Leslie.

She let out a big sigh but remained on her back with her eyes firmly shut. 'You're just like my Granny.'

'Your Granny?'

She opened her eyes a fraction. Leslie's smiling face. Beyond it, Nano's clock display read 09:02.

'Granny. My cat.'

She closed her eyes again. The light was much too bright.

'She never lets me sleep in either. And it's my birthday.'

'I know, old girl. That's why I've brought you breakfast in bed.' He put the tray down at the foot of her bed. 'Bon appetit, mon ami. And many happy returns.'

He gave her a peck on the cheek.

She stretched under the cover. The horror of the day sank in.

'Oh, Leslie, I'm no longer twenty-one. I'm getting old.'

'Twenty-two is not the end of the world. Take it from me. I'm living proof.'

He strode to the porthole and flung the curtain aside. More light flooded in.

'Glorious day out there. But decidedly chilly.'

Ruby grabbed her T-shirt from the floor to make herself decent for Leslie. As she slipped it on, she was dimly aware of some odd memory. Something to do with the T-shirt. She couldn't think what.

She pulled the breakfast tray onto her lap and gulped down the freshly squeezed orange juice.

'Up at dawn, me,' said Leslie.

'Whatever for?'

She poured milk over the muesli.

'There was a bit of a rumpus in the night. Around our end, anyway. That terrorist escaped.'

'No! Did they find him?'

She munched. She was beginning to feel a bit more human.

'Seems not, but they had a good look round. Wonder you didn't hear it. They think he went overboard, but can't be sure. Could be hiding somewhere on the ship.'

Ruby thought of the lower level. What was down there? She had to interview the captain. She would ask him.

Leslie was staring out of the porthole.

'Oh, and icebergs have been spotted. That cranky friend of yours got the first sighting.'

'Barbara?'

'Yup. Won the prize. Dinner with Lord Straker. Course, you know what the second prize is?'

Ruby looked at him blankly.

'Breakfast with Lord Straker.'

He threw his head back and whinnied.

Ruby smiled. She attacked the tomatoes and mushrooms. Things weren't so bad. Perhaps life was possible after twenty-one.

Leslie plonked himself down on the end of the bed and grabbed a slice of toast.

'If icebergs have been sighted,' said Ruby, 'then today's the day Mike Brack will be starting his iceberg carving and – '

Ruby stopped abruptly, remembering.

'What's the matter, Rubes?' Leslie's large face was all concern and toast crumbs.

'Just broke a dream I had last night. I was climbing an iceberg. Mike Brack's face carved in it. I think.'

'Mmm, a dream about climbing Mike Brack? You know what that means, don't you?' He reached for the marmalade. He was settling down for a gossip.

She put the tray to one side and sidled out of bed, pulling her T-shirt down to cover her bum.

'I'm sorry, Leslie, I'd offer you coffee, but I mustn't miss the sculpting. I have to cover it or Lord Stanley will kill me. I must get dressed.'

'You haven't opened your present.'

'Present?'

Leslie plucked something from the tray. It had been hidden behind the coffee jug.

'From me and Diana. Well, Diana chose it. I only paid for it.' He snorted and tossed her a small, neatly wrapped package. 'Only joking, Rubes. Happy birthday.'

'Leslie, how sweet.'

She tore off the paper to reveal a jeweller's box. She snapped it open. Inside, on dark blue velvet, lay a ruby pendant attached to a fine gold necklace. It was not her usual style, but the thought was touching. Her eyes misted over. She gulped down the lump in her throat and reached out and gave him a hug.

'I'll wear it tonight. At the ball.'

'That's the idea. Diana got a card for you as well. Says you'll get it later.' He patted her thigh. 'I'll let you get ready. I must get on as well. Your boss is popping in to see rehearsals today.'

'Lord Stanley?'

'Yes, old thing. He's flying in by helicopter to open the ice sculpting season. Didn't you know? Then he's master of ceremonies at the ball.'

'Oh, no,' cried Ruby, 'and I haven't done any work yet.'

'And I've got a song to learn, my dear, so we'd both better get on with it.'

He moved towards the door and chortled.

'Tin man from *Wizard of Oz*. Just as well I've got a tin ear! Enjoy your birthday.'

The door closed. His cheerful whistle faded down the corridor. Ruby replaced the necklace in its box. She grinned to herself at the thought of her funny, sweet friends.

She poured a cup of dark steaming coffee.

If she could really get some work done during the day and manage to keep out of Straker's way until the evening, she might be able to face him at the ball.

She went to the porthole. She could see the scattering of icebergs. Some of the distant ones were like flecks of foam on the vast stretch of blue, but a couple were close. Their size astounded her. Massive, flat-topped mountains.

She shuddered. There was gooseflesh on her arm. She turned to the wardrobe. She would need to wrap up well.

The helicopter hovered for a moment above the uneven motion of the deck. A bulky figure was hanging half-out of its open door, smiling widely, a plump hand graciously extended in almost papal greeting to the applauding passengers who thronged the deck.

The helicopter came to rest. With an energetic bound which defied his corpulence and age, the man was on the deck and engulfing the waiting captain in a suffocating bear hug. Large as life and twice as irrepressible, Lord Stanley Straker had arrived.

By the time Ruby had emerged into the cold brightness of the sun deck, swathed in a woollen scarf and heavy jacket, the Nanocom clipped to her pocket and the Holocam hanging round her neck, Lord Straker's coarse Australian voice was blaring over the ship's public address system. He stood beside his helicopter, microphone in one hand, pointing with the other at the laser gun mounted on top of the bridge.

'. . . first ever iceberg to be sculpted anywhere in the world,' he was proudly announcing. 'Carved by that artist extraordinaire, the fearsomely gifted Mike Brack. His magnificent tool,' he went on with a wicked leer, 'the powerful turbo-pulse laser gun developed by the US Army.'

The crowd was laughing and applauding. Straker worked himself up to a ringmaster's roar.

'Ladies and gentlemen, it gives me great pleasure to tell you that today you will be witness to an event which has never before been experienced in the entire history of the Earth. A genuine world first!'

It was claptrap, of course, and so the passengers clapped and cheered.

Ruby remained beyond the steps of the bridge, out of Lord Straker's direct line of sight. Her boss boomed on, ever more grandiloquently. Ruby ceased to pay attention. She was transfixed by the spectacular view.

The ship was pounding into the channel formed between

119

the two nearest icebergs. They dwarfed the ship. In the watery blue distance beyond, numberless crags of white broke the surface. On the far horizon lay the continent where these gigantic snowy cliffs sheered off and crashed into the sea. If she shielded her eyes, Ruby could just make out a line of brilliant white. Antarctica.

She felt a hand gripping her shoulder. She turned with a start.

'Mike!' Her voice was breathy with the shock.

He said nothing. His eyes narrowed.

'I haven't seen you for a couple of days,' she said.

He remained silent. His hand withdrew from her shoulder.

'So how are you?' she tried again.

'Gutted,' he grunted.

The scowling mask of his face reminded her of one of his own caricatures. She smiled brightly.

'I wondered if I could talk to you about the ice sculpting? You know, for the *Sunday Seeker*. And take a few holograms of the action?'

He looked at her for a moment. When he spoke it was almost to himself.

'Ruby Duvall. Investigative reporter.'

The words were slightly menacing, and had a mocking edge.

This was the first time they had spoken openly about her being a reporter. In fact, it was the first time they had spoken since that extraordinary incident in the library.

He turned away to the steps of the bridge.

'The monkey is about to perform,' he called back grimly as he ascended to the roof of the bridge. 'Might as well have a ringside seat.'

She followed him up the steel steps. Once on the roof, he strode out ahead of her towards the gun turret.

The view from up here was breathtaking. As Brack eased himself into the operating seat of the ice laser, Ruby checked the Holocam's power level. It was low. She'd soon have to change the power-pack.

She peered through the eye-piece. Framed in the viewer was the sleek barrel of the laser gun. She panned to the left. One of the icebergs came into view. The sun sparked off the rippling blue water and chiselled ice face. She pressed the exposure button. There was a momentary hum then pszhtt! like magic, a perfect hologram emerged.

She held the transparency to the light. The beauty and brilliance and colour of the scene before her was reproduced with stunning three-dimensional fidelity. Ruby tilted the hologram slightly. Light glinted on the laser barrel. Sun sparkled on crests of waves. The picture had a living clarity, as if she were looking at the actual scene.

Then she noticed the scene was dancing around her feet. The sun was shining through hologram and projecting a perfect 3D image on to the roof of the bridge. It was magical.

'Pretty impressive, huh?' she called out to Brack, pointing at the projected 3D image.

His head was buried in the laser controls. He glanced across. There was a flicker of interest.

'This is all done with lasers, too,' she said.

But he had swiftly resumed his mask of indifference and returned his attention to the laser gun. It had been generating a gentle hum for the past few minutes. He turned a key and pressed a button.

'If this is what they want,' he said with a sudden burst of relish, 'let's give it to them.'

He grasped a joystick set into the operating console. The laser gun slid noiselessly to the left and up. He squeezed a red button on the tip of the joystick. A pencil-thin line of intense orange light streamed from the tapering barrel. A split-second later it made dramatic contact with the closest iceberg.

Where the laser beam touched the ice, clouds of steam billowed, hissing and savage, from a new deep scar. As the ray sliced downward, a chunk of ice twice the size of the *Elysium* was cut adrift. It crashed into the sea with a roar and disappeared under water and foam.

A full minute passed. A long slow wave swelled towards the ship and subsided against the hull. The *Elysium* heaved away and back again. The crowds on the decks swayed and reached for each other to steady themselves. They watched in silent awe as from the water's surface, with menacing slowness, like a sea-beast arising from the depths, the upper portion of the mountainous chunk emerged. It was now much closer to the ship and it reared above the level of the upper decks. The crowd erupted, gasps giving way to cheers and applause.

Brack pulled on the joystick once more, bringing the laser to bear on this iceberg of his own creation. With a few deft passes of the ray, a shape began to emerge in the block of ice. The profile of a human head. A heavy brow, a bulbous nose, a jutting chin. A stub of ice projecting from the mouth.

An excited buzz arose among the crowd as they saw the ice take vivid form. The hum of the laser died. The white plumes of steam melted away in the clear dry air. Brack had completed his task. Before their very eyes, caricatured in ice, floated the unmistakable features of Lord Stanley Straker. Not even the cigar was missing.

A spontaneous roar burst from the delighted crowd. The real Lord Straker looked up to the laser gun, removed the cigar from his mouth, and gave a gracious wave in acknowledgement of the sculptor's skill.

Ruby raised her Holocam. She zoomed in. Lord Straker's eyes, above the wide grin of pleasure, had a crafty look. The passengers would now be willing to pay large sums to have their own features sculpted dramatically in the ice.

The Holocam hummed and a hologram appeared from the base of the camera. It captured Lord Straker's candid expression in all its 3D clarity.

She turned her camera to record the ice sculptor's moment of glory. She focused on an empty seat. She heard a clanging on the steel steps behind her, then saw him striding resolutely, head down, hands in pockets, behind the crowds of people, in the direction of the cocktail lounge.

Ruby pulled at the strip of holograms hanging from the camera. She carefully tore along the perforated edges and slipped the separated transparencies into the wallet.

He was a real puzzle, Mike Brack.

As she descended the steps by the door of the bridge, she saw Captain Trench inside. He was sitting in the rest area, reading the month-old copy of the *Sunday Seeker* and smoking a pipe.

She reached for her Nanocom and tapped on the door.

Wine and wormwood. He threw the green liquid down his

122

throat and placed the glass precisely in the middle of the table.

The cocktail lounge was empty. Many of the passengers were still up on the deck ooh-ing and ah-ing over the chunks of floating ice. The rest preferred non-alcoholic beverages this time of day, halfway through the morning.

So, at this time of day, the cocktail lounge was his favourite haunt. Somewhere to sit quietly, pursue his plans, think out his thoughts.

This business with Ruby Duvall, for instance.

He felt she suspected something. It was impossible, of course, but it nagged at him. There were times when he felt like telling her, confessing all. But that was not the rational thing to do. Or was it?

As he turned things over in his mind, he sketched and doodled on a paper napkin. He ordered another absinthe.

Wine and wormwood.

'Thank you for the interview, captain,' Ruby said, graciously.

'It was entirely my pleasure, Ms Duvall,' said the captain. 'Sorry about the lower deck. Maybe in a week or two.'

Ruby nodded and smiled. The captain disappeared back into the bridge.

So the lower deck was out of bounds, a closed-off security area. The engine rooms were down there. It was also where the terrorist had been held. Nothing else of interest, he had said. Storage, that was all. She would need security clearance and an escort for a visit.

There was nothing less she fancied than being taken around a dingy hold by a creepy FF freak.

She pulled her jacket tight around her and snuggled into the hood. The jacket was old and one of her favourites, stitched together from brightly coloured patches of recycled fabric. It was loud, but comfortable and warm.

She had come to a decision about Mr Mike Brack. She would try the direct approach. She had nothing to lose.

She set off for the cocktail lounge.

Five cocktail glasses were arranged in the shape of a cross at the dead centre of the table. He was allowing his mind to wander. Wormwood and wine. He drew firm lines on his napkin. Calculated. Made connections.

Somebody was approaching his table. He kept his eyes down, pretending not to notice. He refused to sign more autographs.

'I thought I might find you here,' said Ruby.

He looked up and stared at her icily. She had picked up an empty glass and was inhaling the aroma. She squinted at the drop that sparkled at the bottom.

'I love that emerald colour,' she said. 'Liquid jade.'

He stared at her face. The face of Ruby Duvall. He knew it so well. The face of the daughter of the crippled scientist. The face of an up and coming investigative reporter of the *Sunday Seeker*. The face he should have recognized. Before.

It was always a mistake to get involved with people.

She was leaning towards him, gazing at him with those dark, insolent eyes.

'Don't you think we need to talk?' she said.

He stood as if she had not spoken, as if she wasn't there. He pocketed his pencil and dropped his crumpled napkin on the table. Then he just walked away.

Flabbergasted, she watched him go, striding out of the cocktail lounge.

On the table were the empty cocktail glasses and his discarded napkin. He had been sketching something when she arrived. She opened it out and spread it flat on the table.

It was a rough drawing of some kind of complex machine. At its centre was an object the shape of an egg. Parts of the machine were labelled, words such as 'speaker', 'refracting transmitter', 'lights' and most curious of all 'cybernetic controller'.

Her eyes strayed back to that central oval. Suddenly the whorl of lines made sense. The oval had a face drawn on it. A caricatured face. She hadn't seen it clearly at first because the face had been heavily scored through. But now she recognized it. A chill went through her.

The face was hers.

He walked across the deck.

It was not the movement of the ship that made him unsteady

on his feet. The sea was a mirror over which the *Elysium* glided, between the channel formed by the icy cliffs. He looked to the stern of the ship, along the line of the wake. The iceberg with face of Lord Straker was far behind them now, a blur in the distance. He had to blink it into focus.

More iceberg sculpting that afternoon. He could have done without it. He had other things on his mind. But it was a contractual obligation, part of the deal with Straker.

He set off again towards the sun deck lift. He swayed a little. It was not the movement of the ship. It was the alcohol in the absinthe. The wine and wormwood. He liked it too much.

He must control his passions, so his passions would not control him. But as fast as he shot them down his drowned emotions erupted above the surface.

Did she know? Was she on his trail? What if he made a clean breast of it first? Dare he do that? Could he cut through the whole shitty mess? Act courageously for once?

It had control of him. He was in too far. He had a job to do. He must get on with it.

He got into the lift and entered the security code. He descended to the lower level and went directly to the room which contained his machine. It was almost complete. It was ready for the testing.

He flicked a switch. Lights flickered and flashed. There was a small eructation of smoke. That would have to be adjusted. The framework revolved erratically round the central oval sphere. He spoke into a microphone. His voice boomed hollowly, metallic amid the smoke.

She had been up and down at least four times now.

She was pressed against the control panel, Nanocom in hand, already primed. But she could hardly move. The lift was packed.

She'd chosen the worst moment to try bypassing the lift's security lock. It was coming up to lunch time. People were dispersing from the sun deck and returning to their cabins, or going to the restaurant.

For the fifth time she arrived at A deck. The lift doors opened. Its chattering occupants piled out. No one was waiting to get in. Now was her chance.

Behind their departing backs, she extended the Nanocom's aerial and whispered, 'Decoder. Random test.'

The monitor nodule flickered red. Across the Nanocom's screen slid a stream of numbers as the computer sifted hyperactively through all the possible security codes that might give access to the lower level.

The lift doors closed. The lift descended.

'Come on, Nano,' she urged. 'Come on.'

Her little wonder machine had already defined the code as six digits long and had picked out two of the numbers required. Now all she needed was a clear run down in the lift. At this rate Nano should have cracked the code within the next few minutes. The lift passed B deck, C deck. At D deck, her luck ran out.

The doors opened. There was no one there. Someone must have pressed the call button but got impatient and gone by the stairs. She banged her thumb onto the 'close doors' button.

Around the corner ambled a doddery couple, arm in arm.

'Hold the lift for us, dearie.'

Nano's light was flashing. The screen said *code found*.

'I think you've dropped something,' called out Ruby, pointing to the empty floor behind them. They turned, saw nothing, then turned back.

'Sorry,' she called, as the doors closed on their bewildered faces.

'Decoder. Send,' she said to Nano.

There was a flickering of Nano's nodule, an answering beep from the control panel of the lift. The light next to the slot lit up. The lift descended.

Done, said Nano.

The impassive observer monitored the changing patterns of filaments and dials. An alarm was being raised.

The observer focused on the message.

GROUP FIVE TO CONTROL.
THIS IS GROUP FIVE.
Suspect discovery. Reason unknown.
Request guidance.

IMMEDIATE.

Ruby stepped out into an ill-lit corridor, airlessly warm. She unbuttoned her jacket and let it flap open. A rhythmic pounding echoed towards her from somewhere ahead. Its vibrations shuddered through the soles of her boots. She realized she must be close to the engine rooms.

The passageway fell away into almost total darkness. She was suddenly afraid. Twenty-two, and she had still not lost her childish fear of the dark. She switched on the light of the Holocam. It was an effective torch. She forced herself forward. Her heart was pounding.

What was she doing down here anyway? What if the terrorist was still in hiding? Maybe she should have waited for that FF escort after all.

She was moving closer to the pounding noise. She turned a corner. Her improvised torchlight picked out an iron door studded with rivets. Engine room two.

She knew that two of the three original engines were still in use. To judge by the noise and vibration, engine room two was clearly one of them.

She pressed down on the large iron handle and pushed against the weight of the door. It swung open smoothly. She was greeted by darkness and the roar of machinery in relentless motion. And the heat was stifling.

Both the working engine rooms were fully automatic. No operators were needed down here. The engines were monitored and controlled from the bridge via the ship's computer. She pointed her torch at the gloom.

Four gigantic pistons thundered up and around and down in their preordained patterns. There was something brazen in their ceaseless pumping, the baring of glistening steel membranes at each pull and push, the out and in, the roaring and the hissing. Her cheeks were hot. She was almost embarrassed to witness the overcharged calculated frenzy of it all, as if she had caught the machine in *flagrante delicto*. It was an awesome sight, and beautiful.

It was this passionate frenzy of machine on machine which pushed the ship through the water. She gazed at the pounding rhythm of the motion of the pistons, the sheer naked power.

She marvelled that they avoided crashing together, they were so massive and rushed so close.

She raised the Holocam and took a couple of shots. There was a strange sensation, a voyeuristic thrill deep in her stomach.

Suddenly, everything went black. The light of her Holocam had failed. The batteries had given out. She cursed herself for not having brought the spare power pack.

There was a dim light coming from the corridor, enough to find the open door and ease herself out of it. Her heart was pounding louder, it seemed, than the pistons she was leaving behind.

A distant light was shining along the corridor to her right. She had not come that way but she flapped towards it in her open jacket like a brightly coloured moth towards a flame.

Reaching the junction where the light was shining, she saw another lift. She was moving towards it in some relief when a door to one side of her opened wide and a face peered out. Mike Brack. She almost jumped out of her skin.

He looked as shocked as she was. Through the open door of the room behind him she saw a contraption of wires and flashing lights.

Both of them stood unmoving for a second. Then Brack took a step towards her, closing the door behind him firmly shut. She didn't like the expression on his face.

She ran. She banged her fist on the call button. She dare not turn round. The lift doors opened, mercifully soon. She rushed inside and pressed the button for D deck. As the lift doors closed, she glanced back down the corridor.

Mike Brack had disappeared.

15 Where You'll Find Me

Blackness.

The Doctor came round to the clack of footsteps. But he saw nothing. He was lying on his back on a hard surface. His head throbbed. He was in a bad way.

He was sure his eyes were open. He tried closing them tight. He opened them again.

Blackness.

Perhaps he'd gone blind. His head was throbbing loudly. Almost vibrating. He remembered hitting his head on something hard as he came out of the TARDIS. Perhaps he had damaged the optical nerves.

The footsteps were dying away. He still had his hearing.

He sat up.

The vibration was not in his head at all. He could hear a distant pounding. He felt the vibration under his palms on the hard cold surface. The air was cool and smelt of metal and oil.

He got to his feet and swayed in the blackness. He felt for the pulse beats of his double heart. Quite normal. If it was not concussion that made him sway, perhaps the steady rolling motion he felt was caused by effects outside his body. Perhaps he was inside a moving vehicle.

So. He may not be concussed. He wasn't deaf. And now he realized he couldn't be blind. Some parts of the blackness around him were denser than others. He could make out certain vague shapes.

There was a large denseness of black rearing above him. He put out his hand to touch it. A hard, greasy, metal surface. A massive limb extended away and above him. He looked around and peered into the gloom.

Other metal limbs loomed at him out the darkness. He stood

beneath some giant mechanical spider. It watched and waited.

'The further one goes, the less one knows,' he murmured.

Soft flesh

Skin under sunlit warmth.

Moisture. The dampness of bodies clamped together. Moving together.

Rush of wave on a shingle shore. Shock of sea spray.

Lips. Curving in laughter. Bodies shaking together.

Shava.

The beauty of Shava.

And Talaron.

She kisses. Lips to moist lips.

She kisses Talaron.

The impassive observer was aware of the malfunction. Images were manifesting spontaneously from within.

The phenomenon was well established. It was a curious experience, nevertheless. It might only happen once in a hundred years, but when it did, it could be disruptive of efficient working practices.

The technical term was emotional memory, a left-over from the pre-mechanical time. A redundant reflex. An echo of their ages-old, original primitive existence, the organic life.

There was a well-defined procedure for dealing with attacks of emotional memory. Attention was to be directed away from the images and focused on underlying cybernetic principles.

The observer re-ordered the monitoring priorities.

She slammed her cabin door behind her. She leant on it, panting. Her heart was thumping. She did as Barbara had taught her. She sucked air deep to the pit of her stomach and expelled it in a controlled, slow exhalation.

She was such a wimp.

She pulled the power-pack angrily from the Holocam and replaced it with a full one, plugged the empty one into a socket to recharge. Her hands were shaking. This would not do. She had to reclaim some power over herself. She had to recharge her own batteries. She decided on a workout in the gym. She flung off her patchwork coat and set off down the corridor.

The gym was not a large place, but it was fitted out with the most up-to-date equipment. A handful of middle-aged men and women were grunting and groaning as they racked their bodies in self-inflicted torment.

In the changing room she dropped a one ecu piece into the vending machine. Out popped a shrink-wrapped disposable leotard.

She felt dirty and sticky from the morning's escapade.

She was going to get a lot dirtier and stickier in the gym, but she was looking forward to it.

She was feeling more positive already. She had managed to break into the lower level. And there could be no doubt about it now, Mike Brack was definitely up to something.

She removed her clothes and pulled on the leotard. The papery material stretched over her body. It had the sheen of graphite.

Fifteen machines were crowded into the gym, each designed to exercise one specific muscle group. She fitted herself into the biceps machine. The groans of effort, the cries of relief, the hiss of air through tight-clenched teeth, the moans of pain as hard-worked muscles begin to rebel, these sounds were familiar and comforting to Ruby as she worked her own noisy passage from machine to machine. To each was attached a small computer and display screen. She was able to compare her present ability with what it was at the start of the voyage. On average there had been an increase in her stamina, strength and suppleness of thirty per cent.

In the mirrors which lined the walls she monitored herself as she flexed and relaxed, her body taut, her muscles rippling, her brown flesh shiny with sweat. She had never felt so fit. A sensation of well-being pervaded her body. For half an hour she worked against the weights.

When she looked around again, she saw the gym was deserted. The pungent odour of sweat hung in the air. It wasn't unpleasant. It was a feral, animal smell – the soft odour of humanity. It was a reminder we were all animals under the skin. Each of us a bag of flesh and blood.

In the empty changing room she stripped off her sopping

leotard, threw it into the recycling unit, and stepped into the auto-showering cubicle. This was the most delicious moment of the work-out. She didn't have to raise a finger. She could give herself up to the machine.

She shut herself in. Pressurized jets of hot and cold water, soapy then clear, blasted at her from every angle, cleansing and enlivening every part. It made her skin zing. The flow of water had ceased now. Warm air enveloped her. She nudged the temperature control down a touch. Cooler air instantly surrounded her. Goose-pimples rose on her flesh. Soon there was not a trace of moisture anywhere on her body.

She pushed on the door. The mechanism seemed stiff. She pushed again. Nothing moved. The door was jammed.

She couldn't get out.

Emotional memory was to be rigorously distinguished from historical memory. Historical memory was the ever-accessible data store which held the entire record of the race in every detail. All conquests, all defeats, each survival and destruction, were minutely observed. They were recorded in the History Computer.

Efficiency derived from understanding the mechanics of the past. Every action, successful or not in itself, was a guide to successful action in the future.

The goal they pursued was three-fold. Everlasting survival. Absolute efficiency. Total control.

All three were attainable, in time. Eventual success was inevitable. The logic on which it was based was unassailable.

'Spotted them!' shouted Bono triumphantly.

Nike grabbed her sunglasses and swung herself into the cockpit seat next to him, pale and tiny against his solid bulk.

'Great!' she cried. 'Show me. Where?'

Bono pressed a large finger onto the cockpit window.

'Way over there. Do you see it? A definite AXV.'

She peered beyond it out into the blinding wastes of snow and let out a whoop.

'Attagirl! That's some quick going.'

Jude was praying for the journey to be over.

Adler was bugging her. He was a lamebrain, a clunk, a pain in the butt. She stared out through the AXV5's window into the dazzling white and blue. She willed the AXV2 to appear. Nothing. She just wanted to get this operation over with and be back with Gary. Right now, she wanted him more than ever.

Bono came through on the radio.

'OK, AXV2. We've got a fix on you. And you're looking sweet.'

Jude glanced across to Joe. He was looking puzzled, too.

'Receiving you, AXV5,' he replied. 'What you talking about?'

Nike's voice came through. 'We can see you. Great going, you two.'

'Hold it, sister,' said Joe. 'You seeing things. We ain't nowhere near.'

Jude spoke up. 'Hi, Nike. Hi, Bono. We don't have a visual. Are you behind a snow hump maybe?'

'Flat as my chest round here,' replied Nike with a giggle. 'The both of you must have drunk too much last – '

A hiss rendered the rest of the sentence inaudible.

'We got static, Niko.' said Adler. 'What did you say?'

'I said I'd have drunk you under the counter, Joe.'

Joe Adler laughed his raucous appreciation. 'Yeah, well, this time it's you seeing things. What's the Metal Mickey doin' to you in there?'

'Come on, Joe, you're joking us,' came Bono's deeper tones. 'You must be seeing us now. You're coming right – '

Again the voice was lost in a hiss of white noise. This time Adler could not regain contact. The channel was dead.

'What the fuck was that about?' said Adler. 'We're nowhere near.'

'What did they see?' asked Jude.

'Fuck knows. The Orient Express for all I know.'

He powered up. They sped across the empty ice towards the Whitmore Mountains. She knew he was worried. The stream of mindless banter had stopped.

It was a full half hour before they made a sighting. Something was wrong. The stranded vehicle looked twice the length it should have been. As they drew nearer they saw the illusion was caused by a second identical vehicle which was parked nose to nose with the AXV5.

The other vehicle clearly belonged to the base. The matt black letters on the white metal sheen read AXV9.

'What the fuck's going on here?' said Adler under his breath. 'We lost that mother a year ago.'

The two disasters of the past thirty years were setbacks only. Sustainable. Both were recorded in the History Computer.

It detailed the long journey from Planet[14]. The failure of their attempt to invade and conquer Earth. This had been the first major setback of the Post-Organic era.

The remaining units had been forced to disperse. Those that survived had waited for the return of Mondas, the planet of their origin.

The impassive observer, Co-ordinator[38], had once lived on Mondas as a fully organic Mondan, ten thousand years ago. Mondas had orbited the sun with its ancient twin, the planet Earth. Then it had drifted away to the edge of the solar system. The troublesome emotional memories were linked to that distant time. The Organic Era. The time of flesh and blood.

Thirty years ago, following the first major setback of the Post Organic Era, the Co-ordinator and his group had crashed into a polar region on Earth. They had laboured year upon year just to survive, to maintain their strength, awaiting the Return which they knew must come.

Thousands of years ago, the Co-ordinator had belonged to the Faction, the Mondan sect who wanted fully to embrace the logic of the cybernetic way. As Mondas continued to drift to the edge of space, they had dared to leap across to the outermost world of the system, Planet[14], and take it as their adopted home.

The Mondans they left behind had, like the Faction, augmented their failing bodies with mechanical devices. But they could not bring themselves to convert fully. They refused to divorce themselves entirely from their inefficient organic origins.

They turned their attention instead to speeding the Return.

Harnessing the power of the magnetic field, the Mondans steered their world back to its original orbit.

Then the second disaster had struck.

The journey had depleted the planet's electromagnetic reserves. The Mondans sought to replace lost power by transferring energy from Earth. Miscalculations were made. The energy could not be contained. Mondas was torn apart. The planet, its inhabitants and the invasion forces deployed on Earth, shrivelled, disintegrated, and were obliterated.

The Co-ordinator and the other units had observed the disaster from their hidden base. They had retrieved what remaining material they could find. Little was suitable for recycled use. But close examination of one landing craft and its mechanimate Mondan occupants yielded valuable information about their distant cousins.

The same mistakes would not be made again.

She was naked, cold and stuck in the shower. What a way to spend her birthday.

Still pushing on the door, Ruby looked upwards. The cubicle was open at the top. She saw that it might be possible to leap up and grab hold of the top of the cubicle walls and haul herself out that way.

Then something occurred to her. She tried pulling on the handle instead of pushing.

The door clicked open.

She went to her locker and pulled on her clothes. The workout and shower had refreshed her, her body felt good, but mentally she must be still off-balance.

She sighed. She felt moody. She was all tangled up inside. That Mike Brack had something to do with it. He'd got under her skin and now he was acting so strangely.

She cursed her emotions. Sometimes it would be simpler not to have any.

By the time she had returned to her cabin, Ruby had worked out a plan of action. She would go through her wardrobe for something to wear at the ball that night. Then she would combine business with pleasure. She would surprise Diana and Leslie at their rehearsals and take holograms of them at work.

She noticed a card had been pushed under her door. From Barbara. A hand-made card which opened to reveal a pop-up cut-out of a complicated Chinese character. Under the cut-out Barbara had written:

T'AI
(PEACE)
Happy Birthday, Ruby!

She had added in a scrawl, Did an I Ching reading for you. Came out peace (T'ai):

NO LEVEL WAY NOT FOLLOWED BY DECLINE.
NO OUTWARD PATH NOT FOLLOWED BY
RETURN.
CONTINUE MINDFUL OF DANGER. NO BLAME.

P.T.O.

Barbara had told her that the I Ching was some kind of Taoist oracle. It did not foretell the future. It clarified. It outlined a likely course of events.

Ruby turned the card over. The scrawl covered the back. Barbara sometimes got carried away with these things.

She stuffed the card into the hologram wallet for later perusal and set about choosing her fancy dress for the ball.

The theme was the 1950s, to celebrate the decade the *SS Elysium* had been constructed. Ruby stripped off her clothes, put on new knickers and, after rummaging through the odd assortment of clothes she had brought with her, she pulled out a jump suit. Shocking pink, the Fifties would have called it.

With a small pair of scissors she cut off the trousers just below the knee and made a fringe out of the frayed material of the legs by ripping it into narrow ribbons. Then she cut the garment across the waist. Now she had frayed shorts and a shirt. She tried them on.

The shirt she left unbuttoned and tied the two loose ends together under her breasts, exposing her midriff and cleavage, such as it was. The tight-fitting shorts hugged her thighs. Exotic cycling shorts. Fifties pedal-pushers. Her knees peeked out between the shreds of torn pink cotton. Her calves were left bare. On her feet went her little pink socks and her flat white tennis pumps. Very period.

136

She was getting somewhere. The pink went well with her dark complexion. But there was something missing. As usual, her hair was an unruly mass. What could she do with that, she wondered? She had an idea.

She shredded the discarded trouser legs into narrow strips. She grabbed hold of sections of her hair and braided them tightly, dreadlock-style, weaving in the shreds of pink cotton. A homage to her distant West African origins, on her mother's side, of course.

A final examination in the mirror. Yes! Fifties and funky.

She put on her heavy multicoloured jacket, grabbed her recharged power pack and Holocam, and headed for the ballroom.

She had reached the top of the final staircase that led onto the ballroom mezzanine when a familiar voice rang out.

'Ms Duvall!'

Her heart sank. She kept on going.

'Ruby!'

It was no good. She had to turn and face him.

'Lord Straker. What a surprise.'

He removed the cigar from his yellow teeth.

'How are you doing? Hard at it, I hope. Your hair's gone Afro. Is that the sea breeze, or just the good sex?'

He smirked and snaked an arm round her shoulders. His tone became more confidential.

'This feature of yours. How are we progressing, would you say?'

'Coming along, thanks,' Ruby lied. 'I'm getting together a good collection of holograms.'

'Yes, the Holocam's a remarkable piece of technology,' he said, tapping the camera which hung at her side. 'It'll make money, will that one, especially when we've featured the results in the *Sunday Seeker* – along with your ten thousand words.' He gave her a quizzical look and replaced the cigar. 'But that's shaping up, I bet. All you need is an angle. Aren't I right?'

She nodded breezily.

'Remember. Keep it light. Not too much complexity in the ideas department. Less head, more read. Ever heard that little Aussie gem?'

137

As he spoke his eyes had been prying between the flaps of her open jacket.

'Mind if I peek?' He drew open her jacket by the lapels and leered at her Fifties funk. 'Now, that's an interesting outfit.'

Ruby was glad to change the subject.

'Yes, actually, it's for the ball tonight.'

'Very nice. Talking about the ball. I promised to drop in on rehearsals for tonight's cabaret act – Diana Milton and Leslie Laughland. Friends of yours, I believe. Perhaps you could snap a hologram or two. Great for morale. Good for the feature.'

'Actually, I was just on my way to see them.'

'You were? Then let's go together.'

The mezzanine was filled with sunlight which streamed down through a high ceiling of glass. Lord Straker hauled open a tall bronze door and motioned her through.

The ballroom was built on a grand scale. It took up almost the entire width of the vessel and a third of its length. The high ceiling was picked out in golds and blues. Large crystal chandeliers sparkled in the yellow light which spilled from the portholes to one side. Tall mirrors, which lined the other walls, expanded the light-filled space to infinity.

At the far end of the ballroom was a raised stage. Diana was playing at the piano. A figure in a silver suit was performing a little mechanical dance. Its muffled voice was singing a plaintive song:

'Just to register emotion,
"Jealousy", "Devotion",
And really feel the part.
I could stay young and chipper
And I'd lock it with a zipper
If I only had a heart.'

The music ended. The Tin Man looked puffed. He leant on the piano.

Lord Straker started clapping.

'Up there, Cazaly!' he shouted.

Diana looked their way. She gave a little squeal of delight.

'Lord Straker!'

She glided across to him and offered her cheek. He gave it an eager peck.

'How nice to see you! Leslie said you would be dropping in,' she simpered. 'And Ruby, darling.'

She blew over a kiss and put her arm through Lord Staker's and led him back to the piano where Leslie was struggling to remove his headgear.

'Thought you'd want pepping up for tonight,' beamed Lord Straker, entranced by Diana's attentions. 'But by the sound of things, you're onto a winner. Ruby, wouldn't you agree?'

'You're very sweet,' Diana smiled, fluttering her eyelids.

Leslie at last emerged, red-faced. He nodded to his visitors as he clanked the metal helmet down on the piano. 'How do you do, sir. Hello, Ruby. Look, Diana,' he continued in one breath, 'I really don't know whether this idea is going to be on. I could suffocate in this thing.'

'People will love it,' said Diana soothingly, 'and you do it so well. You heard what Lord Stanley said.'

'Yes, but – ' Beads of sweat were standing out on Leslie's forehead. His face had gone white. He put a hand to his mouth. 'I'm sorry, I must just get a breath of fresh air.'

He clanked across to a porthole, pulled it open and leant out. Icy air gusted in.

'He just needs a little time to get used to his costume.' Diana twittered. 'It's splendid, don't you think, Lord Stanley? You don't mind if I call you that do you?'

It amused Ruby to see her boss on the receiving end of such deadly accurate charm.

Before he could respond, there was a fierce scraping sound along the hull. A shriek cut through the air. Leslie sprang away from the porthole, tripped backwards and ended up sprawled on the floor.

'Easy now, sport,' called Lord Straker as they rushed to his side. Diana put a hand to his ashen cheek.

'Darling, you look awful. What was it?'

'Out there,' he whispered hoarsely. 'In the ice.'

Ruby was already at the porthole. Diana and Lord Straker followed her over. Diana pointed.

'That iceberg looks rather close.'

'Nah,' said Ruby's boss. 'It's miles away.'

Leslie joined them. He put his head through the open port-hole and pointed along the hull.

'Look, there it is!'

Ruby peered out. She saw a large bobbing chunk of ice, thudding against the hull. It was freezing out there. She pulled her head back in.

'It's one of those sculpting chippings the captain was worried about.' She slammed the porthole shut. 'Growlers, they're called.'

'Well, whatever it was,' said Leslie, 'it passed right by this porthole. I could have sworn I saw someone. Someone in a metal suit. A deep sea diver. Someone in armour. Trapped in the ice.'

'Perhaps it was your reflection,' Diana put in breezily, taking his arm. 'You know how that can frighten people.'

Leslie stuck out his tongue at her. He looked shaky and perplexed. Lord Straker patted him roughly on the back.

'No worries,' he said. 'Captain Trench is a first-class skipper. He'll get us through safely, no if and buts. Now,' he clapped his hands and rubbed them together vigorously, 'must wend my weary way. We've a couple of surprises up our sleeves for this ball. But before I go, Ruby, it'd be nice to have a couple of snaps of me with the cabaret artistes. Wouldn't you agree?'

After his final departure, the three friends breathed a collective sigh of relief. Diana hugged Ruby and gave her a big birthday kiss.

'Sweetie, sorry about your card. I'll drop it in later. Promise. But look, I do have this.' She produced a folded piece of paper. 'Couldn't give it to you while Lord Stanley was here, for obvious reasons.'

It was a letter.

Monday 29 May 2006

Dear Mike

It was a pleasure spending those few hours with you round at your studio on Friday evening. Of mutual benefit, wouldn't you agree? I must say you have an original cast of mind!

My friends from Panama were impressed by your quote for the arms which they consider quite acceptable.

You say it will be 4–6 months before the consignment is complete. Best to ship them all in one go, wouldn't you agree? If you can get them crated up, I have a plan for getting them over there which will cost us nothing and won't involve Customs & Excise (Heaven forfend!).

There may even be another job in it for you, if you're a willing bugger. Details to follow.

All the best

Stan Straker

Pretty damning, darling,' said Diana. 'Wouldn't you agree?'

The procedure for dealing with the troublesome spontaneous manifestation appeared to have been effective. Images of purely organic origin had subsided. Emotional memory had been quelled, perhaps for another hundred years. Normal monitoring could be resumed.

The Co-ordinator focused on the continuing plan for survival.

Phases One and Two would ensure total control of Earth. Interim experiments using human subjects would lead to the construction of a more effective unit of conquest. Work was proceeding on both fronts.

The Co-ordinator directed full attention to the data images relayed from active units to check that instructions were being carried out.

Recycling Module Group[1] was at work in the central chamber. Routine reclamation work continued satisfactorily.

Engineering Module Group[4] was in the conversion chamber. Suitable humans were being dismantled and reconstructed.

Surveillance Module Group[5] had earlier alerted the Co-ordinator to a possible breach of security on the target ship, the SS Elysium. Interim measures were being implemented.

Sabotage Module Group[7] was pursuing activities of more urgent importance.

The Co-ordinator observed.

A thermal lance was cutting through white metal. A glowing flap was prised aside. Two humans were revealed. One male black. One female yellow. They were exhibiting typical human emotional symptoms of fear. The female yellow was diminutive, of minimal use. The male black was much larger. Promising material for experiment.

Two other humans had been apprehended. One female beige. One male beige. All from STS.

The Co-ordinator issued instructions.

ALERT. GROUP[7]. ALERT.
Phase One of survival plan continues.
Plan will be served by utilization of captured humans.
Disposal as follows:
Small female yellow to be recycled.
Male beige and female beige to be adjusted and allowed to return to STS.
Priority instructions:
Large male black.
This human is suitable for experiment.
Store him.

Where was the Doctor when the lights went out?

In the dark.

And where was the Doctor now?

A dim memory came to mind. He had once landed the TARDIS momentarily in the middle of a cricket game at Lord's one Earth summer during the 1950s. Something to do with Daleks, he was sure. But he couldn't for the life of him remember what. Perhaps for some reason his time-travelling machine had returned him to the same year. But why inside a ship?

Memory was a vortex. A whorl of mental confusion, emotional agitation. Yet it alone maintained the illusion of personality, the thread by which the disparate circumstances of his life might be pulled together.

There was a drawback in living as long as the Doctor had.

Events coalesced in the mind. One's physical body might regenerate, as his had, several times, but his memories remained the same spinning vortex, growing ever larger and deeper. The past became a hopeless jumble.

After a thousand years it had become more and more difficult to distinguish all his many adventures, the quests, the triumphs, the failures, his adversaries, his companions. The different strands of his life tangled together, confusingly, inextricably.

Who was he? Where had he come from? Where was he going?

The way that can be spoken of is not the unchangeable way.
The name that can be named is not the unchangeable name.

The whirling core of memory had been the only thing about him through each of his reincarnations that had not changed. Yet it remained an illusion. Insubstantial, darkly visible, the self that it conjured up only seemed as if it was there.

So where was the Doctor now?

In the light. At sea.

When he had at last found a light switch and flicked it on, he saw that he was in the deserted engine room of a large seagoing vessel. Massive oiled pistons. Complex gearing arrangements. Toothed wheels within wheels. He guessed he had probably materialized in mid-twentieth-century Earth. At least he was not holding up a cricket match.

When he caught sight of the TARDIS he had a shock. He had known he was travelling in a split-off version, a kind of figment generated from within his thousand-year-old unconscious. But he hadn't known what to expect. Its appearance had undergone a subtle change.

The delicate translucent stone of the shrine was pleasing to the eye, at once solid and somehow insubstantial. The effect was pure illusion, of course. The plasmic shell, which was basically all this TARDIS was, had taken on a shape consistent with an earlier connection with Earth, a time when he had been clearer in his mind about the meaning of things.

Or had that been an illusion too?

He stood by the control console. There was a greasy spanner

lying at his feet, but no other tools or sign of activity. Elsewhere, he could hear the pounding of working engines. He had tried the engine room door to investigate further, but it was locked. The room and its engine were clearly out of use.

That was fortunate in a way. The TARDIS was positioned just beneath the poised arm of one of the mighty pistons. Throwing a spanner in the works would be as nothing compared with throwing a TARDIS into this convoluted machinery, had it been in action. Not that the TARDIS would suffer much. But the pistons would certainly take a pounding.

He gazed in fascination at the inert machinery. Primitive propulsion technology, powerful and beautiful. His hands glided over the control board. His fingers itched to press one of the big red buttons, or to pull one of the green-knobbed levers. Why not? The engine was out of action, after all.

He grasped a lever and eased it down. There was a hiss.

To his horror one of the piston arms swung in a slow circle. It smashed against the green stone doors of the TARDIS with a resounding thud.

He ran across to check out the damage.

The piston had survived intact, and of course the doors of the TARDIS were unscathed. The cracks in the stone were natural and purely decorative. But the entrance of the TARDIS was entirely blocked by the piston's huge knuckle of steel.

He was in a locked room. The means by which he had entered was closed to him.

He was trapped.

He remembered the footsteps he had heard when he first came round in the blackness. Perhaps there was a regular patrol. He made for the door, picking up the spanner on the way, and started tapping in morse.

Taptaptap. Tap. Tap. Tap. Taptaptap.

Taptaptap. Tap. Tap. Tap. Taptaptap.

Someone would find him. Sometime.

Wouldn't they?

16 Who?

The bogyman will get you.

Ruby tried to keep the thought out of her mind, but it kept floating back in.

The bogyman will get you.

It was back to the childhood fears again. She was down in the dimness of the lower level once more. The lift doors closed behind her. There was a muffled stillness all around her. The engines pounded in the engine rooms at the far end of the corridor which disappeared into gloom and darkness ahead of her.

There was that strange feeling of excitement and fear at the base of her diaphragm, in the pit of her stomach. Anticipation of the unknown. That feeling you want to pee but know you don't really.

The bogyman –

She started to walk away from the light above the lift. Into the dimness. Towards the door where Mike Brack had appeared. She would not use her camera as a torch just yet. It wasn't dark enough. And she didn't want to announce that she was here.

She stopped at the door. No sound. Just the pounding of the engines, and her heart. Both were throbbing in her ears.

It was an old iron door with an old-fashioned keyhole. She put an eye to the keyhole.

It was not entirely dark in there. Something glowed. She could see an array of lightbulbs on a framework of metal struts and –

She recognized it. Brack had drawn it on the paper napkin. At its centre was the oval shape, like a disembodied head. It glowed with luminescent light. Beyond the machine or sculpture or whatever it was, bomb maybe, were wooden boxes.

145

The light was not strong enough to make out any more. She carefully tried the handle. Nothing doing. The door was locked.

She had an idea. For some technical reason to do with lasers, the light from the Holocam was emitted through the lens. That meant she could take a picture through the keyhole. She positioned the camera and clicked. The hologram transparency shot out at its base.

She tore it off and, putting it in her wallet along with the other holograms, she caught sight of the back of Barbara's card. Out of the scrawl some capitalized letters caught her eye.

HE ARRIVES LIKE A BIRD, HEEDLESS OF HIS
WEALTH.
THE WALLS RETURN TO WATER. NO USE FOR
ARMY NOW.

She heard the whine of the lift. She slipped the wallet back in her pocket and started off down the corridor. As she turned a corner into the real gloom, she swore she heard some kind of animal noise. She stopped and switched on the Holocam torch.

There it was again. Like the soft growl of a lion.

The light of the Holocam picked out a door. Engine room three. The growling was definitely coming from behind it.

There was a key in the door. She tried to pull it out so she could peer through the keyhole. The key turned easily to left and right but would not come out. She turned the key till the lock clicked. She inched the heavy door open and eased her head through the gap.

She had to stifle a giggle.

A metre or so from the door there was a middle-aged man, flat on his back. His mouth was open.

He was snoring. Loudly.

Joe was shaking his head, goddamn it, and staring at her like she wasn't getting madder by the second.

'No sign of anything? No footprints? No message taped to the window? Broken down – back in five minutes?'

She was being unfair on them, she knew. And she was getting nowhere. They must be dog tired, and just as shocked as she was.

Trouble was, she blamed herself. She had to calm down.

But something was badly amiss. The two of them had walked back into the base and calmly announced they'd located the AXV5 all right, but Bono and Nike were missing.

Try a new tack.

'OK, OK, I'm being facetious. I apologize. You need some rest. You're both off-duty as of now. Get your heads down for a couple of hours. De-briefing will continue later.'

'Affirmative, general,' said Joe Adler.

'Affirmative, general,' said Jude Black.

No apologies for messing up. No explanations. No gratitude for being let off the hook. Just a perfect salute from each of them.

The general was perplexed.

There was a spanner just inside the door. It looked heavy enough to use as a weapon if need be.

As she picked it up, the ship rolled. The door swung to behind her with a resounding clang. The man stopped snoring. He shut his mouth and licked his lips. His eyes remained closed.

She looked him over. His cream-coloured suit was crumpled and smudged here and there with grease. His feet were bare and the soles were black. There was a rumpled paisley-patterned cravat at the neck of his cream-coloured shirt. He looked every inch the holiday-maker. Was he a passenger who had lost his way?

Ruby couldn't help the smile that came to her lips. He looked so out of place lying on the engine room floor in his summer suit. He could have been lying by the pool in the sun. He didn't look like a bogyman.

He began to stir. One eye opened. It strayed across in her direction and stopped.

'Kadiatu?' He murmured uncertainly. He opened both eyes and sat up. He stretched and yawned.

'Kadiatu Lethbridge-Stewart?'

She shook her head. There was a strange burr to his voice which Ruby could not quite place. Irish? American? Dutch?

The man rubbed his eyes and blinked at her. He eased himself to his feet and took a step towards her. He was not tall, and did not look threatening, but she tightened her fingers around the shaft of the spanner. She raised it as a warning not to come too close.

He made a sudden apologetic gesture with his hands.

'No, of course you're not Kadiatu. What was I thinking of?' The hair, perhaps. The play of the light. And from the floor – ' He gestured behind him as his words trailed away.

They both swayed in silence with the motion of the ship. He smiled at her.

'I've been asleep, you see,' he said simply. 'I was waiting for you.'

She had no idea what he could mean, but it sounded vaguely ominous. There was silence again. He smiled. She was just about to ask who he was and what he was doing in the unused engine room, when he said something she didn't quite catch.

'Sorry?' she said.

'Ah, you do speak English. Had me wondering. Wu-ming, I said. Ancient Chinese. First thing that came to mind. No name, you see. You were about to ask.'

Ruby nodded slowly. Was he a nutter?

'Who –?'

'Wu-ming,' he said, shaking his head. 'That's just the point. No name. But you can call me the Doctor, if you like. Some people do. I'm just a traveller, really. On holiday, sort of. And you are?' He stuck out a greasy hand at her.

She had to clear her throat.

'Ruby. Ruby Duvall.'

'Pleased to meet you.' He took her free hand in both his and shook it firmly. He pointed at the door behind her. 'You have a key?'

'No,' said Ruby uncertainly, turning to the door and trying the handle. 'The key's in the lock on the other – '

The door would not open.

'Ah, what a pity,' said the man. 'It seems, Ruby, that you've locked yourself in with me.'

148

She didn't like the sound of that. She swung round and faced him again. Anxiety caught at the edge of her voice.

'How did you get in, then?'

He started to chuckle, then laughed out loud.

'The best guard secures without use of key. The best traveller leaves no sign of passage. The first is you, the second me.'

Ruby was suddenly angry at his evasive answers. She was also a little bit scared. Maybe he was the escaped terrorist, or a deranged stowaway.

'Look, forget the wise talk for just a moment – ' she began.

'But how did I get in? It may not be the answer you expect, but here goes. You see that green box in the corner?'

Ruby followed his pointing fingers down into the well of the engine. Pressed tight against the wall by a large piston was an ornate booth of pastel green.

It looked as if it were made of lightweight stone or some plastic imitation. It had a double roof in the oriental style. It reminded her of the kitsch phone boxes of London's Chinatown. She felt almost homesick for the filth of Soho. It seemed ten thousand miles away, as of course it was.

'I came with that,' he said, 'and can't leave without it.'

Four Chinese characters were inscribed on the lintel.

'What do those letters mean? Over the double doors.'

'It says, "No time, no place". Actually rather appropriate.'

'Oh, I see!' said Ruby, the light dawning. It was suddenly clear. The booth was one of the surprises for the ball her boss had mentioned. It belonged to Wu Ming, a traveller in Oz. This guy must be playing him in the show, had stored the booth down here and, in coming to collect it, had got himself locked inside the engine room. Simple. She understood.

Until he said, very matter-of-factly, 'It's my TARDIS, you see. I travel through time and space in it.'

Joe shut himself away in his room. He locked the door.

The general had told him to get some rest. He was not in need of rest. What was required was to increase his efficiency.

The room was untidy. His desk, for example, was littered with unnecessary items. An open newspaper. A half-read science fiction novel. Both were inessential. He dumped them in the bin.

On the wall by his bed were the Page Three pin-ups the general had got him to remove from the rest room noticeboard. She was right. They inflamed the passions, encouraged arousal and dependency and other emotional weaknesses. Greater control was required. One by one he pulled the cuttings off the wall and dropped them into the bin.

Near the bin were the white crumbs of some hurriedly eaten sandwich. He bent to pick them up.

The crumbs were moving. He saw they were bugs. He watched as they moved in orderly fashion with true efficiency.

The Co-ordinator communicated a directive.

ALERT. GROUP[5]. ALERT.
Supplement to previous instructions.
Retaliation unuseful at present state.
Target is dense in processible units.
Lock on.
Maintain surveillance.
Phase One update.
Magnetic flux at low oscillation.
Prepare for activation of Phase One.

It was bugging him. Gary had at least expected a hug from Jude as she'd stepped from the lift and into the tracking room. He hadn't even got a smile. 'Hi, Gary,' was all she had said. Neither was there any of the usual infantile banter from Adler, either. They must be both dead tired.

From her debriefing with the general, Jude had gone directly to her room. After a decent interval, he had followed her. Now he stood outside her door. He tapped on it softly.

'Jude?'

'I'm sleeping,' came Jude's breathy voice.

'Jude, it's Gary.'

'Gary, the general said I had to get my head down.'

Gary smiled on the other side of the door. She sounded like an automaton. She always did when she was sleepy.

150

'Want me to join you?'

No answer.

'Jude?'

'No, Gary. I've got to get some sleep.'

There was nothing in her voice. No irritation. No humour. Just the information.

'That's OK, babe. See you later, then?'

There was no response. Maybe she was too far gone. Maybe she had fallen into solid sleep. He would leave her in peace. He padded off on tip-toe.

Inside the room Jude was sitting upright on her bed, fully dressed. Her eyes were open, as if lost in thought. She was staring into the space ahead of her.

The captain was worried. He and his first officer were poring over the latest satellite print-out. It revealed an increasing break-away of icebergs from the Ross ice-shelf. The *SS Elysium* was currently passing through the Amundsen Sea and would be moving into the midst of the Ross Sea icebergs in less than twenty-four hours.

'This one's a monster,' said the captain, indicating the largest by far of the icebergs.

'It's heading for the Falklands.'

The captain looked up sharply at his first officer.

'At a steady fifteen knots,' the man added. 'It'll break into growlers long before it gets there. Thousands of them.'

The captain returned to a study of the chart.

'Then it's a mercy we got through those waters when we did. But we're still exposed to these damned sculpture chippings. They're as bad as growlers. Must keep an eye out, Jones. They could do considerable damage, taken head on.'

A maintenance hatch had swung open soundlessly behind them. From it had emerged the Doctor. He had listened with interest to their conversation and now peered over their shoulders at the chart.

'Global warming syndrome. It's unmistakable. Look at these data for the rate of flow of the glaciers,' said the first officer, pointing at a series of graphs at the base of the print-out. 'Up from seven metres per year in the early eighties to twenty metres a year now. That's nearly a trebling.'

151

'Yielding, like melting ice,' said the Doctor.

'Quite,' said the captain. Then he swivelled his good eye to the first officer.

The first officer was looking at him.

Slowly, they turned to the source of the unfamiliar voice.

The Doctor put his hands together and gave a little bow.

'Formal, like an uninvited guest,' he said.

Deep below the STS tracking room, in the field loop chamber, Whitehead and Palmer were making adjustments, fine tuning the newly installed machinery.

Private Palmer was fiddling with a tiny washer. It was near impossible to place it neatly into the exact groove. His gloves did not allow him much dexterity. He kept at it, though.

Corporal Whitehead was restless. He'd completed his assigned task. He was waiting for Palmer to finish. He wandered through into the snow lab. He glanced at the stacks of specimen dishes, the bench with its collection of snow dissecting instruments, all neatly laid out in a row. His breath came out white. It was colder in the ice lab than in the main chamber.

He saw something lying on the solid ice floor. He snickered. It looked like a rozzer, a scumbag, a used frenchie. He knew the blossoms shagged like rattlesnakes. But do the do in here? It'd freeze the beef in seconds.

He squatted to take a closer look.

It was a clump of glistening dead bugs. Shiny. Silvery. He poked at it with his gloved finger.

The skin of his shaved head prickled inside his hood. The bugs were far from dead. The clump broke up into milling activity. Like ants they darted this way and that and then headed off away from him in single file to disappear behind the nearby buttress wall.

The bugs had left something behind, something they had been clumped on top of. What it was Whitehead could not quite make out. But he knew what it looked like. It looked like a little lump of flesh. Yellow. And human.

One hundred and five.

Her calf muscles were pumped up. She could feel the blood rushing through them, the veins standing proud.

One hundred and six.

Ruby was still climbing the iron rungs of the inspection shaft. They had found it when seeking a way out of the unused engine room. She had made this Doctor, or Wu Ming, or whatever be was called, go first.

One hundred and seven.

She couldn't make him out. He seemed to think the year was 1959. She supposed it was some kind of extended joke on his part to do with the ball and its celebrations.

One hundred and eight.

At the start of the climb she had begun to count off each rung. At around rung eighty, a light had appeared above her. She had looked up to see the Doctor step off the ladder into the brightness. She could hear muffled voices as she continued the climb, then shouting and the sounds of struggle.

One hundred and ten.

She was slowing down. Despite her training, each new rung demanded an increasing effort. She had to pull the breath into her lungs. The air in the shaft had the smell of diesel. There was an oily coating on her tongue. Almost there. She wondered how the Doctor had been able to clamber up the shaft with so little effort. After all, he must be getting on. He looked fifty, if he was a day.

One hundred and –

At last she emerged into the light of what she was surprised to find was the bridge. The Doctor was being held by two FF security men. He was saying something about Snowcap Tracking Station. The captain had lost his usual composure and was looking rather red in the face.

'And you say it's the year 2006?' the Doctor was asking.

'Look. I don't know what kind of trick you're trying to pull, but if you are indeed known to the general then it's a simple matter to put a call through to STS. If the general denies all knowledge then I'll have no alternative but to have you restrained below.'

'Oh dear. That sounds unpleasant,' the Doctor said.

The washer slipped in beautifully.

He'd got the hang of it now. Only one more to go and then it was back to the rest room for a well-earned break. They were at least an hour over schedule, and Whitehead had been in a sweat for him to finish.

A shadow fell over the machinery beside him.

'OK, Whitey, almost there. Keep your hair on,' hissed Palmer.

The shadow moved directly over where he was working. It was difficult enough to get this job done without some asshole of a corporal stepping in his light.

Palmer whipped round to give him an earful.

'Aw, come on, ya – '

The words stuck. His jaw fell open, rigid with fear. Two metal hands gripped his shoulders and dragged him up. His feet left the ground. His face was brought level to another face. A blank face. A face of metal.

An electric arc crackled between them.

So the Bono/Nike problem seemed to be sorting itself out somehow. That was a relief.

It was all still a bit of a mystery. Hilliard had suddenly spotted AXV2 on the wall screen. The radio link was dead but Bono and Nike were headed for home. There had been some screw-up, that was for sure, and Pam wasn't convinced that Adler and Black knew nothing about it. She would have to send Venning out with Brooks in AXV5 immediately if the field survey was to continue uninterrupted. And she would have more words with the sergeant and corporal.

Dave Hilliard called over. There was a tremble of shock, or disbelief, or something, in his voice.

'General, I've got the *SS Elysium* on the line. The captain's holding a stowaway who says he's known to you.'

He paused. Pam looked at him questioningly.

'He calls himself the Doctor,' he added, significantly.

They held each other's stare for a moment, then Pam picked up her phone.

'Yes?' she snapped.

There was a moment of silence before she heard a tentative voice. 'Erm, I wonder if I could speak in person to General Cutler?'

'This is the general. Now listen, buddy, we've serious business on here.'

'Ah,' the voice said, as though something had suddenly made sense. 'So, obviously I'm not speaking to the General Cutler who died at Snowcap Tracking Station in 1986?'

'What are you trying on, mister? That was my father.'

'Oh, I see! Oh dear, yes. I am sorry.'

Pam had started to shake. This wasn't funny.

'So, what do you know about it?'

'Actually I was there. It was rather a traumatic time for me, too.'

Logically, there could be no doubting that this guy was a screwball. Trouble was, she wanted to believe him.

'How do you reckon you can prove it to me?' said Pam, shocked at herself that she was even entertaining the idea.

'I – er – I could pop over and visit you. Right now.'

He was a screwball.

The door of engine room three was flung wide open.

A couple of FF guards went in first, gave the place a quick once over for booby traps and secured the door in its fully open position, so there was no chance of being locked in again. Two more FF men bundled the Doctor inside. Unnecessarily roughly, Ruby thought.

She had persuaded Captain Trench to allow the Doctor to be proved wrong. Since there was no possibility that he could travel to STS in the green booth as he was claiming, what could they lose? To confront him with reality would bring a decisive end to the whole charade. It would make an excellent story for her feature. Crazed stowaway's desperate escape bid.

The captain motioned Ruby to follow the men in. He and three of his officers took up the rear. Two other men in dark blue overalls, ship's engineers, were emerging from the inspection shaft at the rear of the engine room.

It appeared there was going to be a problem moving the piston away from the booth. It would have to be done manually. The four FF men spat on their hands and put their shoulders to the piston arm. Their faces wore that smug expression of men whose strength was being called on. They were going to

155

prove their macho credentials. Ruby felt they were putting on a show of strength for her. One of the engineers released the gear and the four hunks heaved.

Nothing doing.

The two engineers leant their weight against the gleaming steel arm. Grunts and groans. There was some movement, but not enough.

The three naval officers went to help the others, who were now red-faced with strain and perhaps some slight embarrassment. Even the captain lent a hand.

The combined effort of the ten men brought success at last. The piston was lifted free of the green pagoda. Immediately, the Doctor grabbed Ruby by the hand.

'Prepare yourself for a surprise,' he said, as he yanked her through the double doors.

The ten men exchanged uneasy glances. They were left holding the piston. There was not much else they could do if they weren't to trap the two of them, that idiot stowaway and the journalist girl, inside the absurd green box.

Before the doors swung to behind her and plunged them into darkness, Ruby caught a glimpse of the blank walls of the inside of the box. She hadn't expected the pagoda-like column with the hat on top of it, rising out of a hexagonal console which all but filled the room. But otherwise it wasn't much of a surprise. In fact it was much as she had imagined. A cramped dark space. Like climbing inside a wardrobe.

The Doctor was putting on a creditable performance. He seemed genuinely taken aback. He was muttering to himself in the dark.

'Someone in the main control room has been messing about with the TVG. That means we've got a bit of a rush on our hands. Now where on earth could it be?'

It sounded as if the Doctor was scrabbling about on the floor. She switched on the light of her Holocam. He was on his hands and knees.

'There it is!'

He picked up a black object. It was not unlike a large spark-plug from a car. He opened a small flap under the green stone console. As he continued to fiddle about, he uttered a steady stream of gibberish.

'Sorry about all this. It's the time vector generator. It got disconnected. Probably something to do with my travelling companions. They're in a different spatiotemporal dimension, at the moment. Two different dimensions, I imagine. You see, we're in a plasmic shell. And the inside – where we are now – is no bigger than the outside. Slightly smaller, in fact, as you were probably expecting. But this is actually only part of the TARDIS, a part that's been jettisoned temporarily and – could you just shine that light over here? – that's got it.'

There was a hum. Soft lights faded up. Ruby had been directing the camera light towards where the Doctor was working. When she looked up again she had a shock.

It was not a trick of the light. It could not be. They were inside a larger space. The walls were definitely further away. And they were no longer blank. They were made up of a bamboo lattice-work and hexagonal rice-paper cells. Green light glowed within.

'There,' said the Doctor, wiping his grubby hands on the tails of his suit as if it were a hand towel, 'that's the transdimensional interior matched up again.' He adjusted some dials on the console. 'Welcome to the Jade Pagoda. Now, I'm going to hurry if you don't mind. Here we go.'

He pulled a lever. The central column rose and fell. The cream-coloured felt hat with its paisley-pattern band that was perched on top of the column rose and fell with it.

The ten men still held the piston away from the green stone booth.

The captain was about to shout out and ask what the devil they thought they were up to in there, when he heard a gurgling noise, almost like water going down a drain. It was coming from the green box.

The yellow Chinese lantern on its topmost roof began to revolve, flashing on and off. The stone was fading, becoming transparent. He saw the rusty iron wall of the engine room behind it. Then, as he watched, the pagoda vanished completely.

The box had gone, and Ruby and that dratted stowaway had

disappeared with it. Ten very puzzled men were staring at an empty space.

And they were still holding that blasted piston.

Brooks whistled. His eyes were glued to the periscope monitor.

'Well, I'll be a Chinaman!'

Hilliard was at the other end of the tracking room.

'What is it, private?'

'Take a look at this, will'ya, Colonel. There's a couple of civilians wandering around up there. Large as life.'

'Oh, yeah.'

Hilliard was not in the mood for Brooks' infantile humour. He had more worrying things to occupy his mind.

'No joshing, colonel. There's a green hut or something out there, too. About two hundred metres due east. They've spotted the vent shaft. They're running this way.'

Brooks' imagination never usually stretched this far. Hilliard strode over to take a look. He was almost winded by what he saw on the screen. The man was in a light summer suit. The girl had on a multicoloured coat, but her long brown legs were bare.

'It's ten below out there. For chrissakes, Brooks,' he shouted, 'get up there and get them in! Before they freeze solid. They've come over from *Elysium*.'

Brooks stared at him slack-jawed for a second, before he charged towards the lift.

Hilliard knew that what he'd just said was impossible. He also knew that it was true.

Ruby was not quite sure what was happening. She was in a kind of daze. One minute this Doctor had dragged her from the *Elysium*'s engine room into his pagoda. The next, he'd dragged her out into the freezing cold at the South Pole. It was unbelievable, but equally, it was undeniable.

What the Doctor had said would happen, had happened. Except that his travelling machine, his TARDIS as he called it, had landed a good distance from the STS entrance shaft. The Doctor had said something about having forgotten to take glacial drift into account. The base had moved with the ice. The TARDIS had landed where STS had been in 1986.

Ruby was dazed. But her legs were warming up again. One of the soldiers, a Sergeant Adler, had brought her a fleecy blanket and a cup of steaming coffee. He'd given his name, rather formally she had thought, but had said nothing more. He seemed like a zombie. The word came instantly to mind. He didn't seem in the least surprised at their arrival, unlike the soldier who had ushered them in and the second-in-command, Colonel Hilliard, and the woman general, Pamela Cutler.

From these three there was an air of incredulity, of not quite believing the evidence of their eyes which Ruby understood well. But Sergeant Adler wasn't turning a hair.

Ruby looked around her at the twinkling lights, the flashing VDUs. It was simply, starkly, incredible. They'd arrived like birds, from nowhere, from out of the sky.

The Doctor and the general were deep in conversation.

The colonel smiled across at her. He seemed a nice old bloke.

'Like a tour?' he asked.

The Doctor seemed to be making little rational sense. The general was perplexed.

'From Dave's description,' she said, 'I would have expected an older man.'

'Ah, yes. I was older then. That must sound odd, I know, but I was at the end of my first incarnation. My body was wearing a bit thin. That's how I put it then, anyway.'

The Doctor was pleased with himself. His memory had sharpened up. They were talking about the earlier days, of course.

'Mind you,' he continued, 'that incarnation lasted pretty well. Longer than the other six. Matter of luck, partly.'

The general was just staring at him. She gave herself a little shake as if to make sure she was not dreaming. Then she asked, 'My father, what do you remember about him?'

'Actually, he was rather rude. He called me Grandad, I remember, and when I said I didn't like his tone, he replied that he didn't like my face – or my hair. Come to think of it my hair was pretty awful then.'

The more Pam heard, the more convinced she was that, however, improbable, this bizarre man was the doctor who had been involved in whatever had happened at the base the time her father had met his death. She was prepared to believe anything now, alien invasions, instant travel in green pagodas, even throwing off a worn-out body like a snake sloughs off a useless skin, anything, as she got nearer the truth about her father's death.

She was convinced she was talking to someone who knew.

The two soldiers who came out of the lift looked scary.

They were dressed in insosuits like the one the colonel had provided Ruby with. He'd kitted himself out with one, too. He was taking her deep down to the reactor level where the field loop was installed.

But as the lift doors had opened she had seen another two zombies, one black, one white, both with shaved heads, both with bloodshot staring eyes. They did not say a word. They grunted acknowledgement only when the colonel greeted them.

'Had a bit of a blow-out, last night. We've just got FLIPback up and running,' said the colonel as they descended in the lift.

That explained it.

It was a real scoop to be getting a look at STS at such an historic time. Ruby snapped away with her Holocam.

The colonel seemed to have his mind on other things.

When he brought her to what he called the snow lab, she suggested he go back up. She wanted to spend a bit more time down there and she could tell he was itching to talk to the Doctor himself.

'Well, yeah, I could do with getting back. Er, just in case the general needs me. Are you happy on your own?'

'I'll be fine.'

He left her to it.

The snow lab had been carved out of the solid ice. It was like Santa's grotto. Ruby snapped away.

For a really dramatic shot she could do with a different angle. She found a promising niche and tucked herself into it,

160

pressing hard against the ice wall. The picture framed in the lens was stunning.

As her gloved finger pressed on the button of the Holocam she heard a creaking noise behind her. The wall gave way. She fell backwards into darkness.

When she had got over the shock and had picked herself up, she saw she was in a tunnel which sloped upwards on a slight incline. A tunnel carved out of the ice. An unused part of the base, maybe, which had been sealed off.

She switched on the light of her Holocam. It reflected back from crystalline walls. They sparkled in rainbow colours.

It was beautiful. A rainbow highway.

She started forward. To explore.

17   Suitable for Conversion

She felt sick to her stomach. Panic was beginning to set in. Under her insosuit, she felt the cold sweat trickle.

She should have made some marks somehow in the ice to show where she had come from. It was after that third junction that things had started going wrong.

When she had started out it had seemed easy enough. Walking up the gentle incline she had come to a four-way junction. There was a passage ahead of her and one to the left and one to the right, all curving into gloom. She had turned right.

The curve of the passage was such that she could see no further than ten metres or so ahead. Soon she arrived at another junction, three-way this time. A tunnel led off left from the main curving passageway. She had turned left.

At the third junction she had turned right.

She was pleased with her consistency. Right, left, right. It would be child's play to retrace her steps.

Then she came to a dead end.

She thought as she approached what looked like a blank wall that it was a three-way junction and that she would be able to turn left or right. Left, to keep consistent. But the passage ended abruptly and she had been forced to return to the previous junction. The third junction.

Now she could either go forward or turn left. Which would be most consistent? From the point of view of her outward journey, going forward would be turning left at the third junction and she should be turning right. Shouldn't she? She thought that was right. So she turned left. But at the next junction she turned left again, because turning right would take her back to where she had come from. Wouldn't it? At the next junction she turned left again because that was what she would have done if she hadn't got out of sequence.

She started to feel uneasy at the next junction. She guessed she had been wandering around down here for no more than ten minutes, but it seemed longer and she didn't appear to be getting anywhere. Beautiful though these ice tunnels were in the laser torchlight, did they lead to anything in particular? More importantly, would she be able to remember the way back? Yes, she thought she could. She turned right.

The next junction came quickly. She turned left into a passage that seemed to stretch endlessly into the distance. She started walking.

After five minutes or so, it suddenly occurred to her that she was getting nowhere. She had found nothing. And unless she turned back now there might be a chance that she would forget her plan and lose her way. On a sudden impulse, she turned round and started back.

At the first junction she turned right of course. But it was the next junction that caused her difficulties. This was where she should turn right again. Or was it left?

In fact, now she came to think about it, had she ever been at this junction before?

That was when the panic began. She should have been leaving a trail of holograms, or something, something to indicate the way she had come. When she'd been playing the *Elysium's* Vreal machine, maybe instead of spending so many hours flying about over unreal landscapes, she should have braved the dark labyrinths. It would have been better practice for her current situation. She just hoped there weren't aliens round the corner.

The thought had been a flippant one, but she felt the cold sweat trickle. Her heart began to pound. She turned left.

She soon felt she was going the wrong way. She turned back and went straight on at the junction. At the next junction she realized she had really gone wrong. She knew she had never been this way before. The junction was different from all the others. One passage veered to the left, one to the right. But a metre or so along the right passage was another passage off to the right.

That was when she caught sight of the hand.

* * *

The first officer was on the bridge, guiding the ship through the litter of growlers from the latest iceberg sculpting. He divided his attention equally between studying the radar screen and peering out towards the bright horizon. The white cliffs of Antarctica were away to the left. He could just make out the vast inlet of the Ross Sea bay.

Then, in the distance, he noticed something odd. He knew what it was immediately. But, putting it simply, it couldn't be where it so obviously was. He sighed. He was having a bad day.

It started with the escape of the stowaway in the early hours, was made worse by the nutter who called himself the Doctor, with that journalist girl in tow, and compounded by the disappearance of both in that curious emerald pagoda while the rest of them were left holding the damned piston.

Some kind of practical joke. Must have been. Dreamt up by Lord Straker, wouldn't be surprised. Dry run for tonight's festivities. And what a raucous time that was going to be. No end of tricks and swizzles. Then there was Christmas.

The first officer sighed again. He wouldn't be sorry to see the end of this cruise.

Pretty convincing at the time, though, that vanishing cabinet trick. Amazing, what could be done by magicians and such like, nowadays. Taken them all by surprise. Till anger had overtaken puzzlement, as they finally realized they were being pissed on from a substantial height.

The captain of course was exceptionally enraged. Had every right to be.

The first officer gritted his teeth and ground them together. The captain would not be in a mood to hear about this latest development. But it was extremely odd. He would have to be told.

The first officer reached for the intercom.

She shone the light directly at it. The hand was embedded within the wall a couple of inches beneath the surface. The ice was utterly transparent to that depth. The back of the hand was towards her, the fingers splayed and slightly bent.

It had the hyper-realism of a hologram. Every detail was clear. The curled black hairs, the blueish knots of veins, the ragged nails on stubby fingers. The flesh had the rosy tints and glossy sheen of living flesh.

But this hand was not living. It was severed at the wrist with surgical precision. She could see the two white circles of the sliced-through bones with their brown marrow centres. She felt sick.

She could see there were other objects embedded in the walls along the passage. She forced herself forward. There were disembodied human parts on each side of her. A leg severed at the thigh. A pair of hands, small and clearly a woman's. Slender with perfect painted nails.

As she walked on, the embedded parts became more numerous. There were internal organs, too, all were grouped like with like. There was a row of human hearts and lungs, complete with connecting arteries and airways. Fresh blood glinted on exposed raw membranes.

Nausea was tugging at her guts. It crawled up her gullet like a slug. The gallery of human parts stretched ahead as far as she could see. She was a professional journalist. She had been on the scene of the most appalling accidents. She had reported on the most gruesome examples of man's inhumanity to man. Nothing like this, though. Never anything like this. Whatever it could be. This anatomical chamber of horrors.

Unless it was when she had visited that abattoir. When she had given up eating meat. This was how they 'dressed' cattle, how they prepared a cow for human consumption. Entrails taken out, skin stripped, hooves and horns removed. Nothing is wasted. The skin can fetch up to fifty ecu at the tanner's. Hooves and horns sell on for glue at a fiver a bin. Everything is of use.

She was a professional. She had to see if through. She swallowed and moved on.

The next exhibit was too much, even for her. A naked human figure towered above her in the ice, but it was impossible to tell whether it was male or female. The sexual organs were missing and the wounds obscured in scar tissue. The skin was raw and bloody as though the upper layer, the epidermis, had been somehow scoured or burned right off. The face was featureless. The eyes were gone, leaving just the empty sockets.

Ears sliced off. No head of hair because, above the metal band clamped around the forehead, there was no head. Just the brain, horribly exposed. Undulating folds of whitish-grey.

The greasy lump was rising in her throat. She bent and retched it up. The remains of breakfast spattered onto the floor of ice. It steamed in the cold. Her body convulsed twice more. Thin greenish fluid poured out. She reached for the wall to steady herself and heaved for breath. She wiped her lips with the back of her hand.

Her head felt hot under the plastic hood. The taste was bitter in her mouth. But the nausea had gone. She looked again at the figure suspended in the ice.

The arms and legs had been removed. In their place were powerful limbs of metal and plastic. Their length were what gave the partly human figure its inhuman height and proportions. The front of the torso had been slit from throat to groin. The long wound was expertly stitched.

On closer inspection Ruby saw it was not in fact stitches that held the flesh together, but rather a kind of long zip fastening. The flesh was zipped shut to chest level. There the flaps of skin gaped partly open. Beneath could be seen the rib cage, white bones reinforced by shiny steel. And within the cavity was the glint of other mechanical parts, replacement heart and lungs perhaps.

Ruby was transfixed and horrified. But she had to seek out an explanation. It was her job. Reluctantly, she raised her camera and captured on hologram the ghastly spectacle before her. She forced herself onwards.

Human figures loomed out at her whenever she directed the light of the Holocam at the walls. Some were in various stages of dismemberment and augmentation, or intact and pathetically vulnerable in their naked human wholeness, or fully clothed, as if patiently waiting their turn to be processed and transformed. These were the ones that could still be identified as ordinary people. Air pilots, perhaps, or naval personnel, stewardesses or men and women in business suits, all of them held in suspended life, it seemed, within the aspic of the ice.

She was approaching another junction. She thought she saw lights reflected from the passages ahead of her. She immediately switched off the light on the camera.

It was when she turned the corner that she saw them. The silver creatures. Softly illuminated by the light which shone from a bulge at the top of their heads. It was then that she thought she must be asleep in her cabin on the ship, caught in a nightmare, dreaming of humans embedded in the ice and of silver creatures, like Leslie in his Tin Man costume, walking up and down, inspecting them, embedding them there within the walls of ice. For that was what they must be doing, these silver creatures. What she had seen, what she was watching now, had all the unreality, the casual horror, of a dream. The bizarre and the ordinary welded together by an appalling, elusive logic.

She peered round the corner at them. She dare not use her camera for fear the whirr of its mechanism or the flash of its laser would give her away. Her heart was thumping in her chest. It thumped so loudly she could not believe they did not hear it.

There were two of them. She noted the details. Metal masks for heads. Blank vestigial faces. Two holes for eyes. A slit for a mouth. A tubular excrescence from where the ears should be, extending upwards and inwards to merge with the metal cranium behind the source of light.

They were enveloped in a suit of some flexible silvery metal. A network of thin rods extended along their limbs, as if their skeletons were outside their bodies. Fixed into each of their chests was a flat panel. It had two square vent-holes on either side with a few buttons between, and some other details she couldn't quite make out. From throat to groin was an obvious zip.

Ruby felt immediately queasy again as she made connections with what she had seen of the figures embedded in the walls. She swallowed hard and kept her eyes fixed on what was taking place along the passage.

They were walking towards her. Between them was a man. Uniformed, black-skinned, thickset. He must have been large because he was not dwarfed by their height, which was clearly considerable. She judged it by the roof of the tunnel. The silver creatures must be seven feet tall, at least. The human was shorter by a head, but big. For all their height, their frames

167

were slender. The human's bulk was certainly greater than theirs.

But he wasn't resisting them. He walked between them and appeared compliant.

They stopped. One of them placed something at his shoulder, just behind his neck. The other raised a bulbous tube that could have been a gun and pointed it at a wall. There was a glow of reddish light, a hiss and a massive billowing of steam. They gripped the man by the shoulders and pushed him towards the wall. Into it, it seemed to Ruby, for he disappeared from view. She realized they had placed him within a hollow or niche that the gun had blasted out.

They both stood back. They raised their weapons and pointed them up into the cavity above the man. There was a glow of red, the hiss of steam, and then a flash of intense blue light. The vapour clouds instantly dispersed with a tinkle of falling glass, or icicles perhaps. The niche was no longer there. The wall was solid ice once more.

The silver creatures turned and walked back down the passage. They mounted some sort of mobile platform. There was a distant hum, and then they were gone.

After a minute of utter silence, Ruby finally gathered the courage to see what they had done to the man. She switched her light back on and ran down the tunnel. He was now like the others she had seen, the ones in their various everyday clothes or uniforms, eyes lowered but not closed, as if waiting, waiting for their captors to return. Like them, this huge man stood and waited, fixed in the ice. His uniform was UN blue. Above the breast pocket were the letters STS. Below it, hand stitched in red, one word. BONO.

She raised her camera. She stood back to centre the figure in the frame. There was a sudden hiss, a sharpness in her nostrils. Her arms fell loosely to her side. The camera clattered on the floor. At the corner of her vision she saw a silver arm. Her shoulder was gripped hard, hard enough to hurt. She heard a voice, as though it was inside her head.

'You will come with us. You will not resist.'

Consciousness came and went. She was walking. She was stepping onto a low platform. The ice walls were whizzing past. She was entering a high-domed cavern, full of instruments and twinkling lights. Silver figures stood at consoles, hands attending to controls. Three-fingered hands. She was being strapped inside an upright metal box. The lid closed to.

Darkness.

There was a metallic, buzzing sound in her head.

Ezz amnayn anewal ooway zoon oyoomin drooda.

It repeated itself. It seemed to be making a kind of imposs-ible sense.

Eggs ham and bacon and devaluation of you, man, in true door.

A third time the voice buzzed. This time she understood.

Examination and evaluation of human intruder.

A mild electric current seemed to be coursing through her. The voice droned on, endlessly repeating itself. She knew no more.

He knocked on the door of her cabin. No answer. He tried the handle. Locked.

He'd scribbled a note to her. The envelope was in his hand. Should he leave it for her?

He was exhausted from the sculpting. His head was thick with his morning drinking, the many glasses of absinthe. Somehow he'd carved out the likenesses in the ice. To order. But then he was used to working in an alcoholic haze.

The effects of the wine were fading. But the bitterness of the wormwood remained. It seeped right into him, into the reservoir of bitterness that lay within him.

He wanted to talk with Ruby first. He needed to explain. He pushed the envelope under her door.

Absinthes make the heart grow stronger.

How long she had been in there, she could not tell.

When she came to, her whole body seemed alive, cleansed through. Her head was clear again. She could hear the buzzing voices still, but they were definitely coming through speakers close to each ear.

'Examination and evaluation complete.'

Then came a deeper voice. 'Transfer data to central store.'

There was a rapid pulse of high-pitched whirrs and clicks.

169

When it had stopped, the first voice droned, 'Data transferred.'

After a moment's silence, the deeper voice spoke again.

'Human intruder evaluated as suitable for conversion.'

Icy fingers of fear gripped her insides and squeezed. She shouted out, 'Who are you? What do you want with me?'

The words reverberated inside the box. As though she was speaking to herself. But a reply came swiftly.

'I am the Co-ordinator. You are to be converted. Resistance is useless.'

It was the deeper voice which spoke. It had little or no expression. What it stated was information, pure and simple. It continued to speak. It told her she had been captured and would be put to service.

'In the service of what? In whose service? Who are you?'

'In your language we may be described as – '

There was a whirr as the vibrating, buzzing voice seemed momentarily to be choosing a suitable term.

'Cybermen.'

It came flooding back to her. All the outrageous claims that Isobel Watkins had made.

A different, more distant-seeming cyber voice sounded in her ears.

'Group Five to Control. This is Group Five. The *Elysium* is now within range. Request instructions for proceeding.'

The Co-ordinator responded immediately.

'Control to Group Five. Request received. Proceed as follows. The *Elysium* is rich in processible units. Approximately one thousand human passengers. They are to be captured alive. Use maximum force compatible with minimal fatalities. Human units are to be transported to Cyber Control. They will be processed and stored for use in Phase Two.'

'Group Five to Control. Instructions received. Proceeding with attack on the *Elysium*.'

There was a brief pause. Ruby could hear a background hum, a few clicks and whistles. Then the Co-ordinator spoke again, but not to her.

'This large female brown will be stored and converted. Release her from the humaform.'

Ruby wasn't sure she liked the description. But it was direct and to the point. What was more to the point was how she was going to escape the fate of those she had seen incarcerated within those walls of ice, and how she was going to warn the Elysium of the impending danger.

She was surprised at her clarity and coolness of mind. It was an unexpected bonus in the midst of this nightmare. She would need all her wits about her now.

The door of her box, the so-called humaform, swung open. One of the silver creatures, one of these Cybermen, stood before her. Its silver arms reached out to her. Her straps were loosened. She was pulled out of the box. She did not resist. She would have to choose her moment carefully if she was to survive in one piece.

She screwed up her eyes against the lights until she grew accustomed to the dazzle. The dome of the ice cave was high and vaulted, reinforced with metal spars.

The Co-ordinator spoke.

'Take her to the store.'

She was guided to the entrance of the cavern, where a heavy iron door was wedged open.

The Co-ordinator's voice echoed once more around the dome.

'Return with the large male black.'

That would be the STS man. Bono. The one she had seen placed in the ice, however many hours ago. What were they going to do to him?

She looked round for the source of the voice to see what the Co-ordinator looked like.

There were a number of silver creatures in the cavern. It must be one of them. But they all looked the same. She had thought that the one called the Co-ordinator, presumably their leader, would be distinguished in some way from the rest.

'Co-ordinator!' she shouted out. 'Which one are you?'

Her voice sounded puny. It lost itself in the empty spaces of the cavern. It reverberated thinly off the circular icy walls.

A deep synthetic rumble came from the centre of the cavern.

'I am the Co-ordinator.'

To her surprise it was none of the Cybermen that spoke in reply. The voice emerged from something else. From a machine. A tangle of wires and flashing lights. There was a globe at its centre which had glowed as the voice had spoken.

'You are the Co-ordinator?'

'That is correct,' came the expressionless reply.

'But you're not like the others, the other Cybermen.'

The oval chamber at the centre of the flashing lights glowed in unison with the synthetic voice. It sounded like a priestly litany, intoned as if not solely in answer to her, but as an affirmation of intent.

'I am the Co-ordinator of Cyber Control. I belong to the Cyber race. I am the source of Cyber knowledge. I control all Cybermen under my command. We follow the imperatives of the Cyber race. We will survive. We will proliferate and we will survive.'

Ruby had began to wish she'd never asked. Until abruptly the Co-ordinator ceased its intoning. Then she wished she'd kept the conversation going longer.

'Take her away,' it buzzed. 'Return with the human control specimen. The mobility experiment will now proceed.'

That last bit sounded ominous, thought Ruby. Ominous for Bono, anyhow.

Her implacable guides brought her out of the cavern, holding her in a tight grip, one on each arm. Outside in the tunnel the light from their heads illuminated the low metal platform. It was a form of transport. It was what had brought her here.

The platform was about a metre long, less than half that in width. Two thin tubes rose up at the front and met at a kind of handle, on which were a couple of buttons. They got her to stand on the platform between them. Compared with Bono, she was a slight figure.

Tall as she was, the Cybermen loomed above her. She was clamped between them, held fast. It was far from comfortable. She felt like the filling of a particularly inedible sandwich.

The platform hummed to life. It rose slightly, glided forward, and was soon skimming over the ice at speed. They raced along the curving tunnels. As the walls whizzed by, Ruby was aware that embedded in them were silver figures. Cybermen. Hundreds of them. Waiting. Stored. For what?

Occasionally the vehicle would slow, as a junction neared, and turn off to right or left. Soon they had reached the point where Bono had been stored, the place where she had been gassed, if that was what had happened. It was all very hazy in her mind. But she knew that this was the place. Her camera was still on the floor. And as they slid to a halt, she saw the big man, Bono, held motionless inside the wall of ice. They dismounted.

One Cyberman held her firmly. The other raised its gun to the wall. A glow of heat, a rush of water, a hiss of steam, and Bono was free of the ice. He stood slackly inside the niche, barely breathing. The Cyberman reached towards him and pulled him forward. He came out meekly, blinking slightly, but unresisting.

He must be drugged, thought Ruby. How had he survived the sub-zero temperature? He must have been in there for a couple of hours at least. It would be her turn next to be frozen inside the wall. What should she do? She was rigid to her fingertips with fear.

She felt a pressure on the muscle above her shoulder-blade, then a sudden sharp pain. The Cyberman holding her had jabbed her with an injection gun. The kind of thing you injected horses with. She saw it glint in the three-fingered hand as it pulled away.

A sensation of heat was spreading from the wound and coursing through her body. She was being pressed into the niche. Her back was hard against the wall.

The Cyberman in front of her raised its freezer gun.

Captain Trench had his grave face on. He couldn't explain it. But there was no doubting what it was.

Jones was right to have called him up to the bridge. It was inexplicable, like that disappearing pagoda. Two inexplicable phenomena in the space of a couple of hours.

The captain was weary. He was getting pains in his phantom limb, a sure sign that things were getting on top of him.

'We left it behind us six hours ago, cap'n,' the first officer was saying. 'It should be more than a hundred miles north-west of us now. I can't see how it got ahead of us.'

'Perhaps it has propellers and an engine.'

The first officer chuckled politely at the conceit.

The captain stared at the iceberg with his one good eye.

The face carved into it was clearly Straker's. The *Elysium* was fast approaching it. Or was that an optical illusion? Was the truth in fact that the iceberg was fast approaching the *Elysium*?

The captain was prepared to believe anything now.

A distant noise sounded. Did it? Or was it in her mind? No, there it was again, too far away to be distinguished. The falling in of a roof, perhaps. The grind of collapsing ice.

The Cyberman lowered his freezer gun and turned to the second Cyberman. There was silence. The Cybermen nodded at each other and the first Cyberman turned back and raised its gun again, directing it up into the roof of the cavity where Ruby stood, her back against the solid ice.

She did not feel the cold of the wall through her insosuit. In fact she glowed with heat. Whatever the Cyberman had injected her with, it was certainly effective at keeping the cold at bay. No doubt that was the intention. No doubt that was how Bono had survived, frozen solid in the ice.

She braced herself against the rush of melting icy water from above. She wondered what it would be like to be frozen in a solid block of ice. She would soon find out. That would be something to tell the readers of the *Sunday Seeker*. If she ever got the chance. Pity she hadn't brought her Nanocom.

There was the noise again, nearer this time. It sounded like an animal. Some kind of beast. It sounded again. A roar. Like a lion. It echoed down the passageways.

The Cyberman hesitated once more, turned to its colleague.

Suddenly she realized that if there was ever going to be a chance to escape, this was it.

She ducked down as she slipped out of the niche, going slowly at first so as not to skid on the ice. She was moving noiselessly. They hadn't noticed her. Instinctively, she picked up her camera on the way. Then she started to run flat out.

There was a hum behind her, a brief flash of orange light, and the roof above her dropped in a torrent of water and steam. She felt the weight of it glance off the back of her insosuit. It knocked her off balance. As she crashed to the floor she let herself roll right over and somehow regained her footing once more. She ran.

She ran in the gloom. The tunnels were endless. At junction after junction she blindly charged to left or right. No time to think about direction.

At last she had to stop. Just to catch her breath. She could run no further. Besides, the light of the Holocam was fading fast. Thank goodness she'd brought the spare pack with her. She fished it out from under the insosuit.

In the brighter light she saw she was near another junction. She moved towards it. There were scratch marks on the wall. Three marks, close together. Like the scrape of claws. Three-fingered claws.

Then she heard the roar.

It seemed to come from behind her. Which of the two passages ahead should she take? She started down the left one. Suddenly she stopped. She was rooted to the spot. There was the glow of a distant light reflected off the walls ahead of her. She had to move. She switched off the Holocam. She walked backwards, her eyes never leaving the glow as it intensified, her hand reaching along the wall behind her until she felt the gap where the other tunnel led off from the junction. She hid herself at the mouth of the tunnel, pressing close in to the wall.

The light hummed past her – a lone Cyberman on a skimmer. It had missed her. She sighed with relief. She was breathing hard. But the sounds she heard were not only hers. Something was breathing behind her. Something gripped her.

Her yell of fear was stifled.

18 Bluebirds Fly

She was whining like a dog. It was all she could do.

A hand was clamped over her mouth. It was clammy and very cold. Like mortuary flesh. She wanted to scream and scream.

A voice was whispering hoarsely, 'It's me, Ruby. Ssh. It's all right. Ssh, they'll hear you.'

It sounded like the Doctor.

He had a torch. He shone it up into his face. Lit from such a peculiar angle, it was a ghastly sight. He was deathly white. Sweat glistened over his eyebrows. He was panting heavily.

She was relieved, angry, suspicious, all at the same time. Relieved she was not in the grip of some ferocious cybernetic beast. Angry that he had given her such a fright. Suspicious that he might have something to do with these Cybermen. After all, he got her in to this.

She stopped the whining. He removed his hand. She gulped down a cold breath of air and blew it out slowly, a long white stream in the torchlight. She felt a bit calmer now. At least he had come to find her.

'I don't know whether to thank you or to thump you,' she whispered. 'Was that you, roaring like a lion?'

'I thought it might create a distraction.'

'Well, yeah, it did that all right. What the Cybermen made of it, I don't know, but it scared the pants off me.'

The Doctor grinned a lopsided grin.

She was suddenly worried about him. He'd be about her father's age. He was still in his summer suit. He must be frozen stiff. She pulled off a glove and felt his cheek. It was like touching ice.

'God, you're cold.'

'Yes, I am rather. Still, the hat conserves the body heat. We should be able to trace our way back before too much damage is done. Follow me.'

He seemed to know where he was going. They came to one junction, then another. At each, the Doctor was unhesitating in his choice of direction.

'How do you know the way?'

'The sign of the beast.'

She looked at him quizzically. He pointed to a three-clawed scratch mark on the wall. Then he produced something from his jacket. A small pocket knife. He made scraping actions with it in the air. One, two, three. Ruby understood. Clever old Doctor. She put an arm around him and whispered in his ear.

'Thanks for coming after me.'

'You'd been gone a long time,' he whispered back. 'They didn't seem unduly worried at the base but I came to see what you were up to. When I found the tunnel in the wall I guessed you'd gone exploring.'

'You'll never guess what's going on down here.'

'You'd be surprised. I'm well acquainted with what the Cybermen get up to.'

They turned a corner and came to the grisly row of partly augmented bodies. They walked down the tunnel in numbed silence.

She stopped to look again at the first human figure she had seen embedded in the wall. Was that what they were doing to Bono? It didn't bear thinking about.

'Terrible creatures,' muttered the Doctor.

She examined the scarified face behind the ice. There was something odd about the eyes. When she had glanced at them before, she had been too horrified to look at them closely. She had just seen empty sockets where the eyes should be. But now she saw that embedded in the sockets were dark red jewels. Like rubies.

It gave you a strange sensation to look at them. As if you had dreamt about such things.

'So cruel,' she whispered.

'I don't know that cruelty comes into it,' said the Doctor, moving on. 'They did it to themselves. So they think nothing of putting humans through the process. Gives a new slant to the precept, "Do unto others . . ." '

There was a movement at her feet. Looking down she saw a milling frenzy of small white bugs. They were clustered around a greenish stain on the floor. She realized with distaste that they were feeding on her vomit.

It would have fascinated her mother, but it made own flesh crawl. She ran down the tunnel and caught up with the Doctor.

'You've come across the Cybermen before?' she asked.

'Oh yes, several times. And now, as then, they must be fought. But first I have to get back to the TARDIS. It's in a volatile condition.'

'It looked all right to me.'

'What you saw was a third-generation plasmic shell. A copy of a copy, as it were, of a form it took on hundreds of years ago. Because of the TVG dislodgement – '

'TVG?'

'The time vector generator. Remember? It's what keeps the inside larger than the outside. It got disconnected. The TARDIS will soon become unstable in its split-off state. First, it will reassume its most recent appearance, and then – '

The Doctor had stopped dead. Ruby could see why. There was a tell-tale glimmer of lights, way down the tunnel, reflected off the curving walls of ice. The Doctor turned to her.

'Stay here!' he hissed. He switched off his torch and was trotting down the tunnel towards the lights before she had time to reply. His silhouette disappeared from sight.

A minute passed. Then another. Ruby began to get worried.

A light was twinkling on the walls, getting brighter. She heard the hum of one of the skimmers. It skidded into sight. She turned and tried to run but in her haste she slipped on the ice and went sprawling over the floor. The skimmer was almost on top of her. She covered her head with her arms and braced herself for the impact. She heard the skimmer swerve to avoid her. It bumped into the wall and scraped along it. Something hit the floor and rolled towards her. She peeped out under her hood. She saw a cream fedora.

'Climb on, quick!' the Doctor yelled.

178

She picked up the hat and jumped on the skimmer behind him.

'Hold on tight!' he ordered.

She grabbed him round the waist. The jolt of the vehicle under his inexpert control almost dislodged them both. But they were away. They swerved round to the left at the junction and zipped along the passageway. It was on a slight upward gradient but the machine was picking up speed. With a free hand she wedged the Doctor's hat back on his head.

'Thanks,' he shouted.

The tunnel no longer curved. It stretched ahead of them as far as they could see. The light on the front of the skimmer shone out like a laser. There were no more passageways off to left or right. They raced over the smooth ice, onwards and upwards.

Over the hum of the skimmer the Doctor asked what had happened to her. She told him what she could. She told him about the threat to the *SS Elysium*. He didn't appear surprised.

'I think they'll be after more than the *SS Elysium*.'

'Doctor,' she began, wondering quite how to phrase the question. 'Are these Cybermen an alien species?'

As soon as it was out of her mouth she grimaced at its tabloid tackiness. But the Doctor's answer was not what she was expecting.

'Depends how you define alien,' he said simply. 'They were human once, before they started altering themselves. When you look at a Cyberman you might be looking at yourself, a few thousand years on. Given that you've made certain choices based on the supremacy of logic, and on the survival of the individual. Does that make them alien? One thing's certain, unless we get out of this place, there's a very good chance they'll turn us into Cybermen. Who'll be the aliens then?'

She felt him shudder. And there was a tremble in his voice she didn't like.

They seemed to have lost their pursuers. But they were getting further and further away from the base. It had to be many kilometres behind them now. The tunnel continued to rise on its gentle gradient and had begun to curve again. They

179

must surely be nearing the surface. At any moment they might burst into the open air.

They slowed to a stop. The Doctor switched off the motor.

'Can you hear anything?' he asked, turning back to her. His teeth were chattering. His face was almost grey. She was alarmed. He could wear her insosuit for a bit. She started unzipping it.

'You'll be getting hypothermia. Put this on.'

'Ssh! Listen! Can you hear something?'

It was difficult to be sure. The journey had left her ears ringing. The Doctor turned off the skimmer's light. Reflected along the tunnel behind them they could see a far-away glow.

'Oh, no,' moaned Ruby.

The Doctor switched the light back on and started the motor.

'Get on!' he ordered.

She was half in, half out of her suit. Under it, her heavy jacket was gaping open. Her body heat was evaporating. She wasn't dressed for subterranean ice caverns. But then, neither was he. She couldn't understand how he wasn't frozen stiff. Though to judge from his appearance he soon might be.

She fastened her insosuit and leapt up behind him. The skimmer glided off along the tunnel. She clamped herself to his back in an effort to keep him a little warmer.

'Onwards and upwards,' he whispered. His teeth were clenched against the biting cold.

They swerved this way and that as they negotiated the bends. Ruby looked desperately for sign of a passage leading off to left or right, down which they might evade their pursuers. But the tunnel continued uninterrupted, on and on.

They had taken a particularly sharp curve when the light hit them. The end of the passage ahead was bright with rainbow colours. And a yellow dazzle was at its centre.

The Doctor was not prepared for it. He was fighting to slow the machine down. But they were skidding. Skidding towards the open sky.

'Jump!' the Doctor shouted.

* * *

Everything was under control. Everything was running smoothly and according to expectations.

Pam read the data as it came on stream. The AXV5 was doing its job just fine. Venning and Brooks were proving to be an excellent team. Just excellent.

Magnetic flux was now extremely weak and unstable. It was clear they were into Critical Blue. At any moment they might find themselves in a Critical White. That would be the test. They must be ready.

The conditions for Critical Black might be found in any of the Critical White phases. It could as easily be the first they encountered as the thirty-first. They must keep their wits about them.

Pam was steely calm and in total control.

The Doctor was pulling at her camera. Trying to get the strap over her head. He was saying, 'Holograms? It produces holograms?'

'Yes,' she said, bewildered.

At last he had the Holocam free. He was pointing down into the gloom of passage along which they had come. The reflected lights of the approaching Cybermen were clearly visible. You could hear the hum of their machines.

What was he doing, taking pictures at a time like this? He was snapping away, moving this way and that, as if he wanted the perfect picture. The Cybermen were coming and he was taking snaps. Madman.

There was no hope of escape from them now. She and the Doctor had narrowly escaped certain death by jumping from their skimmer when they did, but they awaited a more gruesome fate at the hands of the silver creatures.

Be they aliens or be they not.

There was absolutely nowhere to hide. The skimmer had plunged out over the abyss. They had reached the end of the passage, where it opened onto daylight, just in time to see it spiral downwards and crash on the lower slopes of jagged ice far below, skittering over the white wastes in several tangled pieces, and tumbling at last into the frozen sea. They were looking out from a sheer ice cliff, high above a wide bay and the open Antarctic sea. The sun was a dazzling spot, low on the horizon. Among the silhouetted icebergs she could see a ship.

She gasped as she recognized the *SS Elysium*.

It must be getting towards the time of the ball, she thought. All those people, crowded into the ballroom. They were going to be rounded up by Cybermen like cattle. There would be no escape.

That was when the Doctor had started pulling at her camera.

Now he was tearing off the individual holograms from the strip he had taken. He selected one and wedged it in the ice at the edge of the tunnel. He ran down into the tunnel and looked back towards her.

'Doctor?'

'You're in the light. Get down!' he shouted.

She dropped to the floor, perplexed. He squinted against the strong sunlight and shook his head. He ran back to the tunnel edge and stuck a different hologram in the ice, at a slightly different angle. He returned to his former position some metres down the tunnel. This time he seemed satisfied.

'The way is shadowy and indistinct, yet within it is an image,' he declared, his arms flung wide.

Madman. Goofball. Now he was spouting Lao Tzu.

The humming was very close. She expected to see them at any moment.

'Doctor!'

'Yes. All right.' He was running towards her. 'Now flatten yourself against the wall.'

He spread himself against the wall, crazily close to the precipice. It's madness, she thought. But she had no better idea. She followed his example and flattened herself against the opposite wall. She swivelled her head to look back into the gloom of the tunnel. A skimmer swerved into view. On it rode a Cyberman. Another skimmer appeared behind it, this one with two more Cybermen on board.

They kept on coming. They did not attempt to stop. They did not even slow down. They just kept on coming. The first skimmer zoomed past them, within an inch of Ruby's feet. It sailed out into the empty air in a graceful arc.

The second skimmer followed almost immediately, passing them with a rush of air and taking its cargo of Cybermen to join the first, which was now breaking up and scattering over the jags of ice. Ruby looked on in sheer amazement.

'They didn't even try to stop. They must have seen us.'

'Knowing when to stop avoids the danger,' said the Doctor in a weird croaking voice. He was trembling all over now. He started down the tunnel.

'But – '

'Look, and you will see.' He turned to her and she ran to join him. He was pointing to the opening.

When she turned towards the opening, it was no longer there. There was no dazzle of sunlight, no rainbow colours. In its place she saw a tunnel curving into gloom, exactly like the one behind them.

'The hologram?'

'Yes,' he said. Talking seemed to demand an effort. He forced out the words. 'The angle of the sun – projected the holographic image of the tunnel – into the passageway. The Cybermen – the Cybermen never saw – '

The Doctor was swaying. Then he collapsed. The cold, thought Ruby. She quickly climbed out of her insosuit and took off her multicoloured jacket.

She had managed to pull the jacket over his arms when she realized she could hear the hum of another skimmer.

It swung round the corner into view and immediately screeched to a halt. The Cyberman dismounted. Ruby backed off towards the opening. The Cyberman increased its speed. They weren't as slow as they looked. It ignored the prone body of the Doctor. Its long legs strode towards her.

She kept looking behind her to check her position. She was almost at the precipice. The Cyberman halted, suddenly uncertain. It looked this way and that, turned to look behind it, then to the front again.

Of course! She had stepped behind the holographic image. From the Cyberman's perspective, she had disappeared.

But she wasn't out of danger yet. The Cyberman was walking forward once more. She remembered her Pah T'wa. She assumed the basic standing position and took long slow breaths.

The blank face was only a metre away. She could see the

peculiar teardrop holes at its eyes as it loomed above her. The Cyberman broke through the image into the light. It saw her.

Time to tango, Mr Cyberman.

The Cyberman lunged for the human female who had suddenly re-appeared directly in front of it.

Ruby caught the swallow by its tail.

She brought the tiger beneath the mountain.

The Cyberman teetered on the edge of nothingness. She was now behind it. She placed her foot in the small of its silver back.

She repulsed the monkey.

The Cyberman toppled out of sight like a colossus.

Ruby paused to bring her hands together. She bowed slightly to the emptiness where the Cyberman had been. Then she remembered the Doctor.

He was still and cold. She felt for a pulse at his neck. It was there, but it was weak and its rhythm alarmed her. It was almost as if there were two hearts beating inside him, not quite in unison.

She had an idea. She rushed to the Cyberman's skimmer and flung open the box that hung like a saddlebag from the handlebars. She was looking for an injection gun like the one the Cyberman had used on her. She saw it almost immediately, held in a pouch to one side of the box.

She had never injected anybody before. She almost lost her nerve as she held the muzzle of the gun against the muscle at the back of his neck. She thought of the intense warmth that had flowed through her body after the Cyberman had jabbed her.

She squeezed the trigger.

Lord Straker was peeping between a gap in the curtains.

The passengers were thronging the ballroom. The electric buzz of excitement had risen with the arrival of the Kinky Gerlinky contingent. Lord Straker found it impossible to distinguish the weirdly dressed men from the women. He was fascinated.

There was an outrageous drag queen, adorned in blood-red wig and magnificent ball gown. There was a pneumatic bunny girl on the arm of a near-naked body-builder. There was an eighteenth-century courtesan sporting such extensive décolleté that her entire bosom was exposed to devastating effect. Then he realized it was just another man in drag. The perfect breasts were merely life-like plastic shells. He suffered a pang of disappointment.

He brought the curtains together and turned to Diana and Leslie who were standing nervously in the wings.

'The roar of the greasepaint, the smell of the crowd,' he declaimed, his arms stretched out towards them.

Diana smoothed down the blue gingham of her Dorothy costume. She was inwardly mortified by his crass behaviour. It was simply unprofessional to peek through the curtains before a show. This may be only a cruise cabaret, but one had standards. She was worried, too, by another aspect of Straker's unprofessional approach. It put a sharper edge on her charm.

'I trust this surprise you mentioned isn't going to put us off our stroke, Lord Stanley.'

'Show me the bloke who puts you off your stroke, Di. You hear what I'm saying? Though it might be a different story with old zinc legs here.' He slapped Leslie's back and guffawed. 'Only pissing about, Les. You know that.'

Leslie had on his Tin Man suit. He felt totally isolated from the world. The helmet had been screwed on. He was fighting claustrophobia. He had made sure there was somebody standing in the wings with a screwdriver, just in case. He swivelled his head inside the helmet. He had found he could peek through the ear-hole. He spied on Lord Straker.

The press baron was in his element. He grasped Diana's hand and gave it a big sloppy kiss. Then he clamped his fat cigar between his yellow teeth and waddled past Leslie, back to where the curtains met. He discharged a parting shot.

'I'll tell you one thing for nothing. That Mike Brack's a wizard. He's the one with the tricks up his sleeve. Don't say I didn't warn you.'

He disappeared between the curtains. Diana looked at Leslie. She couldn't be sure he was looking at her. She raised her eyes to heaven, nevertheless.

Beyond the curtain, the band began to play.

* * *

She was getting the hang of the skimmer now. They were racing along. It was downhill all the way, back to base. No level way not followed by decline. No outward path not followed by return.

The Doctor was hanging on to his hat. His other arm was round her waist. The injection had worked. He guessed it was some kind of molecular antifreeze mixed with a metabolic stimulant to keep processes essential to life ticking over within the solid ice. He reckoned she'd saved his life. One of them, at any rate.

He wore her heavy multicoloured coat with pleasure. It was warm and it reminded him of a coat he used to wear in a previous incarnation. He thanked her for the loan of it.

He'd not stopped burbling in her ear the whole way back. What he said almost made sense, but it was mixed in with things that were out of left field, as her mother used to say.

Yes, he'd known the young photographer, Isobel Watkins. She and Zoe had been great friends. Zoe was his travelling companion at the time, the genius at maths. The guy in the kilt had been called Jamie. The Doctor had picked him up at the Battle of Culloden. And Isobel was right about the Cybermen, too. There was an invasion one summer in the 1970s. In fact, it was Zoe's mathematical skill which had destroyed the Cyber invasion fleet.

The Doctor had also been involved in the 1986 invasion at STS. Though for him, because he could nip about in time, the 70s invasion took place several years after the one in 1986.

He was worried about the current situation. No, he couldn't guess what the Co-ordinator's reference to a 'mobility experiment' might involve. But the Cybermen stored in the ice must be part of an army being held in readiness. And they were certainly intending to boost their numbers by capturing the passengers of the *Elysium* and converting them.

How they would do that, he couldn't exactly be sure. But he had some idea. He rattled off a list of names. Tobias Vaughn. She had heard of him. Then there was Ringhead or Ringway from the twenty-sixth century. There were others, too, all of them human agents to the Cybermen. There could well be a cyber agent on the *Elysium*, feeding information to Cyber Control. There might even be a cargo of dormant Cybermen on board the ship, ready to be revived at the touch of a button.

Images of Brack and his machine and those wooden crates flashed through her brain, but she immediately dismissed the idea. He might be an arms dealer, but surely he wasn't in league with the Cybermen.

It was too much for Ruby to take in at one go. Half her mind was concentrating on steering the skimmer. To the other half, the Doctor sounded like a babbling fantasist. But she could not dismiss what he was saying. The Cybermen were real, all right. And so was the fate of their victims. She had very nearly been one herself.

They had reached the end of the long tunnel and were weaving in and out of intersecting passages, following the Doctor's scratch marks in the walls. There was not a Cyberman to be seen.

They pulled up outside the snow lab and made for the lift.

At the upper level they burst into the tracking room. The scene that greeted them was unexpectedly placid.

General Cutler was bent over a keyboard. Colonel Hilliard was checking off figures from a screen. Other soldiers were quietly going about their duties.

Nobody paid them the slightest attention.

It was as if the monitoring of magnetic flux overrode all other concerns. She and the Doctor had been away for six or seven hours. Nobody seemed bothered in the slightest.

The Doctor cast a knowing glance at Ruby. Then he cleared his throat.

'So, general, when can we expect FLIPover to occur?'

His voice was calm but he was wringing his hands for all he was worth.

The general did not even look up. The VDU in front of her was a wash of light blue. Along the bottom was a dark blue stripe.

'That is still uncertain. Critical Blue is rising. Everything is under control.'

It was a routine answer to a routine question.

'I see,' said the Doctor, motioning Ruby towards the lift. 'Well, we'll just pop outside for a minute. Get some fresh air.'

There was no response to this inanity. All were intent on their monitoring duties. The Doctor bundled Ruby into the lift.

'What's going on?' asked Ruby, as the lift began its ascent to the surface.

'They're under cybercontrol. It's a kind of hypnosis. Makes humans into efficient zombies, programmed to assist with the Cyber plan.'

'What is their plan?'

'The Cybermen intend to sabotage the FLIPback device.'

'But that would mean – '

'Yes, bad news for Earth, I'm afraid. You're destroying the place pretty well on your own, as far as I can gather, but the Cybermen are capable of doing it a whole lot quicker. Now, we haven't got much time. You heard what the general said. An hour at the most. First, we must get back to the *Elysium* and try to warn them of the Cybermen's attack. Then – oh, crikey, it's started!'

The lift doors had opened onto the whiteness of the Antarctic surface. In the distance Ruby could see the TARDIS. At least she presumed it was the TARDIS. It was about the same size and shape, except it had lost it's oriental curves. It had also changed colour. Now it was blue.

They ran towards it. As they got closer, Ruby saw the words 'Police Box' had replaced the Chinese characters above the double doors, and a security light had replaced the Chinese lantern at the top. The dark blue paint was cracking and peeling.

'Like seeing an old friend,' said the Doctor, patting it as he went inside. 'As you can see, it's starting to degrade. But at least it's still here.'

She followed him in. She must tell him about Brack. And his strange machine. It may be of help.

'Now we must fly,' he said.

In the Conversion Chamber a group of Cyber surgeons huddled around a central plinth. Bright lights were directed on the object of their activities. There was a high-pitched whine as the cutting device bit with precision into flesh and bone. The mobility experiment was taking place.

From the Central Chamber the Co-ordinator supervised the process with interest. Information was relayed in the flickering pattern of light and the play of electrical resistances. The experiment was of immense importance. If it succeeded it would represent a great advance for the Cyber race.

And for the Co-ordinator.

The routine phase of the conversion operation was underway. The body of a large male black was stretched out on the metal operating slab. The dark skin had the sheen of burnished metal under the powerful lights. The clothing and other non-organic artefacts had been stripped away at the preparation stage. They had been transferred to the Central Chamber for recycling.

The brain had already been removed, as had the superfluous external appendages. The eyes. The ears. The primary and vestigial sexual organs. These were of no further use in their present form. They had been placed in the catalytic generator.

The unwanted internal organs would follow when the rib cage was opened up.

Within the catalytic generator a colony of Thysanura bugs was feeding on the waste products, converting useless protein into valuable enzymes which were of use in the production of plastic-metal compounds. The discovery of these bugs had led to improved efficiency in the recycling of organic wastes.

Non-mechanical life seldom had use in its unaltered form. The Thysanura bug was the exception that proved the rule.

The whine of the cutting device had ceased. The top of the skull was pulled away and discarded. The brain would be removed in its entirety and fed to the bugs. This was a departure from routine conversion.

The cranial cavity would undergo extensive enlargement and reinforcement. This was of exceptional importance given the nature of the experiment.

The sockets of the eye had been prepared for augmentation. The ultra-low frequency red crystal oscillators were awaiting transplantation into the visual cortex. This was routine.

For a human specimen, the limbs were unusually long and powerful. They would not require removal, merely meticulous strengthening of the ligature and suffusion of the porous bone with plastic-metal compound. The process had advantages over separate limb replacement. It ensured a consistent spread of body strength.

Before any further invasive surgery was undertaken, the largest organ of the body must first be adjusted. A different species of Thysanura bugs had been prepared. The range of their usefulness had been significantly extended by selective breeding. The surgeons positioned them on a patch of the human's skin. They began to ingest the upper layer, exposing the glistening red membrane beneath. In line with recent conversion procedure, the thickness of the dermis was to be reduced over the entire surface of the body.

The Co-ordinator impassively observed the Thysanura carry out their task. It might be possible in future years to mechanically augment these creatures. They might then have more far-reaching uses for the Cyber race.

It was an intriguing idea that in time would be pursued. But for now, all resources must be focused on the conquest of Earth.

And the mobility experiment.

The interior of the TARDIS had undergone a transformation as subtle and as complete as the exterior. Everything had a familiar shape and configuration, but the greenness had evaporated, and the oriental trimmings had been replaced by less cluttered, cleaner lines. The console and its central column would not have been out of place in the control room of a twentieth century nuclear power station.

When they emerged again, there they were, back on the *Elysium*. She still found it unbelievable.

The TARDIS was bang in the middle of the mezzanine outside the ballroom. The ball was under way. She could hear the blowzy sounds of the band and the dancing, the shrieks of laughter and the babble of voices.

The Doctor had reacted with relish when she had told him about Mike Brack. He had seized the fuzzy hologram of the storeroom and studied it closely. They were on to something. They must take a look at this sinister machine.

'What about the TARDIS?' asked Ruby, anxiously.

'Oh, I've checked it out,' replied the Doctor, blithely. 'It'll be fine for a few hours yet. The important thing at present is to put a stop to these Cybermen.'

There was nobody about. Everyone was packed into the ballroom. Ruby led him to the nearest lift. She tapped in the security code. She still couldn't bring herself to see Brack as a Cyber agent. Perhaps, after all, there could be some mistake. They descended to the lower level.

The storeroom door was wide open. The machine had gone. But the curious wooden crates remained. The Doctor whispered in Ruby's ear.

'Within these crates there may be dormant Cybermen. We must be careful.'

Absurdly, Ruby felt betrayed. The crates were stamped 'Panama'. These were the boxes of so-called 'arms' Lord Straker had mentioned in his letter. So, he must be involved in it too. 'Arms' was the cover word for dormant Cybermen.

The Doctor approached the crates and put his ear against the wood. He gave it a cautious tap and frowned.

Suddenly, a vibration juddered through the ship. It was the kind of vibration that had bedevilled the ship at the beginning of the cruise. Like going over cobbles on a bike.

'The engines have gone into reverse,' said the Doctor. 'It's an emergency stop. They must be attacking from the sea.'

He started for the door.

'We must get to the bridge,' he shouted as he ran off.

She followed him into the lift.

'Do you have any gold?'

'What?'

'Gold? Can you lay your hands on any gold? Rings. Necklaces. Teeth? The Cybermen can't stand the stuff. It'll help to keep them at bay.'

'Erm, I've got a ruby pendant. On a chain of gold. It's in my cabin.'

The Doctor jammed his thumb on the button.

'Get it!' he ordered. 'I'll meet you up on the bridge.'

She slipped out of the lift and hurried down the corridor.

She was so hot. Her head was spinning. She had to get out of her insosuit or she would die.

* * *

He saw her. He pulled back out of sight and spied on her from the far end of the corridor.

She was outside her cabin door, fumbling at the lock. She seemed in a hurry. She was struggling out of a white plastic coverall. She disappeared inside.

He waited.

She reappeared. She turned down the corridor and walked away from him, head bowed. She was fixing a necklace round her neck. Held awkwardly in her hand was his envelope, unopened.

The necklace fastened, she shoved the letter into the pocket of her shorts.

She hadn't read it.

He started after her. He had to explain.

19 A Spanner in the Works

She crept up the stairwell and poked her head out of the doors. No sign of Cyberman. No sign of anyone. The deck was deserted. And it was freezing cold. Damn! She was a good hundred metres from the bridge and she was no longer dressed for sub-zero temperatures.

She was at the shallow end of the pool. The bridge was beyond the deep end, past the helipad where Straker's helicopter was anchored to the deck. The diving board cast a long path of shadow across the pool towards her. It was eleven o'clock at night and the sun was still hovering reluctantly near the horizon, refusing to go down. It shone a brilliant ochre yellow, but radiated little warmth.

She retreated down the steps and peered along the corridor. She could make her way to the stairwell in the middle of the ship. But she didn't know who, or what, she might bump into. She turned to the stairs again.

She jumped with shock. Something moved in the recess under the stairs. Light shafted across it between the open metal steps, revealing a humanoid shape. It advanced towards her into the light.

Mike Brack.

He had a funny look on his face. A pleading look. He was holding out his hand to her, palm outwards, like a traffic policeman.

She ran past him to the foot of the stairs and started racing up them. Something caught at her leg. He was gripping her ankle through the stair rail.

'Ruby, don't go out there. We've got to talk.'

She wrenched her foot free and bounded two at a time up the steps. Bursting through the deck doors, she ran flat out along the side of the pool. The freezing air tore at her lungs.

She paused as she got to the stairway leading up to the bridge and turned to see if Brack was following her.

He was halfway across the deck, under the shadow of the diving board, but he was no longer coming after her. He was welded to the spot, staring beyond the prow of the ship.

There, less than fifty metres from the ship, an iceberg loomed. It towered above the level of the deck. It sparkled yellow and orange in the sun. On it was carved the profile of a human head. Heavy brow, large nose, a jutting chin, cylindrical stub of ice projecting from the mouth. Brack's sculpture of Lord Straker.

And it was directly in the *Elysium*'s path.

'Jones, restrain that man and have him clapped in irons.'

Captain Trench was shaking. The vibrations from the propellers, since he had thrown them into reverse, were juddering through the entire structure of the bridge. But he was also shaking with anger. The *Elysium* was within an inch of disaster and all this little imbecile could do was blather on about Cybernauts or some such thing.

The first officer spoke into the intercom, requesting two armed security guards to come to the bridge immediately.

'They control this iceberg, I'm convinced of it,' the imbecile was saying. 'Look, they've already forced you to bring the ship to a halt. They will attack us and capture every person on board. We must be ready for them. Have you any gold?'

The captain knew the Doctor was a psychiatric case. He had contacted STS a second time, an hour ago. The *Elysium*'s compass read-outs were impossibly weak. STS had confirmed what he expected. Earth's magnetic field was close to reversal. The unthinkable was about to happen.

The woman in charge was amazingly calm about it. She assured him that the FLIPback device would work.

She had answered his other question, too. The one about this Doctor. He was almost ashamed to ask it. Mercifully, she had answered without a snigger. No, she said, they had received no visitations. No, there had been no sightings of a green pagoda.

Of course there hadn't.

The captain looked out at the iceberg. Someone was running

194

across the deck towards the bridge. A passenger in skimpy fancy dress. Up from the ball, no doubt. She'd catch her death.

Then he recognized her. Ruby Duvall. The undercover journalist.

There was another figure on the deck. It looked like Brack. He was just standing, staring at the iceberg. Now he too was running this way.

Beyond him, the deck doors opened and the two security guards appeared, responding to the request put out by Jones. They carried automatic rifles.

The captain's attention returned to the matter in hand. The *Elysium* was almost at a standstill. The iceberg was drifting to port. It looked as though they might just miss it.

Ms Duvall came onto the bridge. To denounce this charlatan, he hoped. The imbecile seemed glad to see her.

'Ruby, you tell them. I'm having difficulty getting through.'

The first officer sought to put her mind at rest.

'It's all right, Ms Duvall. We know he's a raving lunatic. The guards will be here any moment to take him away.'

'No!' yelled the girl. 'You must believe him. The Cybermen are about to attack the ship.'

Not her as well. The captain cursed under his breath.

The iceberg was swinging alongside them now. He prayed the *Elysium* was far enough away to avoid its submerged bulk.

There was a muffled boom, like thunder.

From the iceberg, from Straker's carved-out eye, clouds of steam were rising. A hole had been blasted out. Something was emerging from it, glittering in the sun. A long metal platform. A gangplank. It extended out from the iceberg's eye and reached for the deck of the *Elysium*.

The guards had skidded to a halt beside the pool. They stared in stunned belief as a tall silver-suited figure appeared at the hole in the ice and walked along the ramp towards them. Two others emerged, and then a fourth and fifth.

'You see?' yelled Ruby.

'I don't believe it!' said the first officer.

'What in the devil's name are they?' demanded the captain.

'I told you,' replied the Doctor. 'Cybermen.'

The security guards had raised their rifles. They were aiming at the nearest silver creature. It was halfway across the ramp. There was the sharp crack of automatic fire, the clang of metal on metal. High-velocity bullets were making contact with their target. Friction sparks flashed on its head and chest.

The creature faltered as it took the full force of the unexpected attack. For an instant it stood immobile. Then once more it started forward.

The guards let go another salvo. This time the creature did not waver in its steady course towards them. It was as if it merely pressed against a heavy wind. It had the measure of the violent storm of bullets.

As it approached the two men, it raised a hand to the panel on its chest. A dense white vapour streamed out, enveloping them. Their arms fell limply to their sides. Their rifles clattered on the deck. They stood inert, facing their attacker with seeming equanimity.

The Cyberman moved past them, striding purposefully towards the bridge. Two others had reached the deck. The remaining two were making steady progress along the ramp.

Up on the bridge, nobody moved. All were mesmerized like rabbits, fixed in horror at the approaching Cybermen. It was as if the paralysing gas had enveloped them too and taken away their will to act.

The door of the bridge was flung open.

'Captain Trench, what in hell's wrong with my ship?'

The captain faced an irate and breathless Lord Straker.

'What's with all this shuddering and shaking? It's ruining my ball, I hope you realize.'

The captain did not have the words to explain. But the spell had been broken. He stopped both engines. The vibration subsided. He lifted his finger and pointed out towards the deck at the marching Cybermen.

'What, more fancy dress?' asked Straker, seemingly perplexed. He was always good at acting the innocent, thought Ruby.

Outside there was a sudden flash, then a loud explosion.

One of the creatures was on its back, writhing, its chest a smoking tangle of molten metal.

An intense ray of orange light beamed out. It came from above the bridge. There was a second explosion.

One of the Cybermen had been just about to step off the ramp onto the deck. Now it was flying through the air. It slapped into the iceberg, spread-eagled by the force of impact. It remained stuck fast, fixed motionless in the ice.

'The laser,' said the captain, finding his voice again. 'Somebody's using the laser against them. Jones, get them on the monitor. Find out what's happening!'

The first officer flicked a switch. On the monitor an image formed of the crowded ballroom. There was a small figure on the stage, Diana Milton, arms spread wide, at full belt. He pressed a button several times in quick succession. Images of various corridors and decks flashed by. The final image was of the roof of the bridge. The laser gun. At its controls, a man.

'Mike Brack! Doctor, he's attacking them,' exclaimed Ruby, now totally confused.

'Courageous bloke,' said Straker. 'Doesn't give a flying toss for anyone.'

'Maybe he's regretting what he's done,' said the Doctor, 'now that he faces the reality. It's a courage of a kind, I suppose. But he's going to need plenty more of it when the Cybermen finally get to him.'

The laser ray flashed out a third time. It narrowly missed a Cyberman on the deck but made explosive contact with the iceberg. A huge gobbet of ice was flung skywards amid an eruption of steam.

'What the heck are these Cybermen?' demanded Lord Straker.

'You really need us to tell you?' said Ruby insolently, but her boss wasn't in the mood to listen.

'And what in buggeration do they think they're up to?'

'Look and learn,' said the Doctor quietly.

One of the three remaining Cybermen had unhooked something from a belt at its waist. In its open hand the object was not unlike a small shiny egg. The Cyberman drew back its arm and lobbed it like a grenade up in the direction of the laser gun. On the monitor, they saw it strike the laser cockpit and come to rest nearby. It started to smoke. Brack cast an

197

apprehensive glance towards it, shielding his face as if expecting it to explode. Instead, it produced more smoke, white and dense.

'A gas grenade?' suggested Jones.

'Obviously hypnotic,' murmured the Doctor, 'to judge by its effect on those two guards down there.'

Ruby tore her eyes away from the monitor and looked back down at the deck. The guards were still there, standing slackly, oblivious to the commotion around them.

'That's what they must have used on me, that first time,' she told the Doctor. 'It saps your will. You can't do anything but what they tell you.'

He nodded gravely. His eyes were on the monitor.

Brack was trying to get away from the smoke that was drifting towards him. He was at the edge of the roof, hanging on to the barrel of the laser.

Suddenly he was gone. Ruby's heart flipped over. He'd lost his grip and disappeared. A shape dropped past the window. She buried her face in her hands.

'Well, I'll be – it's caught him!' she heard.

She opened her eyes. The captain had his face pressed to the window and was peering down. 'That – creature – caught Brack. It saved him!'

'Human life is a valuable resource,' said the Doctor grimly.

'But to catch a man as effortlessly as that,' protested Jones, as he too looked on, 'it would take superhuman strength.'

'Precisely,' said the Doctor.

Ruby rushed to the window. She saw Brack's crumpled figure stretched across the Cyberman's arms. His leg was twisted under him. The Cyberman had turned and was carrying him back to the iceberg. She felt a misplaced pity at the mutilations his body would undergo. Misplaced because he had brought this on himself. Misplaced because they were all in line for the same treatment. Each of them, including her. But you couldn't control what you felt deep down.

Heavy footsteps sounded on the roof above them.

'Who the devil's up there now?' the captain muttered.

Diana was enjoying herself. Apart from the juddering, things were going well. They'd even worked the vibrations into the sketch.

Everybody remembered the awful first few days of the cruise when the new propellers from the Dutch firm Lip had been playing up. It was the work of the Wicked Witch, they pretended. And now she was back.

Leslie said something about paying Lip service to the Witch. The band launched into a Beach Boys standard, *Good Vibrations*.

'Read my Lips . . .'

'That's enough Lip from you . . .'

The tired old jokes were wheeled out again and were welcomed by the audience like long-lost friends.

'What's Dutch for making love?' Diana shouted out. She cupped a hand to her ear. In unison, the audience shouted the punchline back at her.

'Stiff up 'er Lips.'

Everyone roared with laughter. They revelled in their rudeness. They were out to enjoy themselves.

He was outraged – there was no other word for it – outraged that these silver monstrosities were trying to wreck his cruise.

He yanked at the joystick. He had no idea of how to operate it. But he was jiggered if that was going to stop him getting even. He jammed his thumb on the button marked 'fire'.

The laser blasted out. It clipped the shoulder of the Cyberman holding Brack and swung it violently round.

Got the bugger!

Brack was thrown free.

Lord Straker fired again. A second ray of light went wide of the mark and zapped the pool. Steam and water geysered up and showered the deck, instantly turning to sheets of ice. The Cyberman, minus a shoulder and arm, was striding towards Brack, as though, despite its injuries, it had to recapture its quarry.

A thick green liquid oozed from the shoulder socket.

Lord Straker took more careful aim.

The third blast hit the Cyberman squarely on the head,

flipping it over on to the icy deck. It skidded into the pool, and settled languidly on the bottom, glinting like sunken treasure.

Two to go. They had taken cover beyond his helicopter. He could see that one was about to throw a grenade. He pressed the fire button twice. Two more rays of light shot out wildly in quick succession. They missed the Cybermen completely and blasted into the helicopter, wrenching it free of its anchor and swinging it round on the sheets of ice.

The Cyberman lobbed the grenade. He saw it curve towards him. He fired again. There was a vast explosion of yellow flame as the fuel tank went up. He could feel the searing heat even inside the cockpit. A sheet of burning petrol spread across the deck. The Cybermen were drenched with it and blazing fiercely. They were turning, turning, walking around in circles, circling each other, ablaze.

The helicopter had pushed through the railing and teetered at the edge of the deck. Twisting in slow motion over the side, the tail swung round, smashing into the burning Cybermen, taking them with it, tumbling into the sea.

Good riddance. Pity about the helicopter. But heck, he was getting the hang of this laser.

He aimed at the hole in the iceberg. He'd pull the plug on them for sure.

He fired again and again at the caricatured face in the ice. His face. He kept missing his target. But where the rays of orange light made contact, plumes of steam rose up into the air, chunks of ice were scattered wide, water thudded down. His face was becoming a wreck.

Cr-rash! The cigar went flying.

Boom! That was one in the eye for him.

Zzshupp! There went his nose. Never liked it anyway.

His eyes were running, his own eyes, from the white smoke around him. There was an acrid smell in his nostrils, a sharp smell, like ammonia.

His hands dropped from the joystick.

He sat and watched the iceberg.

He was in a kind of daze.

There was a creaking, grinding sound. The top of the iceberg, the top of his sculpted head, was sliding away. The iceberg was falling apart. The top of his head fell off and crashed into the sea.

Inside, where his brain should be, was a hollow space. There were flickering lights and complex machines. And more Cybermen.

They were walking out of his eye and down the ramp and on to the deck of the *Elysium*.

They were coming to get him.

At first, there had been cheers in the bridge as Straker had wreaked destruction on the Cybermen. Now there was silence.

There must be at least a dozen of the creatures. Ruby tried to count them as they fanned out across the deck. A couple were making for the doors at the far end of the deck. Another three or four were disappearing down into the middle of the ship, no doubt with the ballroom in mind. More were coming up the steps to the bridge. She could hear the rhythmic clank.

She was petrified. But she wasn't the only one. The captain and the first officer were catatonic. The first officer was repeating over and over in a toneless voice, 'I don't believe it. I don't believe it.'

Her hand was at her throat, fiddling nervously with her pendant. Didn't the Doctor say they couldn't stand gold? Maybe the gold in her necklace would save them.

A Cyberman loomed into sight beyond the door.

Where was the Doctor? She needed to know what to do with the necklace of gold.

A silver fist smashed through the glass.

Perhaps it would work like a charm, an amulet.

The Cyberman pressed a button on its chest panel. White gas streamed from a nozzle at the top of the panel. It billowed into the bridge.

'I don't believe it. I don't believe it,' the officer intoned.

This is it, she thought.

She felt a tugging at the back of her head. She was being pulled down into the darkness.

'. . . the wonderful Wizard of Oz!'

Diana's hands were raised in a big finish to the song. Leslie was trying to do the same but his costume hampered him. The audience applauded, long and loud.

The lights flickered and dimmed.

'The witch must be on her way,' Diana extemporized.

The audience laughed. They were eating out of her hand.

She peered into the darkness at the ballroom. She pretended to see the witch in the distance and screamed.

To her surprise, there were responding screams towards the rear of the ballroom. Then gales of laughter. Something funny, and unscripted, was obviously going on at the back. It wasn't Lord Stanley's surprise by any chance, was it?

The follow spot moved away from Diana to illuminate the disturbance. She was left in comparative gloom. She was starting to feel somewhat peeved.

There were gasps and screams, laughter and titters. People were craning their necks to see what was happening.

Diana could see very well. The follow spot was doing a wonderful job. It was lighting a man in a silver suit. Michael Brack, no doubt, after the heavy hints dropped by Lord High and Mighty Straker. And if Michael was another Tin Man, he'd made a mess of the costume. It was nothing like.

A silver hand gripped her shoulder. It was Leslie. He pressed his slit of a mouth to her ear.

'Diana, this is spooky. That's what I saw in the ice. I'm sure of it.'

'Oh, no it's not, Leslie. I know what it is. Or rather who it is. And I'm going to have some fun and games.'

With calm deliberation, she descended the stairs at the front of the stage. Her smile was acid.

'You didn't tell me your big brother was coming to the party, Tin Man.'

She was speaking loudly, for the benefit of the audience.

They hooted.

Diana walked between the crowded tables directly towards the giant silver figure. Must have lifts in his boots. He should use them more often. He could do with a bit more length.

'The arrival of the Tin Twin,' she cooed. 'This is a big event. We'll have to celebrate.'

She grabbed an open bottle of champagne from a nearby

table. The occupants looked on, surprised but game. The audience laughed and cheered.

She sidled up to him. She tried to make out a face through the holes of the eyes. She caught a hint of red. He must be wearing a pair of crimson tights on his head. Now that would suit him.

'My, now that I'm this close, I can see just how big and bad you really are. You could get a poor little girl like me into an awful lot of trouble. I think we ought to make you rusty again. Don't you?'

She reached up as high as she could and emptied the bottle over his head. The golden liquid bubbled and foamed over his silver front. It ran down his leg and onto the floor.

Laughter. Applause. Hoots of derision.

The Tin Monster looked confused and somewhat hurt. Well, he should have known better. He messed with Diana Milton at his peril. He ought to have remembered that.

He was lifting his hand to his heart. Or where his heart would be if he had one. Heartless, that was Mike Brack. He and Tin Man had much in common.

He was pressing a button on the peculiar panel at his chest. Smoke was coming out. Right into her face. The little sod.

Her hand fell to her side.

The champagne bottle smashed on the floor.

There were screams of hysteria. People were scrambling up from the tables in panic.

She was seeing double, treble. There were Tin Men everywhere. A white mist was settling.

People were quieter now.

They were silent.

Standing.

Waiting.

Ruby was desperately trying to find a foothold. It was pitch black. She was struggling to maintain her grip on the iron rung.

Someone had yanked her back by the hair, it must have been the Doctor, and thrust her into the inspection hatch. She had only just managed to glimpse the iron rung and grab on to it before the hatch had slammed to.

He had saved her.

She could hear the door of the bridge being smashed off its hinges. She had to get down the shaft and away. She found a rung with her foot and started to descend, carefully at first, and then more rapidly.

There was a strange sensation at her neck. The necklace was coming loose. It was slipping away. She tried to catch it with her free hand but too late. She felt it go.

Now she was powerless against the Cybermen.

She continued her descent rung by rung. At any moment a Cyberman might open the hatch above her and spot her. She was encumbered by the camera round her neck. The Nanocom was no trouble clipped inside her skirt, but the Holocam hit the rungs and got in the way.

She was aware of an opening to her right, a horizontal shaft. She decided to explore.

She felt her way forward in the blackness until she came to a dead end. Her hand came into contact with a handle. She pressed down on it and pulled. An iron panel swung open.

Directly ahead, near the floor, was a red glow, and beyond, a low wide opening. She ducked out through it.

She stepped into a book-lined room. Before her was a long mahogany table. Behind her was a mantlepiece with a heavy sword above it. She was in the library. She laid her camera down on the table.

It was just as she'd always fantasized. There was a secret passage from the library, leading away into the darkness. And she had just emerged from it.

For a split second she thought she had seen a Cyberman in the corner. Her heart missed a beat.

It was the suit of armour.

She went to the open door. Her heart flipped over. There was a Cyberman patrolling the corridor. It was coming her way. She was rooted to the spot.

'Stay where you are. Do not resist.'

She backed into the library. She couldn't get back through the fireplace in time. It would follow her into the secret passageway and, knowing the Cybermen, they could probably see in the dark. She ducked down behind the armour as the Cyberman strode in and crawled on her belly behind a high free-standing shelf.

She peered at it between the dusty volumes. It approached the suit of armour.

Dust was in her nose. She was going to sneeze.

It raised an arm above its head and slammed it down.

Crash! The armour shattered into metal shards.

Atchoo!

The Cyberman spun on its heel and saw her.

She put her hands against the heavy wooden shelving and breathed out. The structure was moving, crashing down on the Cyberman. She turned and sprinted out of the door and down the corridor. She had no idea where she could go, where she might hide. She looked back. The Cyberman was following her.

At the amusement area she paused to think. She had a crazy idea. She felt in her pocket and was relieved to find a one-ecu piece. She went to the Vreal machine and dropped the money in. She grabbed the visor. She selected 'Lucid Dreaming' on the menu.

The Cyberman came into view. She dropped behind the machine. She knew it was coming her way. She could feel the heavy thud of its feet reverberating through the floor.

It stopped. She had a peek. It was turned away from her. This was her chance.

She leapt up and jammed the visor over its head. The Cyberman's hands went up to remove the obstruction but froze midway. Slowly its arms drifted forward and out. Its body swayed as if in flight. Her crazy idea had worked. The creature was soaring above a gorgeous landscape, caught in cyberspace. That should keep it out of mischief for a bit.

She knew now where she had to go. She dashed off in the direction of the nearest lift. The Cybermen would not know the security code. The lower level would be the safest place. Unless there were Cybermen in those wooden crates.

A Cyberman was striding past the lift. She hid for a moment, then tiptoed over and pressed the call button. The lift hummed to life. Her eyes were glued to the Cyberman. It was walking down the corridor away from her. She held her breath. The lift doors opened. The Cyberman turned the corner and disappeared.

But from behind she heard a buzzing uninflected voice.

'Stay where you are. Do not resist.'

She leapt into the lift and pressed the button to close the doors. It took an age to operate. As they slid shut she caught a glimpse of silver. She jabbed in the security code. There was a heavy banging on the outer doors, but the lift descended. Just as it reached the lower level, she heard a wrenching of metal. The doors above were being prised apart.

There was an almighty thud on the roof of the lift.

The Cyberman had jumped. God, it was scary! A silver foot punched through the flimsy metal. She yelled out in blinding fear.

She got out of the lift not a moment too soon. The roof was being ripped apart like cardboard. She heard the Cyberman thump down into the lift as she ran into the storeroom and slammed the door. It was pathetically flimsy. Wooden. No key in the lock.

Heavy footsteps were clanking down the corridor. Clack! Clack! Where could she hide?

A fist smashed through the door, splintered the lock. The door swung towards her on damaged hinges. Ruby was hidden by it. The Cyberman strode in, making straight for the wooden crates marked 'Panama'. Ruby edged round the door. The Cyberman pulled at one of the crates and brought it crashing down. The wooden planks burst apart. The objects within scudded across the floor.

Ruby took off. She felt a sharp jab of pain in her thigh as she scraped past the twisted metal of the damaged door-frame, but the sensation was momentary and, undeterred, she pelted down the corridor.

She had seen what the boxes contained. It didn't make sense.

She ran to the unused engine room, unlocking the door and bolting it back in its open position. A desperate idea was forming. Across the floor of the engine room, beyond the massive piston arms, was the control console. Ruby squeezed past the stationery shafts and cogs of the engine well and grasped a green-knobbed lever among the controls. She held it tight. She was shaking. Her knees were trembling, weak.

The silver figure was framed in the doorway. The blank face scanned the room. A flash of red from the eye holes. Its quarry was located. The Cyberman moved towards her, between the edge of the giant engine and the rusty iron wall. It was closing in.

She carefully judged the moment, then eased the lever downwards till it clicked. There was a hiss. The piston arm moved downwards and towards the Cyberman. Right on target. Her metal adversary would be pressed against the engine room wall, as the TARDIS had been. Even if it wasn't smashed to pulp, it would be trapped or badly damaged.

But the Cyberman had turned. Its arms were extended towards the falling piston. Its hands made contact with the knuckle of steel. Pressed flat to the wall it was straining against the weight, trying to hold back the tremendous bulk of the piston, which had taken the strength of ten men to lift.

To her horror she saw that it was succeeding. The piston had slowed in the Cyberman's hands. It was centimetres away from its head but the creature was supporting the weight. Not only that, but, if her eyes were to be believed, the piston was now moving up and away. The Cyberman was pushing it back.

She daren't hang around to see what would happen next. She rushed for the door, a heavy iron slab ten centimetres thick. She could lock the Cyberman inside. As she unbolted it from its open, secured position, she heard a hiss of hydraulics. The Cyberman had let go the piston and was on the march again.

The iron door swung to with a leaden clang which reverberated along the gloomy corridors. She twisted the key in the lock. There were heavy bolts at top and bottom. She slammed them home. She felt safer, but her heart was fluttering. A sparrow in a chimney. She was feeling faint. She leaned against the wall to draw some breath and slithered down it. She sat on the floor, her back supported by the wall. The rivets pressed into her flesh through the thin cotton shirt.

Ponderous footsteps approached the door. There was a resounding thud against it. If this thick slab of metal could not stop the Cyberman, what more could she do? Where could she hide? If only she had the necklace of gold, it would give her some hope, some reason to think she might get out of this nightmare alive.

Her left thigh was itching. She rubbed it. Her hand came into contact with something sticky. In the dim light it looked black on her fingers. Oil or grease. The leg of the shorts was ripped apart and hanging loose. It was soaked and blackened.

She heard the metal feet clanking in retreat on the other side, then coming at the door again. There was a louder thud. The door bulged in its iron frame.

It was blood, of course. Her thigh was throbbing now and hurting deep inside. Blood was oozing from a tear in her flesh. Her leg was wet. She, after all, was only flesh and blood. The creature had metal limbs and an armoured body. It was programmed to get her. That was its goal. And only a door between them.

The metal feet clanked away again.

She felt so weak, so tired. She should be on her feet and running away. Away from this malevolent man-machine, this cyborg bent on her destruction. No, not destruction. Something worse. Conversion.

It would be so very easy just to stay there. Let the creature come to her. Pick her up in its arms like an old rag doll. Take her away to oblivion.

Without warning, a series of quickening vibrations shuddered through the ship. From along the corridor she heard a familiar churning pulse. The engines had throbbed to life. It roused her from her torpor. She must get away.

The other engine rooms. There must be inspection hatches leading from them. Perhaps she could escape that way, if she could only get to one in time. She struggled to her feet and stumbled down the corridor, as the metal feet of the Cyberman charged towards the door. There was a shriek of rending metal and a deafening bang as the iron door was torn from its hinges and slammed to the floor.

She limped into engine room two. The Cyberman had seen her. It was charging down the corridor after her. It was moving fast. It had scented the kill.

The huge engine was in gleaming, confusing motion. The four giant pistons hissed in and out of massive greased sockets.

Elbows and knuckles of steel were rhythmically squeezing together and rushing apart. At the far side was the inspection hatch.

She took the direct route, straight through the heart of pounding engine, a dangerous course to take but quick. It would give her breathing space. Compared with the Cyberman she was small and agile. It would be forced to go the long way round. She ducked and weaved between the great moving parts.

She was through.

She glanced behind and was horrified. It was taking her path. It was weaving and ducking as she had done. She dived for the hatch and pushed down on the handle. It was stiff. She'd lost her strength. She tried again. It wouldn't budge.

She tried not to panic. She took a deep breath, scrutinized the handle mechanism. Above the handle hung a heavy spanner. Of course! The spindle of the handle was secured by a nut. The spanner loosened it. She unhooked the spanner and fitted it over the nut. She started to turn. Almost there. Got it!

She turned to see the Cyberman. It had adjusted itself to the rhythmic heave and shove of the engine's heavy limbs, become one with the larger machine. It was almost upon her.

But Ruby was defiant now. If she could not escape, she would go down fighting. The Cyberman was not emotionless. Its emotions were hidden, that was all. She knew it was secretly gloating at her. Exultant in its prowess. Daring her to oppose its monstrous strength. Across its face was a nasty tight-lipped grin.

In a final senseless act of insolent rebellion, she flung the spanner at that vindictive, expressionless, monkeybug head. The Cyberman raised an arm and caught the spanner in its fist. It tossed its head in pride. It was certain of its supremacy and boastful of it.

There was a clank. A knuckle of steel had glanced across the Cyberman's head. Knocked it off balance for an instant. The Cyberman's arm went forward. It was caught between the pincer movement of a giant hinge. With a crunch the arm fell off, and thumped to the floor.

Now out of synch with the machine that moved around it,

the Cyberman dodged away from a falling piston only to be pummelled by another. It was bounced into the path of a bulky elbow which smashed across its chest and through it. From the slit of its mouth a thick white liquid spewed out.

Suddenly, bits of Cyberman were everywhere. Green viscous liquid coated the moving steel. Ruby thought she caught a glimpse of yellow flesh amongst the carnage.

The massive engine did not falter. It felt no compunction at dismembering a Cyberman. It owed no allegiance to the Cyber race. It had one job to do. To power the ship. To drive it forward. That was its goal. Implacable. If anything got in its way, man or machine, it was a struggle for supremacy. Might was right, as the Cyberman knew well. The strongest always won.

This time the Cyberman had met its match. Torn limb from limb. Discarded. No longer whole. Not even the sum of its parts. Redundant. Decommissioned.

Ruby breathed again. But she was far from triumphant. She was too shocked by the sudden violence of machine against machine.

She was exhausted. She sank to her knees.

Beside her lay the severed arm of the Cyberman, the spanner clutched tight in its three-fingered hand.

The sobs welled up from deep within her. Sobs of relief. Sobs, unfathomably, of regret. All the regrets of her life, long buried memories, bubbling to the surface. She shook from the guts with forgotten sadnesses. The hopes that had turned to dust. The disappointments. Her mother's death. The loss of her father's love. The hate inside her. All of it hurt. Like the deep throbbing hurt in her thigh. She sobbed it all up, all the pain and fears she had suppressed in the whole of her life. She gave herself up to it.

At last the sobs subsided. She wiped the tears from her face with the back of a blood-stained greasy hand. As she did so, something moved inside her shirt. Something small and cold. With sudden repulsion, not daring to think what it could be, she pulled open the knot which held the shirt together at the front. Something glinted and fell limply to the floor.

The ruby necklace.

She started to giggle. Then laughed out loud. Her neck-lace. Now. When it was too late to be of any use.

She picked it up and stuffed it into the pocket of her shorts, along with the envelope, the one she had picked up from the floor of her cabin. Ruby had forgotten all about it. She imagined it was Diana's promised card. She would open it. It was still her birthday, though it might not seem much like it.

It was a note from Mike Brack, of all people. He was apologizing for his recent behaviour.

> *. . . For 20 years I've lived with a terrible secret. There's something I must explain. Let's talk. As soon as we can. Today. Before the ball . . .*

Twenty years a Cyber agent. He would have joined them at the time of their second invasion. How could he? And why did he turn against them in the end? After twenty years of service? It didn't make sense.

Nor did the contents of those wooden boxes.

It was not hand-guns or rifles or automatic weapons that had tumbled out when the Cyberman had smashed them open.

Nor was it dormant Cybermen.

What had scattered across the floor was, literally, arms. Waxy artificial arms in the colours of human flesh. Black, pink, yellow, brown and white. She recalled the cascade of biceps, forearms, outstretched hands.

Were these a consignment destined for the Cyberman? Was the connection with Panama just a blind? And why had Mike Brack so desperately wanted to talk to her?

Her back was resting against the hatch. Suddenly, she felt the handle move against her side. Something was trying to open it. She leapt away. They were coming through.

In desperation, she pulled the necklace from her pocket and held it out in front of her.

It was all she had left to do.

211

20 Lemon Drops

The Doctor pushed open the inspection hatch. The light of the engine room made him blink. Then he saw her. He shouted above the hiss and clank of the engine.

'Ruby! Thank goodness!'

She was holding a piece of jewellery out at him, a ruby pendant. Her shirt was hanging open. Her eyes were wild.

'Doctor.'

Her arms were about his neck. She was sobbing.

Naked human emotion. Sometimes it quite took him by surprise. Its forcefulness. The deep mysterious well from which it sprang. No wonder the Cybermen found it disruptive, had sought to eradicate it in themselves. Emotion was weakness. Powerful and unpredictable.

Softly, he patted the back of the weeping girl.

'There, there, Ruby. It's all right now.'

Simple words, but they came from the heart.

The girl clung on to him.

Heart, the Doctor pondered. The Cybermen had replaced theirs with a mechanical, more durable, more dependable substitute. But the heart was more than a pump. It connected with the body in more subtle ways. *Heart* had a deeper meaning.

He suspected that even the Mondans, before they began to augment themselves, would have known this double sense. If they had, they had certainly forgotten it now, as Cybermen.

The Doctor was curious about Cyber psychology. He wondered if somewhere in the tangled recesses beneath the neural interface of their augmented brains there did not lurk the vestige of their former selves. An echo of a memory. A tantalizing sense of something lost, just beyond the realm of consciousness, existing but nameless, like a word on the tip of the tongue, like a dream that is never quite recalled.

Ruby still clung. She was quiet now. He rocked her gently. 'Mustn't lose heart,' he said.

She looked up at him and gave him a bleary-eyed smile.

There had been so many times when everything had seemed to be lost. When those who were his companions were close to despair. When those who had depended upon his greater knowledge, had felt their trust in him betrayed.

There were times when he had betrayed them.

As he had grown older, he had become more devious, seeking the larger goal, the greater good. And sometimes he had not even that excuse. As one grew older, it was harder to act from the heart alone. Harder to attain emptiness, to hold firmly to stillness.

Going home is known as stillness.

Had he said that once? Or was it some other, close to him?

How to regain what was lost. Perhaps it was impossible. One cannot step in the same stream twice. Perhaps, after all, the Cybermen were right to make going forward their only choice. Logic demands we look to the future. The past is unredeemable.

Ruby's nose was running. She sniffed.

He pulled out his silk handkerchief. Dust speckled the air around them. There was a musty smell. It reminded him where his journey had begun, at the heart of the TARDIS.

She blew her nose loudly. The engine slowed to a stop behind them.

Ruby looked startled. They glanced at each other and laughed.

'Was that me?' she asked.

'More likely to have been the Cybermen.'

Their voices sounded thin in the sudden silence.

'What's been happening up there?'

'They're searching the ship for remaining processible units. To you and me that means – well, you and me, I'm afraid. They've got everybody else under their control.'

'Why did the engines start up again?'

'Oh, that was me. Before I pushed you through the hatch, I made a mask of this thing.' The Doctor was untying his cravat, which was back to front and hanging like a bandit's bandana below his chin. 'It helped filter out the gas. The rest was down

213

to careful breathing. They didn't seem to notice. Not prioritized for it, I imagine. As soon as I could, I slipped back and got the ship moving full steam ahead. Then I climbed down the inspection shaft. They must just have worked out how to stop the engines. Still, they'll have to dock again. It'll give us some time to think.'

'I'm glad to see you,' said Ruby suddenly.

The Doctor grinned and put his hand to her face. His thumb brushed the old scar on her cheek.

'And me, you,' he said.

He felt in his jacket pocket.

'Like a lemon drop?'

Her camera was still there, on the mahogany table. She picked it up and lifted the strap over her head.

'This is where he was reading a book about cybernetics.'

The Doctor emerged through the fireplace, holding his hat in place.

'I find his behaviour somewhat bizarre,' he said, looking around with surprise at the unexpected surroundings. He noticed the shattered pieces of metal in the corner and cast a puzzled glance at her.

'It was a suit of armour. A Cyberman thought I'd got inside.'

He nodded and continued his train of thought.

'That note of Brack's. You've seem to have got inside his armour. His emotional armour, I mean.'

Ruby said nothing. She felt vaguely embarrassed.

She looked down. She was a mess. Her funky costume for the ball was torn and stained with patches of grease and blood. The Doctor had bound the gash in her thigh with his scarf. Petals of drying blood augmented the paisley, creating a rich heraldic pattern. He was her knight in off-white. She wore it as his favour. He had worn her colours too. The coat she had lent him in the ice tunnels. She had saved his life. He had saved hers. And battle was enjoined upon the Cyberman.

The remains of the lemon drop melted on her tongue. Troubles were meant to melt like that, weren't they? Somewhere over the rainbow? She wondered if theirs were about to melt. She couldn't see it somehow.

Still, the Doctor had shown her how to use the gold from

the necklace. They had that as a weapon. They had prised it apart, link by delicate link, and then took half each. She checked that the fragments of gold were still in her pocket.

It would take only one link slipped into the vent of a Cyberman to cause them trouble. But first you had to find your Cyberman. And then get close enough to pop in the poison.

The Doctor was almost out of the door.

'If we could find a back way up to the ballroom – Ruby, what are you doing?'

She was heaving the broadsword off its wall-supports.

'Well, we've got the gold. I thought this might come in handy, too. Something to beat them about the head with.'

'Oh, I see,' said the Doctor. 'A kind of carat and stick approach.'

She was plucky. And strong. In body and will.

The sword must have weighed a ton, but she'd refused his offers of help. Now she was limping ahead of him, up the spiral staircase from the kitchens, with it balanced over her shoulder.

There was a defiance in her that was remarkable. He called to mind other companions from Earth whom it had been his privilege to know: Zoe, Sarah Jane, Polly, Victoria. Kadiatu.

He was suddenly curious.

'How old are you, Ruby?' he whispered.

She stopped and turned to him. She let out a long slow breath.

'Twenty-two. Today.'

'Oh, many happy returns. Though in the circumstances – '

'Yes. I don't want another like this one, thanks.'

'Parents?'

She eased the sword down from her shoulder and held it out in front of her, squinting along its length.

'My mother's dead. The plague.'

'The plague?'

'That's what the tabloids call it. All the different diseases that are killing people nowadays. Some say its linked to pollution. The hole in the ozone layer.

'What do you think?'

215

Ruby didn't know she thought anything. Especially at that moment. But the words came out despite herself.

'There are too many people. The Gaia effect. You know? The planet's self-regulating process. Ensure that life continues, whatever the cost to humans. That's a cybernetic process, isn't it? Being cruel to be kind?'

A cynical edge had crept into her voice. She reminded herself of Mike Brack.

'Well, certainly the Cybermen had a similar problem, thousands of years ago. You can see how they survived.'

'I'd rather the plague,' she answered flatly. 'It's poetic justice in a way, isn't it?'

'What is?'

'Oh, I don't know. Live by the sword, die by the sword. The destroyers destroyed. You get back what you give. Is that cybernetics, too?'

'Sounds more like ancient wisdom.'

'The Tao?'

'Something like that.'

There was a silence. He was looking deep into her eyes. He saw the sadness and pain within her. The isolation.

Was it right to tell her the future. What little he knew of it? He chanced it.

'Things will get better, you know,' he said.

A still small voice.

Ruby wanted to ask the question again. Who was he really?

'What about your father?' the Doctor asked. 'Is he still alive?'

'My father?' Ruby snorted. 'Well, yes. He's alive. In a way. A brilliant cripple. All head, no heart. The bastard!'

Her rage was palpable.

'You're angry with him, aren't you?'

'Yeah,' she nodded.

Her sword hand was shaking. She rested the sword on the step. She looked suddenly surprised.

'Yes, I am, aren't I? And I thought I felt nothing. When it came to him, I thought I was an iceberg. Then I guess most of it's under the surface. Don't you think? The bulk of what we feel.'

She frowned for a moment. She was going over some detail

in her head. There was a faraway look in her eyes. When she spoke, it was not exactly to him.

'I sort of blamed him for mum's death. You know? I've been remembering stuff while I've been on this trip. Stuff about him when I was little. He had a hard time, I suppose.' She leant on the pommel of the sword. 'But, yeah, I am angry with him. So I do feel something for him, after all. I'm not an iceberg.'

'Melting ice, perhaps.'

She met his gaze. Her insolent look had come back. She couldn't believe she was having this conversation. A guy who says he travels through time, on the back stairs of some old liner, broadsword in hand, about to do battle with metal EBE's. It wasn't real.

'So, how old are you? His generation, I would guess.'

'Well, seventh generation to be precise. I'm not from your planet remember, but in Earth years I'd, erm, let's see – ' He did a quick calculation. 'Yes, that's right. I'd be approaching my second millennium.'

'A thousand? A thousand years old? Come off it.'

'Yes, it's hard for me to believe entirely. But it happens to be true.'

She snorted again and swung the sword up on her shoulder.

'Pull the other one, it's got bells on.'

He glanced down at her leg. At the wound which he had helped to bind to staunch the blood.

'It's got my scarf on, actually.'

He grinned at her. She was stony-faced.

She turned to climb up the spiral steps once more.

He thought she might be angry with him, but then she looked back and flashed him a toothy smile.

'You and Leslie ought to get together,' she said. 'He likes bad jokes, too.'

They walked onto the stage. Everything was eerily quiet. The heavy curtains were closed, blocking off the view of the auditorium, and muffling every sound. Even their footsteps.

The staircase had spiralled up from the kitchens to the backstage area of the ballroom. They had seen no sign of Cybermen, or passengers.

217

The Doctor was centre stage.

'Perhaps they're all on deck,' he suggested.

Suddenly, Ruby caught sight of Brack's machine. It was suspended two or three metres above the Doctor's head. They located, among the many other ropes secured in the wings, the one which held the machine aloft. As they lowered it to the stage, the metal framework began to swivel around its central oval core. Lights fixed on the framework flickered on and off.

'Would you say that's a Cyber communicator?' Ruby asked the Doctor. 'Look, it's even booby-trapped.'

Smoke was starting to billow from underneath the contraption.

'It looks somewhat primitive.'

'Probably had to knock it together himself. Look, I've got a sketch he drew.'

She pulled out the crumpled napkin and handed it to the Doctor. As he studied it, the smoke was drifting towards them.

'Doctor, hadn't we better move away before we get gassed?'

The Doctor seemed engrossed in the sketch.

'I can't be sure,' he mumbled, ambiguously. He was walking on to the stage towards the machine. White smoke curled about him.

'Doctor!'

He disappeared behind the machine.

At its heart, the egg-shaped object glowed with light. Above, amid the smoke, a giant ghostly face appeared, hovering disembodied in space. A huge voice boomed out hollowly, metallically. It sounded as if it came from beyond the curtains. The lips of the hovering face moved in unison with the voice.

'I am Wu Ming, the great and powerful Wizard of Oz. Do not be alarmed. I only seem to be what I am.'

Ruby was taken aback. It took her a moment to realize that the voice was the Doctor's. So was the face. Both were enlarged and distorted. By Brack's machine.

That was the surprise Straker had up his sleeve. Mike Brack had secretly cobbled together not a device to contact Cybermen, but a harmless contraption for creating a bit of stage magic.

The smoke had dispersed. The huge face had gone. The Doctor appeared from behind the machine. Compared with the illusion, he looked and sounded so small and insignificant.

'Speaker, yes.' He ticked off the items on the sketch as he inspected the machine. 'Refracting transmitter? Yes, that's this crystal ovoid. Cybernetic controller? That's right. The C & C system responds automatically to the performer's input. Simple but effective.'

'So that would explain the book on cybernetics?'

'It appears so. It would also appear that your mysterious Mr Brack had nothing to do with the Cybermen. The only thing I can't understand is your face at the centre of his sketch. Sure he didn't have a crush on you?'

'Doctor, please!' whined Ruby, flushing a little. 'Save me the amateur psychology.'

'Not so much of the amateur,' protested the Doctor. 'I studied under Adler.'

Ruby tried a bad joke of her own.

'Joe Adler? That zombie back at STS?'

'Alfred Adler, nuthead. Psychology of power. Helped me understand why the Cybermen – '

The Doctor's voice died in his throat. From beyond the curtain came the unmistakable twanging tones of a Cyberman.

'You will all follow. You will not resist.'

They peeped through the curtains. The sight was extraordinary. The ballroom was still crowded with the hundreds of passengers in their fancy-dress. Some near the back were filing out behind an intoning Cyberman.

'You will all follow. You will not resist.'

The rest were standing motionless, patiently waiting their turn to leave the ballroom.

'Get these curtains open,' whispered the Doctor furiously. 'I'm going to try to put a stop to this.'

She had no idea what he might be thinking of, but she rushed to the winch in the wings and started cranking. As the curtains parted, Brack's machine was already belching smoke. The Doctor was playing the wizard. His disembodied voice boomed around the auditorium.

'You will obey my voice. Stay where you are.'

He repeated the words again and again. The Cyber voice was submerged beneath the barrage. The departing passengers were faltering and turning to the stage.

Ruby was about to return to the Doctor when she froze. Three Cybermen were striding out of the back-stage darkness on to the stage. They had not spotted her. They were making for the Doctor.

One of them raised a gun. There was a flash. The central glowing oval shattered. The Doctor jumped back in shock.

The Cyberman spoke.

'You are known to us. We have encountered you before.'

The Doctor raised his hands above his head and turned slowly to face the intruders.

'You are recorded in our history computer as hostile to the Cyber race.'

'I bet I am,' muttered the Doctor.

'We have captured your travelling machine. It has extensive interior dimensions. We will utilize it for the transportation of our captives. You will co-operate.'

'I shouldn't be too sure,' said the Doctor.

The Cyberman continued regardless of the interruption.

'You will meet the Cyber Controller.'

'Oh, yes?' said the Doctor with some surprise. 'I thought he wasn't invented yet.'

The Cyberman seemed to pause for thought, as if confused by the Doctor's weird time-travelling syntax. Ruby wondered who or what this Cyber Controller was. As if on cue the Cyberman spoke again.

'The Cyber Controller is a new conversion,' buzzed the Cyberman. 'We will survive. We will proliferate and survive.'

As the synthetic voice droned on, Ruby crept up behind one of the other two Cybermen. She was concealed by the black drapes hanging in the wings. In her palm were the deadly links of gold.

She picked one up between finger and thumb and, hardly daring to breathe, snaked her hand round the Cyber chest. She dropped it neatly inside the metal mesh of its vent. She moved back and waited.

Nothing happened.

She thought she might have missed. She tried a second time. She heard the small tinkling noise of the link dropping down inside the workings of the panel.

The Cyberman looked up into the black space above the stage, as if something had fallen from there. Then it pressed a button on its panel. There was a small rush of air and the link was ejected onto the stage.

What a pain, she thought, beginning to panic. The Doctor was wrong. It doesn't affect them in the slightest. What to do now?

She remembered the sword she had dragged up from the library.

She crept into the shadows and picked it up, grasping the handle firmly with both hands. Its weight was reassuring. Its broad flat blade gleamed like a Cyberman.

The passengers were again obediently filing out of the ball-room into the mezzanine beyond. The Cyberman was leading the Doctor down the steps into the auditorium. The other two Cybermen took up the rear, striding one behind the other.

Ruby pushed her body into action. The sword moved with her. It swung in a pendulous arc. She unleashed a massive war cry.

'Paaah Dwaaaah!'

The sword hit the Cyberman squarely on the neck, between the shoulder and the handlebars. There was a sound of crunching. The impact jarred her hands and travelled up her arms. The sword bounced away, edged in green fluid. But it had done its work. The head split off and was dangling loose on a tangle of wires which erupted from the neck.

The Cyberman was a pathetic sight. It had caught its head in its hands. It rocked this way and that. It was attempting to replace the head on its ravaged shoulders. It was frothing at its vents.

A sudden hum and the chest panel exploded in flames.

The second Cyberman was coming at her. She swung again. But the Cyberman stepped neatly back. She missed. The heavy sword pulled her off balance. She fell. The sword jolted out of her hands. It scooted across the stage.

The Cyberman was over her. Its hands were under her armpits. The metal digits dug into tender flesh. She was hauled up. Her feet had left the floor. The Cyberman's blank face was staring into hers. There was a crackle. Sparks of blue static danced across its forehead. There was a smell of burning flex.

A voice rang out.

'No!'

It was the Doctor, still in the grip of the other Cyberman.

The Cyberman spoke to its colleague.

'You will not harm her. This female is valued by the Doctor.'

'Yes?' intoned her Cyberman, as though demanding a better reason not to zap her.

The other Cyberman turned to the Doctor.

'She will be harmed only if you refuse to transport us to Cyber Control. Do you agree?'

The Doctor seemed to wilt. He gave a reluctant nod.

The sparks dancing inches from her eyes subsided. Her feet touched the ground once more. But the Cyberman kept her shoulder in a painful grip.

The other Cyberman spoke again to the Doctor.

'You will transport the captured processible units. They will be altered. They will become like us. We will survive. We will proliferate and survive.'

She and the Doctor were led out of the ballroom.

They were just in time to see the last of the passengers pass through the open doors of the TARDIS. Ruby was flabbergasted. A thousand humans had filed into that small blue box.

Inside, they stood and waited.

The mobility experiment had proved successful.

The Co-ordinator had been altered, had undergone another transformation, the third conversion in ten thousand years.

The Co-ordinator was now to be known as the Cyber Controller. The name denoted a new improved design and function within the Cyber race.

soft under sunlit kiss

The Cyber Controller was now acutely aware of having been trapped for a thousand years. Survival had been but a semi-existence.

At the original conversion, in the distant time of the first

222

experiments, the artificial neural network had interfaced with a first class organic brain. The delicate augmentation had produced an organ of purely rational thought. Emotional scouring was effective.

In those pioneering days, the modification from organism to mechanimate construct utilized a primitive conversion process. Yet for intellectual capacity and expansion potential, this particular unit had seldom been bettered. The CyberMondan that this Organic Mondan had become was one in a thousand. A true representative of excellence.

laughter shock of curving together lips and

It was the bodily augmentation which had caused the problems. The original conversion techniques were not dependable. And when it was decided that the greatest contribution to the Cyber race would be attained by immobilization, the Controller, in that earlier mechanimate form, submitted. In deference to the cause. In preference to a decommission. To avoid complete recycling.

That was the –

shava talaron on shava

That was the second conversion. The mobile mechanimate became immobilized as Co-ordinator[38].

The incorporation into the History Computer of the neural remains of that original organisms had been a major advance for the Cyber race. Other suitable units were configured in a similar way. The Network of nodal command and communication was now inaugurated. Co-ordinator[38] was inextricably linked.

Within the parameters of the Network the Co-ordinator functioned impeccably. But with the failure of the First Invasion and the breaking of the Network, the restrictions of immobility became more onerous. For thirty years Co-ordinator[38] pursued a long-term goal.

That goal had been attained. At last. The Co-ordinator had become the Cyber Controller. That was the third conversion. The Cyber Controller was no longer trapped.

skinfleshwave of bodiesmoist and
shava shavashavashavashavashavashore
rushkiss damp.

Fragments of age-old organic memory were flashing in the

Controller's augmented brain. Normal function had suffered some disruption during the re-grafting process. The images which had troubled Co-ordinator[38] were a degree more persistent.

Considering the scale of the experiment, it was a minor malfunction. Some adjustments would be made. It was purely routine. It was to be expected when embodiment was undertaken.

The newly gained powers could now be explored. The Controller moved towards the Doctor.

Ruby's stomach was churning again. As soon as the Cybermen had escorted them out of the TARDIS, she had known which one the Cyber Controller must be. They were back in the cavern carved out of the ice. The machine which had called itself the Co-ordinator was no longer there. In its place stood a Cyberman, but as different from the other Cybermen as a queen bee was from the workers that served it.

The creature's humanoid shape was clad in an armoured body suit but compared with the other Cybermen it had much more bulk. With growing horror she realized what she saw was Bono's processed body. But what had they done to his head?

Above the large blank Cyber face was fixed a glowing ovoid. The object that had been at the Co-ordinator's active centre. She saw it clearly now. A human-like organic brain, set into a filigree of glass and metal and flickering lights.

So that was the mobility experiment. Ruby swallowed down the bitter phlegm that was rising in her throat.

The creature shuffled unsteadily towards them. A paraplegic learning to walk again. Ruby was reminded of her father, strapped into a power-frame, the flaccid muscles of his legs jerking fleetingly to life in a ghastly parody of walking. He had tried so hard to make it work. He had been so bitter when it hadn't. Her eyes stung with sudden tears. She blinked them away.

The Cyber Controller loomed over them. There was a metal shutter at the mouth slit. It slid out of view as the creature spoke.

'So, Doctor, we meet at last. Face to face.'

The glowing ovoid at the head pulsed with light on each stressed syllable. The voice was close to human speech in tone. It had a slight sing-song inflection. There was no emotion in it.

'It may be the first time for you, Cyber Controller,' replied the Doctor, 'but I've met you and your like, face to face, on many occasions now, and I can't say I enjoy the experience.'

'Enjoyment is a notion we consider superfluous.'

'Ah, yes. Of course. However, I do not.'

The metal mouth shuttered to. There was a moment of internal whirring. Then it flapped open again.

'You are known to us. You are an enemy of the Cyber race. You interfered with our functioning on Planet Fourteen. You have twice disrupted our attempts to utilize Earth resources. This time you will fail to stop us. Phase One of our plan is reaching its climax. Our conquest of Earth is now inevitable.'

'You will destroy it. You know that, don't you?'

'It will become our – '

There was a further moment of whirring as the Controller searched for the appropriate word.

' – our second home, since our first, Mondas, was destroyed.'

'But you do intend to strip the planet of life, don't you?'

'We will intensify a process already under way on Earth. The planet is dying. The humans on it are sickening and dying. As we once were. On Mondas. But to die is unnecessary. We survived. We will allow humans to survive. We will convert those which are suitable. We will save them from misery and destruction.'

Ruby was finding this conversation appalling. The Controller spoke so matter-of-factly. She couldn't keep quiet any longer.

'And what about the rest? The ones who aren't suitable?'

'They will be recycled.'

'Recycled? Oh, I see,' she laughed, bitterly. 'You'll take them to the flesh bank, I suppose.'

The Doctor winked at her. 'Send them to the organ grinders?'

'Yeah, off to head office with them.'

'The second-hand shop.'

225

They were in paroxysms. They couldn't help themselves. Her Cyber guard gripped her even tighter.

The Controller looked from one to the other. It couldn't see the joke of course.

That was its problem. The problem of the Cyber race.

The Controller's large hand came at her. It grasped the Holocam and pulled. The strap gave way. The camera looked small in the Cyberman's palm. Its three fingers closed on it. There was a cracking sound. It tossed the camera back to her. It was crushed to half its size.

'Everything is of use,' the Controller said. 'But not necessarily in its original form.'

It pointed a finger to where, at the other side of the cavern, several Cybermen were moving back and forth around the steaming vat.

'Take them to the form extruder.'

This is it, thought Ruby.

As they approached the weird tangle of machinery, the Doctor grew animated. He seemed to understand the technology and find it fascinating.

The huge vat was being filled with an assortment of metal and plastic items. A Cyberman dropped in a piece of white sheet metal marked with the letters STS. Already in the vat were seat belts and wristwatches, crushed Cyber chest panels and shattered windscreens. She glimpsed a plastic chess set and a stainless steel lavatory pan stamped 'Nikkei 5'.

Over this odd collection, a Cyberman scattered a handful of wriggling white capsules. Maggots or bugs. Like the ones she'd seen digesting her vomit. But larger. Much larger. One had caught on the side of the vat, fleshy and plump with a bristling, squirming tail. It sizzled on the hot black metal and fell into the seething pot.

The acrid smoke caught at her lungs. An intense heat pricked at her face as she leant over and watched. The various bits and pieces were beginning to melt together.

'Throw in that object,' ordered the Controller, pointing to her squashed camera.

She did so. It joined the heap. Everything was puddling together to create a viscous molten substance of uniform colour and consistency. It had the sheen of some dull metal. A blue spark danced over its surface. There was the smell of burning electricity.

'Extraordinary,' said the Doctor as he too peered in. 'You're deferring crystallization, I take it?'

'That is correct,' replied the Cyber Controller.

'What?' asked Ruby.

'Well, if I understand it correctly, they're creating a single crystal artefact.'

'What's that when it's at home?' she asked sullenly. She wasn't sure she liked the Doctor's enthusiasm. He seemed genuinely impressed by their technological wizardry.

'You see,' he went on, 'solid metal is made up of millions of crystals, arranged in perfect order. As molten metal cools it crystallizes, just like a salt solution. You must have done it in chemistry at school. You add a grain of salt to a supersaturated saline solution and, lo and behold, it turns to a solid mass.'

What Ruby had done in chemistry was carve into her desk the names of teenage heart-throbs. Mike Brack among them, probably. She'd never quite gathered what a supersaturated saline solution was.

'That's what would happen to this peculiar mixture,' the Doctor continued. 'If it weren't for the electric current which is making it impossible for crystals for form. Any crystal which begins to solidify immediately short-circuits and melts again. As you can see, the most unexpected assortment of scrap, incompatible in its crystalline form, will melt together.'

'Including the glass and plastic?'

'Yes. Any plastic which isn't vaporized in the heat will add elasticity to the final product. The glass will encourage vitrification. The process is extremely clever, considering the limited resources they have at their disposal. I imagine the necessary peroxidase is provided by the Thysanura.'

All the rest escaped her, but Thysanura sounded like a word her mother would have known.

'You mean those creepy-crawlies?'

'Yes. They'll form the catalyst. The leucocytes will provide the necessary enzyme. When this lot cools it will form one gigantic crystal. A smooth metallic glass. Opaque, pliable and

227

exceptionally strong. And while it's still malleable it'll be extruded into any shape and texture. A rock-hard chest panel. A flexible body suit. Remarkable.'

The Doctor by this time was walking around the various machines, his voice raised in an exultant shout.

'Am I not right, Controller?'

'You are correct. Your knowledge is commendable. You will be a valuable addition to the Cyber cause.'

Ruby's heart went cold. It was back to basics again. But the Doctor's reply made her blood run even colder.

'Yes, I can quite see the potential.'

'Doctor!' she cried horrified. Three fingers dug dutifully into her shoulder.

'I have something else to recycle here, Controller.'

The Doctor reached into his pocket and produced a palmful of the separated links from Ruby's necklace.

'This is gold. That's a metal, too. Extremely unreactive. Shall I throw it in?'

There was a whirring as the Cyber Controller pondered.

Clever old Doctor, Ruby thought, so he hasn't gone across to them. He's up to something.

'Gold will be of use. Throw it in.'

The Doctor did as he was told.

Ruby waited for the explosion, or for the crystallizing process to seize up, or for something dramatic to happen. But nothing. Nothing at all.

'Can I make any other contributions to the cause?' asked the Doctor, cheerily.

So he was going over to them. She felt so alone.

'You possess a machine which will be an important addition to Cyber technology,' intoned the Cyber Controller. 'The laws of instant travel through space and time are unknown to us. You will – initiate us – into the mystery.'

'Of course. Anything to oblige,' said the traitor.

'But first we must pass into Phase Two.'

The Controller seemed better co-ordinated now. As if he was learning to walk as they watched. He confidently strode over to an upright metal box. It was a larger version of the humaform.

'Reversal of the magnetic flux is due. I shall now undergo orientation.'

'Oh, I see. You need to adjust your mechanism to the changed polarity. Otherwise you would cease to function efficiently.'

'You have some understanding of our ways, Doctor. When you become like us you will understand them better.'

Turning to face them, the Controller stepped backwards and fitted himself into the box. It was a tight squeeze.

'Essential operations are now on automatic. Everything is proceeding according to plan. All units will submit to re-orientation,' he instructed. 'Enter the induction forms.'

Apart from their two guards, all the Cybermen in the chamber, about eight in all, moved to boxes set round the walls.

'What's going to happen to all those people in the TARDIS?' yelled Ruby. Her rage had returned. It was rising up within her. All tame creatures had grown up wild. The Doctor was betraying her. It was unbearable.

'They will remain – in waiting,' the Controller replied. The usage was rather odd, but Ruby got the point. 'They will be converted during Phase Two. We have an army in the ice. They have been adjusted for realigned polarity. The humans in the TARDIS will – swell their numbers. Nothing will be wasted.'

'No one,' corrected Ruby angrily.

'No one,' agreed the Cyber Controller.

'And what's going to happen to us?' she screamed.

'You have fear. We will eliminate fear from your brains. You will be made like us. You will be frozen and placed in the ice until we are ready to use you. Put them into the humaforms.'

Ruby tried to resist but the Cyberman was too strong. It pushed her towards one of the smaller metal boxes. The Doctor needed no persuading. He was already positioning himself inside his box and doing up the straps. He called across to her.

'Ruby, don't resist. You'll only make it worse for yourself.'

'That is correct,' said the Cyber Controller. 'Information will first be extracted from your brain. It is a lengthy process. Co-operation is required if pain is to be avoided.

'Immortality, here I come,' said the Doctor. His Cyberman lowered the lid of the box. His voice was fading from her.

'Ruby! See you on the other side.'

Not if I see you first, she thought.

The Cyberman was hurting her. The straps were lashed across her chest, constricting her breathing, biting into her flesh. She yelled with pain as the thigh strap was tightened over her wound. The lid closed down on her.

She was in darkness. And despair. A warm trickle of blood ran down her leg.

A click. A low hum. A pressure inside her head.

She must resist. She would not give in. She must keep her head from emptying. She must have a focus for her thoughts.

Her Nanocom was still clipped inside her shirt.

'Newfile story,' she whispered.

There was an answering beep from the Nanocom.

'Log,' said Ruby.

There was a second beep. Ruby breathed a little easier. She started to tell the story of what had happened.

She told it to Nano.

21   Behind Me

The lid was being raised. Silver arms were reaching in. The light was dazzling. Her eyes hurt. She kept them screwed tight.

Had she told her story? Had she fallen to sleep? Had her brain yielded up its information?

Her head was pulsing with a deep dull pain.

She winced as the strap around her thigh was loosened roughly. She was pulled out of the box. She felt the jolt of the injection gun at her neck, the sharp pain and the spreading of the heat through her body.

The Cyber guard pushed her forward. Each step thundered in her head. She opened her eyes for a second. They were leaving the cavern, passing the armoured door of its entrance. She was bundled onto a waiting skimmer. Its light seared her eyes. She jammed them shut again. The Cyberman stood behind her. She felt its arms reach forward to each side of her. She shuddered. The motor hummed to life. They slid forward.

She felt she was in a dream. There was a voice in her head. It was the Doctor's voice.

'They plan to destroy the FLIPback device. That's the goal of Phase One.'

She could see him in her mind. The image was as vivid as day. His face was hovering in the smoke which rose from the extruder vat. He was the all-powerful wizard, Wu Ming. But eager, excited, filled with child-like glee.

'They're going to use a bomb, I'm sure of it. It'll be sited above the field loop. We must find it and destroy it.'

'It's no use,' she mumbled. 'No use.'

'It's our only hope. The only hope for Earth.'

'No. It's all over now. You betrayed us. You went over to them. I trusted you. And you betrayed me.'

There was soft laughter. The wizard's face was laughing at her through the smoke.

'You're feeling fragile. You'll feel better soon.'

'They're putting me on ice,' she murmured.

The wizard's face was craggy and white, carved in ice, floating away to sea. The face lit up. The smile was splitting the ice. Enthusiasm was turning it to steam.

'Sorry about the gold. I got my Cybermen mixed up. Each type seems to have different strengths. And weaknesses.'

He was floating disembodied in the steam of melting ice. A gigantic gold chain was twined around his neck in place of his paisley scarf.

'The Cybermen from Mondas hated radiation. It seized them up. But this lot are from the first invasion, from Planet Fourteen. Radiation doesn't bother them. Never occurred to me they might be impervious to gold.'

The Doctor's head was going round and round. Ruby felt sick. She opened her eyes. The dimly lit tunnel rushed towards them. Her head was clearing a little. But the voice was still there.

'Feeling any better?'

'Mmm. A little,' she grunted.

The Cyberman squeezed her gently between its outstretched arms. She saw that its hands were five-fingered, human. Naked human hands. Sticking out of the armoured silver sleeves.

'Almost there,' said the Doctor behind her.

Behind her?

'Doctor?'

'Yes, Ruby?'

'I'm dreaming that you're the Cyberman behind me.'

'I am.'

Bewildered, she looked over her shoulder.

He was wearing a Cyber body suit.

'The suit was stacked by the side of the form extruder,' he explained. He kept his eyes fixed on the twists and turns of the tunnel ahead. 'I borrowed it in case I met with opposition.'

She wasn't dreaming. It really was the Doctor.

'It doesn't fit you very well.'

'No, but its warm. Thought you might catch a chill, too. In those pathetic rags you're wearing. So – '

'So you injected me with anti-freeze. Sweet Gaia! I thought they were preparing me for the ice. Oh, Doctor – '

Words stuck. Tears of relief were pricking at her eyes.

'Why did you encourage them like that? How did you get free?'

'If you would have a thing weaken, first allow it strength. If you want a thing destroyed, first build it up. If you would take, first you must give. It's called subtle discernment. Soft over hard, weak over strong. The fish must be kept in the tank.'

It sounded like Lao Tzu on speed. She sort of guessed what he was getting at.

'They thought I was a willing subject,' he went on, 'so they didn't even bother to secure me in the humaform. I gave myself up to the probing and after a decent interval, I simply pushed the lid open and stepped out. No one to stop me. They were all in those boxes.'

He hesitated. Something was bothering him.

'Unfortunately, I think I gave away one or two of the Time Lord's secrets. Not much more than gossip, I'm sure. But I would rather it went no further than these ice walls. Which is another reason we must foil their plan of conquest. Keep the fish in the tank. It's not just the Earth that's at stake. It could be the nature of everything.'

They skidded to a halt. They were outside the snow lab. They ran through to the reactor chamber. The bomb was just where the Doctor had predicted. It had the appearance of a foil-wrapped Easter egg.

'It looks rather puny,' said Ruby. 'Will it be powerful enough to do some damage?'

The Doctor was on his hands and knees, inspecting it closely.

'Some Cybermen I met in the future, oh, years ago, boasted that their Cyber bombs were the most explosive devices in the Universe. The Vogans had given them a hard time. They were loosing track of reality. They were even susceptible to gold.'

He had his ear to the egg.

233

'But the ones who put this together are still in their prime. I'll be powerful enough to do its job. I must defuse it.'

'What's this machine it's bolted to?'

'Looks like the charge transformer. Destroy this and you deprive the loop of its power. It ceases to function.'

He rolled up his sleeves, took from his pocket something that might have been a screwdriver, and set to work.

Ruby's head was almost clear again. There was little she could do down there. She ran for the lift.

'I'll find out what's happening in the tracking room.'

'Geneva calling. Geneva to STS. Are you hearing me, STS.'

The woman's accented European voice was assured and strong. It sliced into the studied silence of the tracking room.

The overhead lights were dimmed right down. Faces were lit by flickering VDUs. Adler, punching in data. Whitehead and Palmer following the wild fluctuations of the green dot on the wall. Jude Black reading out the correlations as they were calculated by the FLIPback software. Her voice was flat, uninvolved, dutiful. The faces were watchful but unexpressive.

'Geneva calling. Geneva to STS. Are you hearing me, STS.'

There was something at the back of Colonel Hilliard's mind. A vague feeling of anxiety. The FLIPback operation appeared to be proceeding perfectly. But something was not quite right. Perhaps it was too perfect?

No, he was tired. He wanted it to proceed perfectly. Of course he did.

'This is Geneva calling. Geneva calling STS.'

A voice buzzed in the colonel's ear.

'Answer them.'

Three silver fingers gripped his shoulder and pressed him into the chair by the radio transmitter.

That's right. He should answer them. He should sit down and answer them. Of course he should.

Colonel Hilliard switched to transmission.

The lift doors closed to behind her. Just as before, nobody had noticed her arrival. Just as before, their focus was entirely on the operation. What was not just as before was the presence of the Cyberman.

It stood behind Hilliard, hand on his shoulder. It looked almost chummy, but Ruby knew the discomfort of that grip. The colonel was speaking tonelessly into the radio mike.

'We're above high-level Blue. We're moving into Critical White. FLIPover takes place within the hour.'

Ruby wondered what would happen to the Cyberman, then. Would it flip its lid? Sacrifice itself in the Cyber cause?

It had taken no more exception to her presence than the humans. They were not prioritized to certain possibilities. Unless she became a threatening presence, maybe. She existed but remained unnamed. She dwelt in the Cyber unconscious.

But she was careful not to draw attention to herself. She hid as best she could behind the water dispenser globe.

The general was close. She was engrossed in the VDU display. The light blue was now a strip of sky along the top of the screen, and floating in the dark blue sea were lumps of white. Icebergs, crowding the sea towards the horizon. One iceberg loomed larger than the rest.

'Entering Critical White One,' announced the general.

'Critical White One. In transit,' confirmed Jude Black.

Colonel Hilliard spoke softly into the radio mike. 'We are into Critical White phase. On alert for Critical Black. Flipover will occur at any time within the next fifty minutes.'

Ruby's heart raced. She silently willed the Doctor, working far below, to get that bomb defused.

To the general's left was a switch under a transparent cover. It was angled upwards to 'OFF'. Below it was 'ON'. Below that was a small covered panel embedded in the work surface. The general slid the cover aside to reveal two keyholes.

'Prepare to expose activating mechanism,' she ordered.

Sergeant Adler, whose behaviour now seemed no more zomboid than the others, was handed a key by Colonel Hilliard and came over to stand by the general, who had also produced a key.

Ruby suddenly became aware that Adler was looking at her through the water balloon. She tensed. His eyes were roving over her body, seeming to take in the rags she wore, her exposed brown flesh. His gaze met hers. A slight frown flickered across his face, and then it passed. He turned to the duty in hand. He inserted his key into the panel. The general inserted hers. They turned in unison. The transparent cover over the switch lifted away.

Ruby relaxed. She was mercifully nonexistent. A figment of Adler's unconscious. Her mind flipped back to the Doctor. Had he managed to defuse the bomb? Was there anything she could do? Countdown to flipover was in progress and there was less than an hour to go. The balloon could go up at any time. Her head started pounding again.

Oh, help me! The balloon's going up! the voice of the Tin Man in her head, really in her head this time. The wizard in the balloon basket setting out for the stars and Dorothy chasing after her little dog Toto who's jumped out of the basket and the doorbell rings and the balloon begins to rise and she's being left behind and a policewoman says my daddy's bad oh help me the balloon's going up come back come back he's leaving me behind.

I can't come back! I don't know how it works!

The balloon's getting smaller. Disappearing. Gone.

And now she'll never get home.

Ruby shook the images from her head. The ordeal in the humaform was still playing tricks with her mind. She focused on the scene before her.

What she knew for certain was that she couldn't interfere without good cause. As soon as she made a threatening move she would be zapped. If she had chance to act, it would only be the once. If she was going to do anything at all it would have to be quick and deadly accurate.

She was still hazy about how the FLIPback operation was intended to counter the reversal of Earth's magnetic field, how the Cybermen intended to sabotage the operation. She tried to think about it logically and clearly. As a Cyberman might.

She had understood the process when she had done her research. She desperately tried to recall the details. The magnetic flux would weaken. Exponentially, yes, that was it. Until it reached a highly volatile state. At the moment when reversal was established beyond doubt, the FLIPback device would be triggered. At the flick of the switch in front of her, power would surge through the field loop. The reversal would itself be reversed. North would be north again, south would be south. That was the theory.

So what would happen if the Cyber bomb destroyed the field loop? Reversal would happen. Unhindered. Earth would be plunged into chaos. The Cyber forces would be re-awakened. They would turn the catastrophe to their own advantage.

An idea was just beginning to form at the edge of Ruby's consciousness. There was something she could do. She couldn't quite grasp it yet, but it was there, just out of reach. A lateral thought, out in left field. An image was in her head. A Damoclean sword was poised on its thread above a Cyberman. Instead of a head, the Cyberman had an outsize human brain, exposed, a tangle of grey, a Gordian knot.

The lift doors opened. The Doctor entered. He saw her immediately. She threw him a questioning glance. He gave a slight shake of his head and stepped forward. Behind him was a Cyberman. Its gun was pointed at the Doctor's back.

'Intruder,' announced the Cyberman.

Ruby slid down behind the water dispenser. But the Cyberman wasn't referring to her. It was referring to its prisoner. None of the STS staff were taking a blind bit of notice. They were continuing with the countdown. But the other Cyberman was walking towards them.

It stopped a metre away from Ruby. It obscured her view of the Doctor. It was taking in the salient features of the intruder and was measuring them against some internal record. Then it spoke.

'This intruder is known to us. He is an enemy. He must be detained.'

'Yes,' agreed the Doctor's guard. 'He was interfering with the explosive device.'

'Is it undamaged?'

'Yes.'

'Actually,' said the Doctor, 'I did manage to unbolt it from its moorings.'

Ruby felt the information was more for her benefit than theirs.

'This is unimportant,' intoned the Cyberman behind him.

'The bomb is set to detonate in nine minutes six seconds,'

said the one with its back to her. 'Does it remain in effective proximity to the charge transformer?'

'Yes,' answered the other.

The general's voice cut across the conversation.

'Leaving Critical White One.'

'Critical White One. Transit terminated,' confirmed Jude Black.

Out of the fading white wash on the general's screen, the dark and light blue tones appeared once more.

Colonel Hilliard spoke into the radio mike. 'Through the first Critical White. Next Critical White coming up.'

Ruby had no idea what this odd-sounding jargon meant, but as the Cyberman strode away again, the Doctor came back into view. She peeped at his distorted image through the balloon of water. He cleared his throat and spoke.

'Whatever teeters on the edge can easily be pushed. We must work on what is not yet there.'

The Cyberman stopped and turned. The Doctor smiled.

'You will remain silent,' ordered the Cyberman, impassively.

The Doctor put a finger to his lips and nodded sagely. The Cyberman took up its position to the rear of Hilliard.

The Doctor was talking to her. In code. Whatever teeters on the edge is easily pushed. Work on what is not yet there. What did he mean?

She had been on the verge of knowing what must be done. Now the idea had completely slipped her mind. She tried to recall it. Her head ached with frustration.

'The time to instil order is before confusion sets in,' said the Doctor.

The Cyberman behind Hilliard turned and motioned to the other. The guard put a hand on the Doctor's shoulder and squeezed. The Doctor squealed and sagged at the knees.

Instil order before confusion sets in. That was it! Sever the threat. Cut through the knot.

She jumped up. She reached towards the general. She flipped the switch.

The general noticed her now. She turned aghast, mouth hanging open, looking first at the switch in its 'on' position and then at her. Sergeant Alder was coming at her. The others had dropped what they were doing and were staring at her.

238

Adler stopped in his tracks and looked uncertain. He glanced at the general and then back at Ruby. His eyes glazed over.

The puzzled voice of Geneva came over the radio.

'STS, our readings tell us reversal has taken place. Flipover has occurred. STS, please confirm. Please confirm.'

Colonel Hilliard was ignoring the radio. He was staring at Ruby.

'Answer them,' ordered the Cyberman behind him.

Colonel Hilliard blinked. He glanced at the Cyberman and then turned to speak into the mike.

'Behind me – ' he started. 'Behind me – '

'What in hell's name is happening down there?'

But the colonel had stopped again. He looked back to stare at Ruby.

The Cyberman cut the communication link with Geneva. He turned to Ruby and strode towards her. She ran to the lift.

'Hold her,' ordered the Cyberman.

The other Cyberman grabbed her. Steel fingers were closing around her neck. The approaching Cyberman was talking. The syntax was disjointed.

'Two are enemies – enemies of the Cyber – must free.'

'Free,' said the one with its hands round her neck. 'Yes.'

'No, free,' said the first, pushing the Doctor towards the open lift. 'One Doctor to go. Companion to go.'

Ruby had no idea what was happening but she rushed into the lift and jammed her thumb on the button. By the time the doors slid to, the Cybermen were enclosed in each others arms. Locked in combat. Or was it a lover's embrace?

The Doctor's arms were wrapped around his head. As the lift descended he peeped out at her.

'Well done,' he whispered.

'What was happening up there?'

'You activated FLIPback before flipover. In their controlled state, the humans weren't programmed for it. Their normal instinctive response was denied them. They glitched.'

'And the Cybermen?'

'Couldn't cope with reversed polarity. Their logical priorities were inverted. Confused their tiny metal minds.'

239

'So that's why they wanted to save us. Instant schizos. A kind of complete metal breakdown.'

The Doctor looked pained. His hands went back to his head.

'Oh, come on, Doctor. I thought you liked bad jokes.'

'No, it's my head.' He grunted in discomfort. 'The polarity reversal is getting to me. I'm not built like you. I'm more susceptible.'

Now that he mentioned it, she did feel a slight blocked feeling above the nose and a pulsing in her ears, but nothing more.

'Besides,' he continued, trying to smile through the pain, 'I told that joke before, long after you were born, when I was only four hundred and fifty.'

'Time flies,' said Ruby.

'You can't,' he grunted. 'They go too fast.'

Suddenly, he was bending over, howling in pain. It was terrible to watch.

'Anything I can do?'

'No. Nothing.'

The lift reached reactor level. His discomfort eased.

'It can only be temporary,' he said, taking a deep breath. 'It'll go completely when polarity reverses to normal.'

They started in the direction of the reactor chamber.

'So I was right, then,' said Ruby with relief. 'Magnetic reversal will occur naturally, won't it?'

'Yes.'

'And things will be back to normal again?'

'Yes. FLIPback has done its work. Before. Not after.'

The Doctor was kneeling by the charge transformer, reaching a hand under the complex of cables. He was grunting again. His face was screwed up in concentration. Or Pain.

'But we've still got this bomb to deal with.'

He pulled out the silver egg.

'How long have we got?' she asked.

'Seven minutes?'

He placed the bomb on the floor. His hands went to his head. He spat out instructions.

'The TARDIS. Get out via the TARDIS. Drop the bomb on the way. Destroy the – '

He fell to ground, unconscious.

Time was flying. The seconds ticking away. She started counting them. *One Cyberman. Two Cybermen. Three Cybermen.* She pulled out his silk handkerchief. Gingerly, she picked up the egg and wrapped it in the silk and eased it into the Doctor's jacket pocket. Six minutes?

She grabbed his arms and dragged him through the snow lab. Thank Gaia! The skimmer was still there. She manhandled him on to it.

She started the motor and raced away up the tunnel. *Fifty-nine Cybermen. Sixty Cybermen.* Five minutes to go?

Another sixty 'Cyberman' went by, and then another sixty. Then she was whizzing past the real McCoy, the rows of dormant Cybermen, waiting in the ice for the conquest of Earth. This was the place to jettison the bomb. She reached inside the Doctor's pocket and pulled out the deadly package. Eggs away!

The little bundle of silk bounced and tumbled behind her. Two minutes left?

One minute later she arrived at Cyber Control. She drove straight into the cavern of ice and slid to a halt.

She sighed with relief. The TARDIS was still there. Looked sort of faded, somehow. But only seconds to go. No time to get into it and away, even if she could have operated the controls.

She saw the armoured door. Block the openings, she thought.

She caught hold of the wheel lock at the centre of the door and pulled, expecting formidable resistance. To her surprise, the massive slab of metal swung easily towards her and thudded into place. She turned the wheel.

There was a roar as of thunder.

A tremor shook the door and juddered along the bones of her hands, up her arms, along her shoulders. The floor of the cavern shook. Lumps of ice were falling from above.

At last, the tremor ceased. In the dead silence, an occasional snowball smashed to the ground. Peels of thunder rumbled distantly. Walls were caving in, roofs collapsing, in the tunnels which spiralled out around Cyber Control.

The walls return to water. No use for army now.

The I Ching was right. The Cyber army was buried. Useless.

241

The slight discomfort in her nose and ears was gone. Natural magnetic reversal must have taken place. The world was no longer upside down. They were safe. Earth was safe.

She ran to where the Doctor lay on the skimmer. He was still unconscious. She tried some Gong Qi Po. Her fingers caressed and massaged the Doctor's neck. He began to stir.

'Destroy the – destroy the ice maze,' he was muttering.

'It's done,' she said.

He opened his eyes. They were a gorgeous, indefinable colour.

'We can use the bomb – '

She put a finger to his lips.

'It's done,' she soothed.

No, not indefinable. The colour of rainbows.

He propped himself on his elbows and gazed around him. He lifted an arm. He was pointing at something behind her. She turned to look.

The lid of the induction form was opening.

The Controller was stepping out.

22 Once in a Lullaby

'Phase One is complete. Earth belongs to us. We proceed with the conquest of Earth.'

The Controller strode towards them. It was making for the Doctor, who was lying propped on his elbows on the skimmer. Ruby placed herself directly in the Controller's path.

There was not a flicker of hesitation. The Controller's arm swept her effortlessly out of its way. She was thrown to the floor.

The Controller was bending over the Doctor.

'You belong to us. You are now like us.'

The Doctor was being lifted into the air. The Controller had him gripped by the shoulders.

'No, actually, I'm not,' the Doctor was saying, between gritted teeth. 'The processing didn't work.'

The Controller paused. Its glowing head pulsed with light. The Doctor's feet were dangling half a metre from the floor.

'I'm still your enemy!' he shouted in the Controller's face.

Ruby was horror-stricken. Was he out of his mind?

'Enemy,' repeated the Controller almost thoughtfully. 'Yes. You are our enemy.'

The Doctor was slowly lowered to the ground. The Controller's hand bunched into a fist. The fist was raised and placed against the side of the glowing head. As if it felt pain there. When it spoke again the voice was less sure, more laboured.

'You. We are you. Are our. We are our enemy. Belong to you.'

It dawned on Ruby what was happening, why the Doctor had spoken as he did. The Controller had been oriented for reverse polarity. It too was having a metal breakdown.

The Controller turned away from the Doctor and lurched over to a bank of controls in the centre of the cavern. Bono was part of that creature now, Ruby recalled with dismay and loathing, a human body grafted, subsumed, into the service of the co-ordinating, controlling mind.

For a moment the Controller seemed to sag, its fists at its head. It was muttering something. Ruby thought she heard '*skin*' and '*laughter*' and was it '*lips*'? Then two words rang out clear.

'Memory. Remembering.'

It started pulling levers and punching at buttons.

'Destroy. Resist. For you, Doctor.'

Smoke was rising from the console. The Controller raised its fists and smashed them down. Again and again. Each time, the Controller uttered a single word, a war cry.

'Talaron!'

What was focused in that word was terrible. You could not call it passion exactly. A terrible intensity.

Yes, that was it. A terrible intensity.

The fists came down. The console exploded into flames. The tortured voice was loud and almost frenzied.

'We will become like us!'

Ruby was spellbound. She felt the Doctor grab her arm.

'Come on, Ruby!'

He pulled her in the direction of the TARDIS.

The central console was now a furnace. The Controller smashed its fists into the flames, its metal body glowing with the heat. Melting lumps of ice were falling from the roof, hissing into the flames, crashing all around them as they dodged their way to the TARDIS.

He went inside. She followed and slammed shut the TARDIS doors behind her. She leant against them to catch her breath. They yielded under her weight, as though made of cardboard. There were people everywhere. The passengers were waiting for instructions. None had been given, so they waited still.

The Doctor had difficulty getting through the inner set of doors. She saw him squeeze past a couple of ageing, near naked, Kinki Gerlinki enthusiasts. Then he disappeared among the throng of bodies. She eased herself into the crowded control room.

Her patchwork jacket was hanging on the wall nearby. She

reached for it, but there was no room to put it on. As the inner doors closed behind her, she was pressed against the exposed warm flesh of the Gerlinky couple. The one was dressed as Santa Claus, the other as a reindeer.

Dressed was an overstatement. Santa wore a beard. A very long beard. Santa's loins were girded up with it. The reindeer was harnessed in braided red ribbon. A big red shiny nose pressed into Ruby's cheek.

It was like rush hour on the London Underground. She had to be careful where she put her hands.

She heard the splash and gurgle of the TARDIS taking off. Her flesh brushed theirs. There was the dampness of sweat, the warmth of skin on skin. The soft odour of humanity.

They were going home.

It was going to be a while before she could take in everything she'd been through. It was like a dream. All she could do for now was to remain still, like the other passengers.

Lao Tzu came to mind.

Attain emptiness. Hold firmly to stillness.
The numberless creatures rise up together.
I watch their return, the teeming multitude.
Each is returning to the source.
Returning to the source is known as stillness.
That is what is meant by going home.

But where was home?

She wondered about the Doctor. Where did he come from? Why had the TARDIS taken the form of a jade pagoda?

There was a slight bump. The shiny red nose poked her cheek.

'Done it!' she heard the Doctor shout.

There wasn't much time left.

How to get the passengers out, that was the question. How to get them all out, and make sure they were all out. If he was able to subsume this plasmic shell within the greater whole, if he could do it in time, he didn't then want to find that some of these people had wondered off into the labyrinthine innards of the TARDIS proper. There was no knowing when, or where, they might turn up.

The problem was that the passengers had been subject to a hypnotic tranquillizer. They had no autonomous control. That, he realized in a flash, was also the solution.

What was that old hypnotic verse he used to sing, several generations ago? He started to hum. Yes, that was it.

He flipped the switch to power the intercom and put his mouth near the microphone. He could now be heard throughout the TARDIS. Throughout this particular plasmic shell, at least.

Now what were the words? Something like this, he seemed to recall. Softly, he began to sing.

'Slokeda kartha fennan klatch
Alark baraan baroon
Slokeda tonnah sherenatch
Baroon bareen baroon
Aroon araan aroon
Baroon baraan baroon'

The bodies pressing around him stirred. He could feel their attention coming to life, focusing on him. He opened the TARDIS doors. Cold light, fresh air, streamed in.

He spoke into the microphone. Compelling words. They echoed down crowded corridors, they sounded in distant rooms.

'At my command, you will take your turn to leave the TARDIS. Captain Trench, you will go straight to the bridge. You will steer the ship back to its proper course. You will stay at your post until your first officer arrives. The rest of you will go to your cabin and sleep. You will wake refreshed and feeling well at your normal waking time.

'You will have hazy memories of the night before. A good time was had by all. Of the events after the arrival of the Tin Man's bigger brother, you will remember nothing.

'Now, in orderly fashion, I command you to go.'

Ruby was the first out. She emerged onto the cold bright pool deck and quickly pulled her jacket on.

The TARDIS was standing near the shallow end. The curious

blue box had a flimsy, tattered look. It swayed with the motion of the ship. At the seams of its corners and edges, the blue was bleached out, like well-washed denim.

The passengers were filing out. The reindeer took the lead, with Santa holding the reins. The procession snaked along by the side of the pool and disappeared through the double doors beneath the bridge. Somewhere near the middle was Diana in her Dorothy gingham and Leslie in his Tin Man suit. Just passing her now was Lord Straker, and the captain, who was making his way to the bridge. They were all humming in unison, humming the Doctor's haunting little tune.

She saw a bundle of clothing under the diving tower. With a gasp she realized what it was. She ran towards it.

Mike Brack was lying where the Cyberman had dropped him. He'd been in the cold for hours. He'd be dying of exposure. She felt in the pocket of her jacket.

The injection gun was still there.

There was a jolt of pain at his shoulder. Heat was spreading around his heart, along his arms, down his back, into his legs. It was his legs that hurt the most. He must have smashed them in the fall.

He remembered falling, but why he had fallen and where he had fallen from, he could not remember.

He felt a hand under his head. They were trying to help him. Someone must have called an ambulance.

'Mike. Mike, can you hear me?'

It was a familiar voice. The face was silhouetted against the brightness of the sky.

'Mike, it's Ruby. You're going to be all right.'

Ruby. Ruby Duvall. He wanted to speak to her. Tell her.

Incredible images flashed through his brain. The carved iceberg, the marching Tin Men, the blasting of the laser gun, the white smoke, the fall. Hallucination. All of it. Except the fall. The fall was real. He must be smashed up for good, he reckoned. Just like her father, Ruby's father, twenty years ago.

The sky was going black. He was losing –

He had to tell her. Unload the guilt.

Twenty years ago. His anger. A motorbike.

* * *

He'd been mumbling something. Ruby could make no sense of it. Then he'd gone again.

As she bent over him, her Nanocom fell from inside her shirt and clattered on the deck. Her Nano. It had kept her going when things were really bad. She picked it up and put it to her ear and shook it. Nothing broken. Pretty tough was Nano. She put it in her pocket and turned her attention to Brack once more.

She laid her head on his chest. His breathing was deep and steady, his heartbeat strong and regular. The injection would do its work. Cyber technology at its best. She gripped his hand. Warmth was surging back into icy flesh.

He started to snore. He was going to be all right. The leg was twisted badly but that would mend. He was going to be all right. All sorts of things were going to be all right. She felt strong and free. A weight had fallen from her. She could do anything she wanted.

She stood and took off her jacket and laid it over him to keep the warmth in. She looked around her. The passengers were still filing past and into the ship. They were humming the Doctor's tune. Snow White's seven hundred dwarfs. And some hundreds more.

The tune was the sort to keep you awake at night. It was catchy, but she wasn't sure she liked it. It went round and round and round in your head.

She started walking against flow of passengers towards the other end of the pool. She hummed along with them. She couldn't help herself. The Doctor appeared at the entrance of the TARDIS.

'Whatever is this tune?' she shouted across at him.

'Oh, a kind of – well, a kind of lullaby.'

He looked a little awkward.

'Ruby, I'm going to have to go.'

He held his arms wide. She went to him. They hugged. Passengers pushed past them through the doorway, humming the lullaby.

'Are you going home?' she asked. She wanted to ask him where that was.

'The TARDIS is fading fast,' he said. It wasn't an answer. 'I'll be lucky to get this lot out before it gives up the ghost. I

248

must get it back in one piece. Or my companions would never forgive me.'

'Companions?'

'My fellow travellers. They're with the proper TARDIS. This one's a kind of echo, really – and as you see the echo's fading rather quickly – but without it the TARDIS couldn't function as a whole. So –'

'Take me with you.'

It just came out. Until she said it, she hadn't realized how much she wanted to be away. To find a new home.

'I want to forget.'

'Not a good idea,' he answered pointedly, but there was a twinkle in his eye. He was looking intently at her. Into her eyes. She stared back at him defiantly, daring him to refuse.

'But if you'd like to join us,' he continued at last, as though weighing the possibility in his mind, 'if you really want to, you'll find there is so much else to think about. And to remember.'

Ruby nodded. There was a broad grin on her face. The Doctor grinned too. The last of the passengers emerged into the sunlight.

'And about time too,' the Doctor said, rubbing his hands together. He turned and glanced at the state of the TARDIS.

'We really must hurry.'

He went inside.

Her jacket! It had her Nanocom in the pocket. She'd left it draped over Mike Brack. She couldn't leave her Nano behind. Not after all they'd been through together.

'Doctor, don't go without me! I'll be right back.'

She was running fast, catching up with the last of the humming passengers, passing them. It wouldn't take long.

The Doctor was shouting after her.

'I can't hold on much longer, Ruby. The TARDIS has a mind of its own.'

She'd got to the coat. She reached inside the pocket. She grabbed the Nanocom. She turned and ran.

The TARDIS doors were closing.

'No!' she shouted.

The light was flashing. There was the familiar sound of take-off.

249

'No!'

The TARDIS was fading, reappearing, fading again. Fading. Gone.

She ran to where it had been.

She stood at the spot where it had been.

And she wailed. She wailed her heart out.

The Doctor held his hat to his head and picked up his umbrella from the floor. It looked a bit worse for wear. Two thousand feet had trampled all over it.

The TARDIS had returned to its source, the centre of stillness. The TARDIS had returned to the heart of the TARDIS.

He left the empty room. The door swung to behind him. The door without a handle.

The smell of mustiness was almost overpowering. He had grown used to the clean bite of Antarctic air. He reached for his handkerchief to cover his nose.

Gone. He must have left it somewhere.

A black shape flapped past him. A bat. It fluttered down the corridor. He followed it.

No, he wasn't going home.

23 Why Oh Why Can't I?

LogOn 00:00 Wednesday 31 January 2007   File: Cruise
Midnight, Nano. Sailing away from Panama City.

Just been out on deck. It was packed. Stifling. Never been so many of us crowded together since –

Well, you know what I'm on about, Nano. Won't spell it out.

The sight was certainly spectacular. On the Balboa Heights, way up above the Panama Canal, the thousand candles, all massed together, lit up the night. And the stars were sparking back as if reflecting the candles. As if in sympathy with their message.

If you looked hard enough you could almost imagine you saw the outstretched hands in the flickering lights, the arms reaching out, imploring, for themselves, for humanity, for the dispossessed, for the suffering, shouting out to us, to the heavens, 'Save us, save our sickening planet, for Gaia's sake!'

Perhaps I'm overstating the hype, Nano. But you get the picture. It was a moving spectacle. The crowd were emotional. Donations pledged to the Preserve Our Planet Fund were topping ten thousand ecu by the time I left. It'll make not a blind bit of difference.

Naturally, the world's press was out in force, transmitting the images to an estimated billion people around the globe. All in all, a marvellous media coup for Lord Straker.

Arms For Humanity. That was the name of exhibition. The latest and greatest of Mike Brack's statements. Sponsored by Panama Projects Incorporated.

In case you haven't heard of PPI, Nano, it's a huge multi-national that's into almost everything on a global scale. Including – so my sources tell me – gun-running, drug smuggling and cash diversification. Laundering to you. So sponsoring an exhibition like *Arms For Humanity* is sort of appropriate. Wouldn't you agree?

And thus, the mystery of the wooden crates is also solved.

The crowd enjoyed themselves. As ever. I snapped away with Leslie's single lens reflex, since my Holocam is irretrievably gone. That's something I had difficulty explaining to Lord Straker. And though I have an extremely interesting set of holograms, I can't admit to having taken them. No one would believe me.

Now I know how Isobel Watkins must have felt.

Not being able to tell. That's the worst of it. Not Diana or Leslie. Not Barbara. Certainly not the captain or Lord Straker. Though they know something strange was up that night. Nobody can really account for the loss of Straker's helicopter. Spontaneous combustion is the best the FF can do.

As for Mike Brack, well, it seems I saved his life. Course, nobody knows about that. He was 'coptered back to the Falklands to have his leg put right. But even if he were here, that cynic'd be the last to believe me.

Am I beginning to sound like him, do you think?

Only you know my terrible, wonderful secret, Nano. Only you. The rest is silence, as someone said.

Things will never be the same, of course. Only today I read in the Panama equivalent to the local gazette that there's a scheme afoot to provide the mega-cities of South America with fresh water. Headline: Water by the million gallon block.

PPI has realized that an iceberg is really an extremely large packet of frozen drinking water. A fleet of ships is on its way now to tow a dozen back to relieve the drought. There's money in them thar ice hills.

But what I can't get out of my mind is that – if what I went through was real – inside those thawing icebergs they might find more than they bargained for.

But that's it, isn't it, Nano? It isn't just the keeping silent that's a pain. It's the doubt nibbling at the back of my mind. Eating away at what I thought was real. Ingesting it, like those awful little Cyber bugs.

Perhaps it never really happened. Perhaps it was all a vivid dream. So vivid that real life becomes dull by comparison.

And if it was real, if I'm not going mad, and this man with no name really does exist, somewhere, nowhere, then –

He's flown beyond the rainbow.

And me? I'm lost in now and can never be found.

But I have my Lao Tzu. And you, Nano. Both on permanent loan. Oh, and I have this bloody scarf. My blood, his scarf.

His scarf. So that must make him real, mustn't it?

So, we're on our way home. I'll see Granny again. And I've been thinking, Nano. I'll get back in touch with my dad. See how things work out.

Mmm. So sleepy. Hardly keep my eyes open.

You know, one thing the Doctor said keeps coming back. Like a voice in a dream. Sometimes I'll have forgotten all about it, then back it comes, surfacing into consciousness.

It's not so much the words. It was the way he said them. That still small voice.

'Things will get better, you know.'

I'll believe you, Doctor.
Night night, Nano.
Sleep tight.
Don't let the bugs bite.

Already published:

TIMEWYRM: GENESYS
John Peel

The Doctor and Ace are drawn to Ancient Mesopotamia in
search of an evil sentience that has tumbled from the stars
– the dreaded Timewyrm of ancient Gallifreyan legend.

ISBN 0 426 20355 0

TIMEWYRM: EXODUS
Terrance Dicks

Pursuit of the Timewyrm brings the Doctor and Ace to the
Festival of Britain. But the London they find is strangely
subdued, and patrolling the streets are the uniformed thugs
of the Britischer Freikorps.

ISBN 0 426 20357 7

TIMEWYRM: APOCALYPSE
Nigel Robinson

Kirith seems an ideal planet – a world of peace and plenty,
ruled by the kindly hand of the Great Matriarch. But it's
here that the end of the universe – of everything – will be
precipitated. Only the Doctor can stop the tragedy.

ISBN 0 426 20359 3

TIMEWYRM: REVELATION
Paul Cornell

Ace has died of oxygen starvation on the moon, having
thought the place to be Norfolk. 'I do believe that's unique,'
says the afterlife's receptionist.

ISBN 0 426 20360 7

LOVE AND WAR
Paul Cornell

Heaven: a planet rich in history where the Doctor comes to meet a new friend, and betray an old one; a place where people come to die, but where the dead don't always rest in peace. On Heaven, the Doctor finally loses Ace, but finds archaeologist Bernice Summerfield, a new companion whose destiny is inextricably linked with his.

ISBN 0 426 20385 2

TRANSIT
Ben Aaronovitch

It's the ultimate mass transit system, binding the planets of the solar system together. But something is living in the network, chewing its way to the very heart of the system and leaving a trail of death and mutation behind. Once again, the Doctor is all that stands between humanity and its own mistakes.

ISBN 0 426 20384 4

THE HIGHEST SCIENCE
Gareth Roberts

The Highest Science – a technology so dangerous it destroyed its creators. Many people have searched for it, but now Sheldukher, the most wanted criminal in the galaxy, believes he has found it. The Doctor and Bernice must battle to stop him on a planet where chance and coincidence have become far too powerful.

ISBN 0 426 20377 1

THE PIT
Neil Penswick

One of the Seven Planets is a nameless giant, quarantined against all intruders. But when the TARDIS materializes, it becomes clear that the planet is far from empty – and the Doctor begins to realize that the planet hides a terrible secret from the Time Lords' past.

ISBN 0 426 20378 X

DECEIT
Peter Darvill-Evans

Ace – three years older, wiser and tougher – is back. She is part of a group of Irregular Auxiliaries on an expedition to the planet Aracadia. They think they are hunting Daleks, but the Doctor knows better. He knows that the paradise planet hides a being far more powerful than the Daleks – and much more dangerous.

ISBN 0 426 20362 3

LUCIFER RISING
Jim Mortimore & Andy Lane

Reunited, the Doctor, Ace and Bernice travel to Lucifer, the site of a scientific expedition that they know will shortly cease to exist. Discovering why involves them in sabotage, murder and the resurrection of eons-old alien powers. Are there Angels on Lucifer? And what does it all have to do with Ace?

ISBN 0 426 20338 7

WHITE DARKNESS
David McIntee

The TARDIS crew, hoping for a rest, come to Haiti in 1915. But they find that the island is far from peaceful: revolution is brewing in the city; the dead are walking from the cemeteries; and, far underground, the ancient rulers of the galaxy are stirring in their sleep.

ISBN 0 426 20395 X

SHADOWMIND
Christopher Bulis

On the colony world of Arden, something dangerous is growing stronger. Something that steals minds and memories. Something that can reach out to another planet, Tairgire, where the newest exhibit in the sculpture park is a blue box surmounted by a flashing light.

ISBN 0 426 20394 1

BIRTHRIGHT
Nigel Robinson

Stranded in Edwardian London with a dying TARDIS, Bernice investigates a series of grisly murders. In the far future, Ace leads a group of guerrillas against their insect-like, alien oppressors. Why has the Doctor left them, just when they need him most?

ISBN 0 426 20393 3